HUNTED

A STALKER'S MOON NOVEL

ELLIE FERGUSON

Hunter's Moon Press

Print ISBN: 978-1-949901-00-9

E-book ISBN: 978-1-949901-01-6

Cover design by Sarah A. Hoyt

If you enjoyed this novel, please check out my blog, Nocturnal Lives, for more titles.

Thank you for your support.

To my dearest cousin Clarice, who encouraged me to follow my dreams and reminded me that writing ran in the family, whether we wanted to admit it or not. I miss you and wish you were here to see this day.

She will run no longer.

CHAPTER ONE

T hey were here.

Despite all my precautions, despite all the times I'd moved and left no forwarding address, they'd found me. Again. I'd done everything possible to live off the grid and for what? All it took was one small mistake or someone catching my image on a cell phone video and there they were.

Damn it. I didn't have any choice. I had to move and move fast.

Assuming I lived long enough.

My heart thudded and a bead of sweat ran down my spine. Every instinct screamed for me to run. I pushed the urge down. Running would only make it easier for the trackers to pinpoint my location. People might hurry down the streets of Fort Worth but they rarely ran and certainly not without a destination in mind. No, I had to continue walking as if nothing was wrong.

A few hours ago, I'd been thinking about the upcoming weekend. I looked forward to a couple of days off after working without a break the least two weeks. I didn't even mind that my roommate, Dana, had set me up on a blind date with her cousin. Not that I expected anything to come of it. Nothing ever did. Either my demons interfered or the trackers did. Like now.

Damn it, what's a girl got to do to have a nice dinner and maybe some good sex?

Who was I kidding? I'd settle for having something close to a normal life and never having to look over my shoulder again.

Without breaking stride, I merged into the early afternoon foot traffic. A quick glance right and then left didn't reveal my pursuers. But they were there. I felt their eyes on me. The back of my neck prickled. There was that *itch* between my shoulder blades I'd learned long ago not to ignore.

Instinct had kept me alive this long. Would it be enough now?

I'd been foolish to believe Michael Jennings had forgotten about me. Even if he hadn't, I'd hoped he finally decided it wasn't worth the effort to keep looking for my latest hiding spot. I should have known better. I'd embarrassed him when I refused his advances. Worse, I'd done so in front of others. Unfortunately, he hadn't been so easily dissuaded.

Bile rose in my throat at the memory of that long ago night. If I closed my eyes, I could still feel his hands on me. I smelled his scent as he'd pulled me close. He'd been over-confident and hadn't expected me to fight back. It was over almost as quickly as it had started. That night I'd fled the only home I'd ever known, leaving behind family and friends. I knew it was the last time I'd see them. My only consolation was the sight of Jennings lying on the cold tile floor, bleeding and nursing what I hoped was a very sore pair of balls.

I might not have looked back, but I did keep a look out. I knew Michael wouldn't just let me go. But I'd never expected him to keep up the chase this long. God, would I never get my life back?

I jogged across Commerce Street. Less than a block away was the county courthouse. There would be plenty of police there who could help me. But that assumed the trackers let me get that far. Unless they were fools, the least thing they'd do was let me near the courthouse. That meant I needed another plan, one with a better chance of success.

Hoping I wasn't making a mistake, I turned right. One more block. If I made it that far, I'd be at the Bank of America Tower. The building offered several advantages. I had reason to be there. I knew the building. It offered thirty-eight floors I could lose myself in and, better yet, it had a parking garage I could use to get away.

If I was lucky.

Fort Worth had been lucky for me, at least until today. I'd pulled into town almost a year ago, hoping to lose myself here. After close to ten years on the run, I was tired. I wanted nothing more than to settle down, find a mate and have a life. The thought of moving again, of having to establish yet another identity was almost more than I could bear.

Had I gotten careless because I was tired of running?

How it happened didn't matter. Jennings had found me and this time there'd be no escape. In his mind, he had to bring me back. Otherwise, he'd lose face with the rest of the clan. They'd believe he wasn't strong enough to control a mere female. If he couldn't control a female, how could they trust him to be a strong enough of an Alpha to protect the clan?

None of that mattered. Only one thing did. I had to get away. The next person to bump into me could be one of the trackers. I'd never been one to act like a lamb awaiting the slaughter and this was no time to start. I might not be the Marine my father had been, but he'd taught me well. He and my mother, God rest their souls, had taught me how to act under fire, real or metaphorical.

It was time to remember who and what I was. I was the daughter of the clan's previous Alpha and his mate, an alpha in her own right. Let the fools Jennings sent for me learn just what that meant.

If they wanted to play, I was more than happy to oblige.

I paused before the main display window for Vintage Gallery and glanced around, careful not to be too obvious about it. Yes, someone was definitely there. Again. As much as I'd like to believe whoever was watching me was more interested in my good looks—hah!—or even in stealing my backpack, I knew better.

I'd screwed up. I'd felt their presence for a week now. Never at the same place and never at the same time—and never this close. Each time, I'd told myself I was imagining it.

Damn it, I had gotten careless.

Fortunately, so had they. They were close enough now I could scent them. Yes, them. There were at least shapeshifters close by. I should probably be flattered Jennings decided a single tracker wasn't enough to bring me in. Hopefully, three wouldn't be enough either.

I didn't have time to wonder why Michael had changed tactics. Had something happened within the clan to force his hand? Or had he, like me, grown tired of the hunt?

God, why couldn't this be over? I like a good hunt as much as the next person. But only when I'm the hunter. This being the hunted didn't sit well. One way or another, I needed to end this game of cat and mouse. But I had to bide my time. Downtown Fort Worth wasn't the place for a confrontation, at least not the sort this could quickly turn into. So, unless I wanted our secret made public, I needed to find some place secluded and I needed to find it soon.

Fortunately, Fort Worth, even downtown Fort Worth, wasn't without out-of-the-way areas where I could put my plan into action. All I had to do was get to one before my unseen trackers made their move.

I started down the block. Attorneys and their clients hurried down the street in the direction of the courthouse, briefcases swinging like weapons to part the crowd before them. Men and women in business suits strolled only slightly more leisurely back to their offices after lunch. One or two may have staggered, a bit worse for wear after one too many margaritas at lunch.

As the crowd pressed on down the street, I paused near the entrance to the Bank of America tower. I carefully shifted my backpack, settling it more comfortably over my left shoulder, leaving my right hand free. I wanted to be able to drop the backpack, or use it as a weapon, when the time came—and something told me that time would be soon.

I had to get off the streets.

A man bumped against me and I stiffened, relaxing only as he mumbled a quick, "'Scuse me" before moving on. One thing about Fort Worth, it's a polite city. Even though I looked like the average college—okay, post-grad—student wandering the streets, people still greeted me and begged for forgiveness for whatever minor breech of etiquette they thought they might have committed. Strange town this.

A slight smile touched my lips as I ducked inside the building. It was a risk. There were any number of security cameras here that would capture my image. But they'd also capture the image of whoever followed me. It might not help me but, in the long run, it would help whoever looked into my disappearance. That was the best I could hope for.

The glass doors closed. For one moment I relished the cool air that greeted me. But I couldn't stand there enjoying it. Too many others wanted inside, politely but insistently pushing past me. Then there were the trackers. I could feel them even if I couldn't see them.

"May I help you, ma'am?" the uniformed security guard asked as I approached his desk. Then he looked up and grinned. This was the third delivery I'd made there this week. "Hey, Finn."

He really did have a nice smile.

"Hi, Gil. I've got a delivery for George and Chandler from the Jessup Firm. They're expecting it."

I waited as he called upstairs to confirm my story. I hadn't realized when I took the temporary job as a runner for a local law firm that it would come in handy as a way to keep alive. It had surprised me enough when it led to some very interesting propositions for dinner and *more*. Now it seemed I had another reason to be thankful for those bottom feeders called lawyers.

"Twenty-fifth floor, Finn. Sign in and put this on."

He pushed a clipboard across the desk in my direction with one hand and handed me a guest badge with the other. He glanced at the page as I scrawled my name on the first available line. I handed him back the clipboard and then attached the badge to the right front pocket of my jeans. There, I was official.

"When you finally going to agree to go have a drink with me, Finn?"

"When you don't have a family to go home to, Gil." That was one of my only rules. No married men, and especially not married men with kids.

I gave a little wave and moved toward the elevator bank. I needed to be smart now. More than my future depended on it. I didn't want to be the one responsible for letting the world-at-large know that shapeshifters do exist and that we walk among them. Jennings might be willing to risk it but I wasn't.

Ten minutes later, my delivery made, I stepped into the twenty-fifth floor corridor and glanced around. No one else was visible. But didn't mean anything. My pursuers could be waiting in the lobby. It would be easy enough to flank me as I stepped off the elevator. Then all they'd have to do was get me out of the building.

I lifted my face and sniffed the air. All the smells I'd come to associate with the building, particularly this floor, assailed me. Cleaners and perfumes, too many perfumes. Someone was nuking what smelled like enchiladas or tamales nearby. The one thing I didn't scent was another like me. That meant the trackers hadn't discovered what floor I'd gotten off on. I didn't know whether to be relieved or not. All I knew for sure was I had to get out of the building without being forced to either surrender or reveal much more to the public than any of our kind wanted.

The elevator doors slid open and I tensed. Instead of the demons from my past appearing, two well-dressed women stepped out instead. From their whispered conversation, I guessed they were discussin a different kind of assignation than the one I'd been expecting. They were comparing notes on their love lives, oblivious to all around them.

As they walked down the corridor, inspiration hit. I reached out and stopped the door before it closed. Holding the door open, I leaned inside and punched the buttons to make the elevator car stop on the twenty first, nineteenth, tenth, sixth and third floors before coming to a stop in the lobby. Unless I missed my guess, the car would stop on at least one other floor along the way, which was all to the good. The more stops it made, and the more people who got on and off, the more difficult it became for my pursuers to realize where I had gone

Now, to get out of the building. Then I could make sure that any confrontation happened on my terms and not theirs.

I resisted the urge to run as I made my way to the stairwell door. I could hurry once there. Then I'd take the stairs up six floors and then take the elevator down. Since the building's last remodel, everything above the thirtieth floor used a different bank of elevators than the one I'd come up on. Those elevators opened out of sight of the main lobby. Even better, they opened almost directly across from the stairwell door leading to the parking garage. If I could get to that door, I'd be in the garage before anyone knew it.

Of course, that was a very big *IF*....

The elevator doors opened, and I let myself be swept out by the other passengers. I glanced around, every sense alive and seeking. Much as I'd hoped my shadows had given up, at least one was still there. I could scent him. He was close, too close for comfort. But where?

Praying the explanation was as simple as whoever it was waited on the opposite side of the elevator bank and was, therefor, blind to my return, I gauged the distance to the stairwell door. All I had to do was get to it. That's it. Less than ten feet separated me from potential freedom.

With my backpack thumping against my side, I hit the door at a dead run. Now we'd play it my way. Let's see just how good he—or she—was. I'd bet my life—hell, I *was* betting my life—that he wasn't nearly as good at this as I was.

I pelted up the drive, climbing, climbing until I saw daylight.

Cars lined up at the gates, waiting for their tickets to enter or to pay so they could exit. I slipped between them, emerging onto the street. Even then I didn't slow. I couldn't. Not when I could hear someone behind me. Running feet, labored breathing. Good. He wasn't in as good physical condition I was and he'd pay for it. Then he'd tell me what I wanted to know or else.

I veered to my right into another parking garage, an above-ground one this time. We'd already run more than a city block, not counting the time in the bank's parking garage. I could sense my pursuer flagging. Good. Just a little longer. I had to be careful about where I confronted him. But soon, very soon, this would be over.

There's something about the hunt that excites at the primal level. It doesn't matter if you're the hunted or the hunter. At least it doesn't matter to me. My senses sharpen as my pulse increases. My mind clears and a calm settles over me. I know how good I am. I've survived combat situations and too many situations like this one because my parents trained me to be ready for any situation that might arise. This hunter, if you dared call him that, was no match for me.

I raced up the ramp, one level and then two. My running shoes, carefully selected for just such an emergency, cushioned my steps. Only a muted slap-slap-slap with each footfall betrayed me. A slight smile touched my lips. I didn't pant and my heart didn't race. I was born for the hunt and welcomed the challenge.

I reached the door leading to the stairwell and shoved it open. Time to add some distance between us. The door slammed shut behind me, just as I wanted. I wanted him in the stairwell. I wanted him to wonder which direction I'd gone. When he started up the stairs, he'd be even more tired. That would make him an easier target when the time came.

Three flights up, I slammed through another door. I didn't think about anyone who might be on the other side. This was between me and the man following me. The world shrank to just the two of us. There wasn't time to worry about anyone else. Not until this was over.

Until he was over.

Then I'd worry about consequences.

I slowed, my eyes scanning the level. Cars and vans, not to mention the huge pick-up trucks I'd come to associate with Fort Worth, filled almost every parking space. The deep shadows, relieved by too few lights, made it easier to hide. And hide I would. Now was the time for patience and cunning. Maybe it was even time to play with the fool a bit before pouncing. This *mouse* had very sharp teeth and the cat had better be battle-hardened before going after it. Otherwise, he'd be in for a big surprise.

He was close. The scents of sweat and frustration hit moments before I heard him. The fool. Why wear boots when you're trying to stalk someone? Every step he took reverberated on the stairs, even through the closed door. A slight smile touched my lips as I took my position to wait.

I crouched behind a van near the top of the ramp, hidden in the shadows. My backpack rested on the concrete beside me. Down the aisle, the stairwell door clanged open, followed almost instantly by a sharp curse. I couldn't help smiling. It just kept getting better.

I remained where I was, secure in the knowledge the shadows were, as always, my friend. For a moment, the only sounds were those of my heart beating and my slow, steady breaths. There! A step. Then another. His pace quickened. He wasn't running, but it was close. Any doubts I'd had about being followed disappeared.

Listening as he moved up the aisle, memory intruded. Something was wrong. There had been at least three trackers when I ducked inside the BoA Tower. Smart money had them splitting up to try to cover the building's different entrances. But where were the others now? Jennings wasn't a fool. He'd have sent a team that worked well together. That meant the tracker following me should have let the others know where we were headed. So, where were they?

Leaving my backpack, I edged around the rear of the van. The backpack, if the tracker found it, would delay him. It would divert his attention and give me the chance to act. But I had to take care not to blow my chance before it arrived.

I crept behind another vehicle, this one big and black. Some sort of SUV. I really didn't care what it was as long as it offered me cover. Now was when hunter became the hunted and the thrill of it raced through me. If only we were away from town where this could become a real hunt. It had been too long since I'd allowed my panther out. Now it strained against my control, confident it was better at this game of cat and mouse than I.

Hell, it probably was, not that I dared do anything about it now. The trackers might be willing to risk exposing our existence, but I wasn't. I couldn't. There were too many others who'd suffer if the normals discovered the things of their nightmares walked among them.

Footsteps neared. Slower now, more relaxed. It was almost as if someone was taking a leisurely stroll down the aisle. Had I misjudged? Was it possible my stalker had been playing me? No, I didn't believe that. There had to be another explanation.

I pulled my hood up, hiding my face, and shrank further into the shadows. My heart hammered. Fear clawed at my throat. For one moment, I closed my eyes. I prayed this was all some horrible dream I'd soon awaken from. But it wasn't. I'd learned long ago that the real nightmares are the ones we're forced to live, day after day after day.

A car door opened a few yards away and I started nervously. My hands flew to my mouth in a desperate attempt to silence my gasp. It wasn't him. By all that was holy, it wasn't him. Whoever it was, they weren't a part of this. All I had to do was wait for them to leave. Then I could finish this once and for all.

If I had time. For all I knew, the tracker heard my gasp and even now was using the sounds of the car starting and backing out of its space to distract me as he closed in on my location. Dear God, what should I do?

Patience. I had to stay patient and not move too soon. I couldn't risk getting careless now, with the end so close.

A red sedan slowly drove past my hiding space. Behind the wheel sat an attractive, gray-haired woman. From where I crouched in the shadows, I could see she hadn't locked her doors. It would be so easy to slide into the backseat as she drove past, to force her to drive me out of there and away from my pursuer. It was so tempting.

. . .

No! That wasn't the way. It was far too dangerous to involve someone else, someone not of our kind. In this day and age of lo-jack tracking on cars and global positioning software in cell phones, I didn't dare risk it. One phone call to the police and they'd know within minutes where the car was. I might be willing to do a lot of things but risking a police shoot-out wasn't one.

The car disappeared around the curve and I sank back against the wheel of the SUV. Where was he? My ears strained and my heart pounded. No matter how many times I'd been in this position—and I'd been there more times than I cared to count—it never got any easier. But this time was different. I could feel it. For whatever reason, the tracker was alone and a one-on-one fight suited me just fine.

I wouldn't kill him unless he forced me to. Not that I didn't plan on doing whatever it took to find out how he'd found me. Once I learned that, I could disappear into the shadows again and move on, another town and another identity.

Again.

Leather scraped concrete and my muscles tensed. I waited, ready to pounce. All he had to do was come a little closer.

A nagging voice inside my head reminded me this was all happening too easily. Was it possible I'd fallen for some elaborate trap they'd laid to capture me?

Fear licked at my confidence and I glanced down, frantically searching for that telltale red dot of a laser scope. Nothing. If anyone besides the two of us were there, they hadn't tagged me, at least not yet. Maybe I was worrying for no reason.

I dropped to my stomach and looked under the cars, searching for another set of feet, for anything to prove or disprove my fears. Nothing. Only the boots and jeans of the lone tracker.

I sat back up and drew a slow, deep breath. My lips pulled back, baring my teeth and a low, primal growl fought for release as my panther struggled to take control. Not now. This was my fight. Mine. My muscles all but quivered in anticipation as each step brought the tracker closer, ever closer.

From where I crouched, I saw his legs first. Faded blue jeans. Black, worn boots. Interesting. That wasn't a tracker's usual attire but it made sense if this one was trying to blend in. Maybe he wasn't quite the amateur I first thought. Or maybe not. Although he moved slowly up the aisle, checking first one direction and the other as he scanned between the parked cars, his hands were visible and very empty. My well-trained eye saw no hint of a weapon anywhere on him. Good. That made things much easier.

I slipped further into the shadows cast by the SUV and the wall behind me. All I needed was for him to take another couple of steps forward. That's all. Then I'd be in his blind spot and could move. He'd never know what hit him. By the time he figured it out, it would be too late. I'd deal with him and I'd be well away from there.

I rose from my crouch and stepped into the aisle, ready to attack. The tracker, barely three feet ahead of me, seemed unaware of my presence. That didn't make sense.

Run!

My head jerked up, the scents of the other trackers suddenly assailing me. Damn it! It had been a trap. I'd played into their hands. But how? How had they known this was where I'd come?

My mind may have frozen, but my body reacted on instinct. I turned and took first one step and then another. I had to run. It didn't matter where. All that mattered was getting out of there. I'd made the worst mistake possible. I'd become over-confident and I'd fallen into their trap.

"Going somewhere, little cat?"

A man stepped out from behind a red Dodge Ram pick-up. As he did, I swallowed hard. Unlike the other tracker, he had a good half a foot on me in height and probably seventy-five pounds, all of it muscle. In one hand, he held a Smith & Wesson 1911. I recognized the gun because I'd dreamed of owning one. In the other, he carried something that scared me even more – a knife. Bullets hurt but a knife -- a knife was the tool of torture.

Fighting down the panic threatening to overwhelm me, I glance around. The first tracker still stood behind me. They chosen well by setting him up as prey. He still stood behind me, unarmed as far as I could tell. The third tracker must be near but where?

"Just out for a run."

Okay, probably not the smartest thing I could say. But it did what I hoped. The first man looked at me in surprise. For a moment, he dropped his guard. That's all I needed. But I knew better than to run. He still held both gun and knife. I needed to relieve him of at least the gun. Hopefully, the second tracker was as inept as I thought. I didn't need him trying to help his buddy before I managed to get one of the weapons.

A split-second was all it took. My muscles tensed. My toes dug in against the concrete of the floor. A moment later, I launched myself at the armed tracker. His breath exploded in a loud *OOF!* as I drove him to the ground. His head cracked against concrete, stunning him. I moved fast, scrabbling for the gun. Even as my fingers closed around it, I felt the man regaining his senses. His body tensed and he tried to roll. Cursing, I pulled back my right fist and drove it into his face. My left hand grabbed the gun. For a moment, I hesitated. The knife rested in the man's loose grip.

The sound of a step behind me made up my mind. I rolled to the left. As I leapt to my feet, the sound of cloth ripping filled the air. Pain seared my side almost instantly. Turning, teeth bared in a feral snarl, I faced off against the second tracker. Sweat shone on his face. A knife glittered in a hand that trembled slightly. Idiot! He hadn't been unarmed after all.

I might be an idiot, but he was a fool. A gun would beat a knife any day, especially if I didn't let him get any closer.

"Drop it," I growled, motioning with the 1911 toward the ground.

Before the tracker could respond, the screeching of tires filled the air. A black Mustang slid around the corner at the top of the aisle and sped in our direction. I watched in disbelief as it neared. Then the driver slammed on the brakes. Smoke billowed out behind the car. A loud thud, followed by the tracker flying up and over the hood, snapped me back into the moment. I stared in disbelief as the Mustang slid to a stop next to me.

"Get in!" the driver yelled as the passenger door swung open

For a moment, hope flared. Escape was at hand.

Three sharp jabs hit my back, like needles or nails, as I dove into the car. Then my system lit up. It felt as if a thousand—no, a million—hot needles suddenly pierced me. Every nerve seemed to catch fire. No longer would my body answer my commands. Muscles tensed, spasmed and I slumped forward. There was pain—I think there was pain—as I hit the dashboard face first. Then I fell back against the passenger seat as the Mustang sped off.

Breathe. I had to breathe. But my lungs wouldn't work. Panic filled me. This is what Hell must be like. A mind alive and terrified in a body that does nothing but scream in agony. Dear God, was this really the day I'd die?

CHAPTER TWO

"Don't fight it. I know it hurts like hell, but it will pass."

The voice was deep and reassuring. I wanted to turn my head to see who my rescuer might be but could no more do that than I could right myself in the passenger seat. My muscles refused to cooperate. My nervous system felt as if it were on fire. There was no way I had gotten the full jolt from the Taser. It shouldn't still be affecting me. What was going on?

It's funny what your mind will do when your body refuses to work. Instead of worrying about the trackers—or even who my mysterious rescuer might be—I wondered how he'd explain my condition if the police pulled us over because I wasn't wearing my seatbelt. *"Gee, officer, I was just driving through the parking garage and saw this nice lady being hit by a Taser and thought I'd bring her home. Is it my fault she didn't buckle her seatbelt?"*

I fell against the door as the car veered to the right. It dawned on me my rescuer must have leaned across me to close the door even as we'd sped away from the trackers. Otherwise, I'd have gone tumbling onto the pavement. The sudden rush of light told me we'd emerged onto the street. I ought to be at least a little worried about where we were going, but it was hard to be when it was all I could do to breathe.

"Once we're away from here and your nervous system is no longer lighting up like a Christmas tree, maybe you'd be kind enough to explain what the hell is going on. Why are trackers working in my territory without permission and why are they after you?"

There was a bite to his voice that spoke volumes. The part of my mind that still worked latched onto the fact he had identified himself as the local clan leader. Shit, damn and fuck. The trackers weren't the only ones in his territory without permission. When he found out why I was there—and why the trackers were after me—would he hand me over to them? God, this just kept getting worse and worse and there was not one damned thing I could do about it. By the time my body started working again, it might just be too late.

I'd made the conscious decision to keep my presence in Fort Worth a secret from the local pride and clan. I didn't know the pride or clan leaders. For all I knew, they were best friends with Jennings and wouldn't bat an eye as they handed me over to him. Would that decision wind up biting me in the ass?

There are reasons, good ones, why our laws require us to present ourselves to the local clan leader when we move into a new area. There might not be nearly as many of us as there are normals, but there are enough that our ancestors learned we needed a set of laws to govern us' Many of those laws are designed to protect us from detection. One way was to form clans in areas where there were more than three packs or prides. In those areas, the individual packs and prides merged under the single leadership of the strongest alpha in the region. Even now, the clans are all but autonomous—as long as our laws are followed.

One of our most basic laws is that a shapeshifter must report to the local clan leader upon entering his territory. It is up to the clan leader to determine if the shifter may stay. I'd never heard of anyone being denied permission, at least not in a very long while. But that didn't change the fact I'd never reported to any of the clan since leaving home so long ago. I hadn't wanted to risk them contacting Jennings. Now I didn't have any choice. I'd have to tell the clan leader I'd broken one of our most basic laws. All I hoped was he understood I'd done it as much to protect those I cared for as I had to protect myself.

What sort of forfeit would I be forced to pay if he didn't believe me?

Damn it, how long would it be before my body started working again?

I closed my eyes and focused on breathing. It was pointless to worry about anything else until the effects of the Taser wore off.

After what seemed like an eternity, I sat up. When I reached for the seatbelt, it felt like I was moving through molasses. Residual pain echoed through me. It was tolerable, at least I told myself it was. But it seemed to be lasting too long, especially since I suspected the leads had been torn out of my back as the Mustang sped away from the trackers. Had they somehow modified the Taser to be more effective against our kind?

Dear God, that was a terrifying thought. If they'd done that, what else had they done and what else were they willing to do to get their hands on me?

"T-thank you," I stammered.

As I spoke, I realized we now drove down a neighborhood street. Even though my companion kept a close eye on the rearview mirror, he seemed more relaxed than he had earlier. Had he given the trackers the slip? God, I hoped so. I needed time to recover before facing them again.

Who the hell was I kidding? I had no desire, and certainly no intention, of facing them any time soon. Just as soon as I could move without falling on my face, I'd be on my way out of town. I didn't have to have a destination in mind. All I needed was to put time and distance between us.

My rescuer glanced at me and nodded. Then he turned his attention back to the road. A short time later, the car slowed and we turned into a driveway. How long we'd been driving, I didn't know. It might have been just a few minutes, or it might have been longer. Judging by how I felt, at least twenty minutes had passed since I'd been hit by the Taser. But, since I haven't made it a habit of letting myself be used as a living lightning rod, I couldn't be sure. Besides, what did it matter? We were away from the trackers. That was all I cared about.

A grinding filled the air as the garage door lowered behind us. Still moving slowly, I carefully sat up. Muscles protested as I fumbled with my seatbelt. Then my rescuer was around the car and opening my door. Strong hands helped me out. Something told me not to protest as he swung me up in his arms and carried me inside.

"T-thanks." The moment he set me on my feet, I dropped onto a chair at the battered kitchen table. My muscles protested any instructions I gave them. That should not still be happening. What the hell had the trackers done to slow the fast healing shapeshifters usually enjoyed?

He paused halfway between the table and the refrigerator and looked at me in concern. Without a word, he closed the distance between us. A gentle hand touched my forehead. Before I could protest, he pushed back my hoodie and lifted my tee shirt. His mouth tightened into a grim line. When he looked up at me, worried clouded his expression.

I watched as he turned. He rummaged in a drawer. When he turned back, he held several dishtowels in one hand. He put all but one on the table. That one he folded carefully before once again lifting my shirt. I hissed in pain as he pressed it against my side. Then, as he reached for my hand and held it over the folded towel, I remembered the kiss of the tracker's knife. Pain washed over me and I swallowed hard.

"Hold that in place," he said as he climbed to his feet. "The cut's not deep but it is long. I'm calling our doctor. You shouldn't be having this much trouble still."

"P-please. No doctor." I struggled to form the words.

He looked at me as if I'd lost my mind. "You don't have any say in this." He pinned me with such a firm look I fought the urge to drop to hands and knees in submission. As if realizing how he'd sounded, he rubbed a hand over his face and blew out his breath. "You don't need to worry. I give my word. The doctor's my uncle and he's one of us."

One of us.

That answered one question. He knew what I was even if he didn't know who I was. Instead of arguing, not that much argument was possible just then, I nodded. The continuing weakness scared me. Even worse was the burning sensation in my back where the barbs had struck. The only good thing, if you could call it that, about it was they kept my mind off the gash in my side.

I wrapped my hands around the glass of orange juice he placed on the table in front of me and watched as he fished in his pocket for his cell phone. Suddenly thirsty, I debated the best way to get the glass to my lips. Not trusting my muscles, I ducked my head so all I'd have to do was tilt the glass. The juice, tart and cold, was just what I needed. By the time I'd taken a few sips, I could carefully lift the glass without spilling its contents down my front.

I turned my attention to my host, relieved my brain was starting to work. He'd moved across the small kitchen and, with his back to me, was staring out the window over the sink. Watching him, my panther stirred—as did a lust I'd not felt in a very long while—and I swallowed hard. Long, muscular legs led up to one of the finest examples of a male ass that I had seen in a very long time. They led up to a narrow waist and broad shoulders. Then he turned, and I fought the urge to lick my lips.

Oh... my.

My panther was so close to the surface, I was surprised to look down at my hands and not see the shift starting. I'd been drawn to other males of our kind before. There were too few of us for our animal aspects not to be attracted to one another. But this was different. Never before had the pull been so strong. If I had to guess, my cat not only recognized his shifted form, but she was willing to admit his dominance. That was something new and something I'd have to think about—later.

No, that wasn't quite right. It wasn't that she recognized his dominance. She recognized him as her equal and that was—interesting. It was also a complication I didn't need. Nor did I need him guessing what was going through my head. That would be more than embarrassing.

"Thank you," I whispered as he ended his call and dropped the cell phone on the countertop. "I apologize for bringing trouble to your territory, clan leader." And I was. Our kind had enough to worry about without causing trouble for one another.

He leaned against the counter, his head tilted to one side. Lips pursed, he studied me. As he did, I took the time to study him. Deep blue eyes set in what the romance novels would call a ruggedly handsome face. A nose that had been broken at some point. A thin scar bisected his left eyebrow. Thick, dark hair the blue-black of a raven's wing. Younger than most clan leaders, yet there was a confidence to him most young alphas did not possess. Was it any wonder both my cat and I responded to him?

"I'm just glad I got to you before the trackers did." He pushed off from the counter and crossed the kitchen in three quick steps. "You can answer my questions after Stefan has a look at you. He should be here soon. In the meantime, he left instructions to get you flat."

As good as that sounded, I couldn't agree. Not yet. I needed to warn him. The trackers wouldn't go away simply because he'd thwarted them. If they had a single working brain cell, they would have taken down his license plate number. That meant they'd know where he lived. I had a sick feeling they wouldn't care if he was the local clan leader or not. Jennings sent them to complete a mission and complete their mission they would. It was better to risk the wrath of another clan leader than to incur Jennings' wrath. I knew that first-hand.

"I can't stay." I struggled to my feet only to fall heavily back onto the chair. Damn it. What the hell had they done to me? "They'll trace your car."

"Who the hell are you, lady? While you're explaining that, you can also tell me why a female alpha is on her own and why trackers would risk breaking the peace with my clan to get you?"

I closed my eyes. He'd asked the question I'd spent years doing my best to avoid. But I owed him the truth. He had at least postponed my *return* to the clan—and Jennings. I couldn't sit here and put him and his people in danger without at least telling him why.

"My name's Meg Finley." I waited, wondering how he would react. "I expected the trackers would show up, sooner or later, but I never thought they would do so without informing you of their presence."

That much was true. I knew Jennings would do just about anything to force my return to the clan, but I'd never thought he would allow his people to operate in another clan's territory without permission. Fear spiked at the realization that he was willing to violate one of our most basic rules in his search for me. If he would do that, what would he do if he ever got his hands on me?

Then something else the man said struck me. *Female alpha?* I shook my head. Had I been on my own so long I'd not realized how strong I had become? If Jennings knew I was an alpha, he'd never stop until he hauled me back to the clan. If that happened, I'd never be free again.

God, I had to get out of here before the trackers tried for me again.

"Finley?" The man's brow creased, and his fingers drummed an impatient beat against the tabletop. "Any relation to Jason and Patricia Finley?"

For a moment I didn't answer. I wasn't sure what to think of him making the connection so quickly. My parents had been well-known among the clans and their deaths—their murders. There was no way they would have killed themselves—would have been something the clans talked about for a long time. There had been so many questions, even among our own clan, about what happened. Still, it had been years since their deaths and my host wasn't that much older than me. Why should he have made the connection so quickly?

"My parents."

Now it was his turn to fall silent. I sat there, wishing I knew what he was thinking.

"Well, Meg Finley, you present me with a problem. When you went missing, your new Alpha sent word to the rest of the clans asking that we let him know if you showed up. He said you were distraught and he was worried about you. Over the last few years, he's sent out further requests for information, suggesting you might be working against the best interests of our kind."

"What?" I surged to my feet, this time without instantly dropping back onto the chair. Amazing what anger can do for you. "I swear I would never put our people in danger and Michael Jennings damn well knows it."

"Sit before you fall," he said. "And quit looking like you're going to make a break for it. I said that's what he told us, not that it's what I believed. Besides, if I'd had any doubts, your reaction—as well as the fact the trackers did something to taint their blade or the Taser. Otherwise, you wouldn't be as weak as a kitten still—is enough to reassure me."

"Then you understand why I've got to get out of here." Desperation filled my voice. I hadn't been this scared in a long time, but it was more than that. This man had risked a great deal by helping me. I didn't want to bring trouble to him or to his clan because of it.

"What I understand is that, for the moment at least, you are under my protection." His expression gentled and he nodded for me to sit. When I complied, he knelt before me. "Nothing is going to happen to you, not as long as you are here."

God, why wouldn't he understand?

"They'll know I'm with you." I ran my hand over my face, wincing as pain shot across my side and through my back.

"Trust me, they won't come here." Now he smiled and something in his expression reassured me. "If they trace the car's registration, it will return to a holding company owned by the investment firm I work for. It's one of several other cars the company owns. Short of hacking into the system, they'll never know who the car is checked out to. So relax. You're safe."

I wanted to believe him. But, when a knock sounded at the back door, I started nervously. Only his hand on my arm kept me in my chair. Looking up, I saw him tense and then a smile touched his lips. At almost the same time, I scented another of our kind on the other side of the door. I blew out a breath to realize it wasn't one of the trackers. Perhaps this was the uncle he'd spoken of earlier.

The door opened and a small, almost non-descript man stepped inside. His blue eyes, not as deep a blue as my host's but reassuring nonetheless, swept the kitchen. He started to say something to my host only to turn and look at me in surprise. Before I could react, he was standing before me. His hands took mine and he looked into my eyes. I swallowed hard, feeling as if he was looking into my very soul. Then he shook his head, a look of bemusement on his face.

"Stefan, I need you to make sure she's all right. She's got a knife wound to the side. It's long but not deep. She was also tasered and I think the leads were ripped out as we drove off," the clan leader said. "That was maybe forty-five minutes ago and yet she's still having problems."

The older man's mouth drew into a disapproving line and I fought the urge to squirm in my seat.

"I'm fine," I began and stood.

"The hell you are!" The clan leader jabbed his finger at my chair, leaving no doubt what he expected me to do. Well, he was about to find out this was one shapeshifter who didn't automatically obey.

Before I could respond, Stefan spoke up. "You can begin by making the introductions, Matt." The look he gave the young man spoke volumes. There was no doubt in my mind he'd just given the clan leader a verbal spanking.

"Sorry." He ran a hand over his face and then gave me an apologetic look. "My apologies, ma'am. I am not usually this obtuse. Put it down to finding those trackers after you and then learning who you are. We've not had this kind of encroachment on our territory in a long time."

"Trackers?" his uncle interrupted.

"Yeah." He shook his head before Stefan could say anything else. "I'm Matt Kincade, and I've led the Texas clan the last three years."

I took his proffered hand, trying to not to show my surprise when a shock went up my arm as our palms touched. I'd had more than enough of nervous system overloads to last me a lifetime.

"This is Dr. Stefan Kincade. Think of him as not only the clan's doctor but our conscience as well. He's my uncle and one of my closest advisors. I trust him with my life and promise you can as well."

I looked from Matt to Stefan and back again. Matt's meaning was clear. He would not reveal my identity to Stefan, but he hoped I would. I had already taken a huge risk telling him who I was. Did I dare trust yet another stranger with that information?

Did I have any choice? Our kind usually heals very quickly from all but the most serious of injuries. But the wound in my side still bled, as did the puncture wounds in my back where the Taser's barbed projectiles had torn into my flesh. Worse, each wound felt inflamed, as if something prevented my system from healing. I would be foolish to turn down treatment from someone familiar with shapeshifter physiology.

"Doctor, my name's Meg Finley." I waited for recognition to show on his face. Either he didn't recognize my name or he was a superb actor. No matter which, I felt better telling him the truth. "My friends call me Finn." At least they did now. It hadn't always been that way.

"Well, Finn, I'm pleased to meet you. I'd be very interested in knowing why a nice alpha female like you was being hunted and why you hadn't told Matt you were in town." There was no hint of censure in his voice, but I still felt as if I'd just had my knuckles rapped. "But that can wait until I've had a look at your injuries. I'm sure Matt has more than enough to keep him busy while we're gone."

With that, he held out a hand and waited until I took it. Then he helped me to my feet. As we slowly walked out of the kitchen, he told Matt that he was taking me into the guest room. We would be back when we were back. Until then, Matt might want to consider calling Gillespie and having him make sure security was in place not only here but at my place.

Matt's only response was to lift one eyebrow. I shrugged and rattled off the address for my apartment. Before he could ask, I dug in my pocket and then tossed him my keys. As I did, I remembered my backpack. I doubted it was still there but, if it was, I wanted it, if for no other reason than I'd like to have my cell phone and laptop back. When I asked if he could have someone look for it, Matt nodded and promised they'd do their best to find it.

Five minutes later, I lay face down on a wide bed in a room off the kitchen. The fact I was nude and a stranger was poking and prodding didn't matter. All I cared about was that he was, hopefully, going to make the pain go away. Since my first shift at thirteen, I'd been injured more than most people would be in their entire lifetimes. It was part of our culture. You fought for your place in pack or pride. You hunted with the full moon and often the prey didn't take kindly to becoming dinner. But I'd long ago learned that only the worst injuries took more than a few hours to heal enough to be almost forgotten, at least the pain of them. This constant neural firing I'd suffered since being hit by the Taser, as well as the burning pain from the wound in my side, was something new and something I could do without.

Stefan's bedside manner was gentle and reassuring. He spoke softly, explaining what he was going to do before he did it. In a lot of ways, he reminded me of how my father used to act around horses. He would talk to them, gentling them with voice and hands. I didn't know the term then, but now I knew he was what folks might call a horse whisperer. Of course, he could do it with almost any animal—or shapeshifter. It was a valuable skill for a clan leader.

"This might hurt," Stefan warned just before he did something to one of the places where the probes had hit.

Pain flared and nausea rose. Tears filled my eyes. I'd have cursed except I was afraid to open my mouth. Instead, my hands fisted on the sheet under me and I whimpered weakly.

"Easy, child." A cool hand touched my cheek, settling me. "I know it hurts but it will be over soon."

"W-what did they do to me?"

"My guess is that they dipped the probes, and probably the knife, in something meant to slow you down even after the effects of the Taser wore off. Whatever they did, we'll figure it out. I promise." He paused and a cool cloth replaced his hand as he bathed my face. "I need to make sure the other probes are out. Then I'll clean and stitch the wound in your side. I'm sorry, but it's going to hurt."

Damn, but the man had a way with the understatement. When he finished removing the next probe, I was shaking and sweating. I'm pretty sure I'd dug holes into the mattress with my fingers. By the time he removed the third probe, I knew I'd gone to Hell. I think I cursed. Maybe I'd cried. Then everything went mercifully dark.

CHAPTER THREE

"You're sure?"

There could be no mistaking the anger in the clan leader's voice. It penetrated the fog that held me, and I opened my eyes. I lay in a darkened room, a sheet covering me. My mouth felt like cotton and my head throbbed. But the pain in my back and side had subsided. Better yet, my neural system no longer did its imitation of the worst electrical storm imaginable. Whatever Stefan Kincade did, it seemed to have worked.

Thankfully.

Another voice murmured something. From the sound, they weren't in the kitchen. They were further away than that. I carefully leaned up on one elbow and lifted my face, sniffing. I caught the scents of five shapeshifters: Matt Kincade, his uncle and three others. So much for having a few minutes alone with the clan leader to find out what he planned to do about me.

Swinging my legs off the bed, I sat up. For a moment, the room swam around me. When it settled, I carefully climbed to my feet. This time, at least, I didn't instantly fall back. Better still, I felt my strength returning. All I needed to do now was get dressed and get out of there before the trackers found me.

I looked around the bedroom, searching for my clothes. Wonderful. They were nowhere to be seen. Well, I couldn't go traipsing through the house in nothing but skin. Surely there was something in here I could wear.

Before I could start searching, a soft knock sounded at the door. It opened a moment later. The reprimand that formed on my lips for entering without waiting for permission died as Stefan slipped inside. A blush that I swear started at my toes and went all the way to my hairline replaced it. Damn it, I shouldn't be embarrassed. He'd already seen me without a stitch of clothing on. Hell, he'd undressed me.

God, I'd been away from our kind too long. There had been a time when being nude hadn't bothered me, at least not when I was with other shapeshifters.

"I thought you might be awake." He smiled and moved to the closet. A moment later, he turned, a thick white robe in his hands. "Feeling better?"

"Much. Thank you."

He waved away my appreciation. Then he motioned me back to the bed. "I'd like to take another look at your injuries."

Even though I felt better, I agreed. Without prompting, I stretched out, rolling onto my stomach. A moment later, he sat on the mattress at my side. His hands, gentle as before, checked each wound in my back. He gently applied a salve of some sort and then fresh bandages. Soon enough, he helped me roll onto my back. I lifted my head to watched as he checked the long and fortunately shallow wound in my side.

"Good." He smiled and lightly patted my shoulder before helping me sit up. "You're healing nicely, Finn. Give it another day or so and you should be good as new."

"Thank you."

I reached for the robe and slipped into it. I felt better, less vulnerable, as I belted it about my waist. It really is amazing how much more capable you can feel once dressed.

"If you're up to it, Matt would like you to join us in the den."

I ran my hands through my hair, hoping it didn't look as bad as I feared—okay, I admit it, I can be as vain as the next person. But it was more than that. I remembered my parents' lessons from my childhood. You didn't present yourself to a clan leader looking anything but your best. Not only could it be considered an insult to him and to his people to come looking like a slob, but it put you at a disadvantage. Unfortunately, all I could do was hope Matt understood.

What was one more insult after all?

At least I knew the first thing I needed to do. When we entered the den, I moved in Matt's direction, stopping several feet from where he sat on a comfortable looking over-stuffed chair. As I dropped to all fours, I felt everyone's eyes on me. More than that, I felt my panther protesting this show of submission. I shushed her, reminding her we were trespassers and that, until I was stronger, we needed the clan's protection. If that meant playing this role, we would do it—for a little while at least.

I crawled forward, head down. I stopped and waited, my heart pounding. This was the first test. If Matt accepted my act of submission, there was at least hope he'd keep his word to protect me. But it was a very big "if".

Before I could speak, he reached down. I swallowed hard and put my hand in his. When he drew me to my feet, I glanced down, making sure my robe was properly closed. Then I looked up at him, wondering what would happen next.

Without a word, he turned me to face the others. Then he slid an arm around my shoulders. "Meg Finley is welcome in our clan and has my protection. You each are witnesses to this." He paused, his eyes sweeping the room until the others nodded. "I know her reasons for not reporting her presence to me, or to any of the rest of our kind, and I approve. Between what she's told me and what Stefan had to say after examining her, she had more than enough reason to want to remain hidden."

"Thank you." My voice was little more than a whisper. Now it was my turn. "Clan leader, I thank you for your welcome and for your understanding. I apologize for being the reason others have trespassed on your territory. I owe you a penalty for that and for not reporting to you when I first arrived. I offer myself up to you for judgment." Having said it, I turned to face him and once again sank to my knees. The others watched, all but holding their breaths as they waited for what would happen next.

Once again, Matt Kincade surprised me. He dropped to one knee in front of me. His right hand reached out and cupped my chin, tilting my head up so we looked into one another's eyes. As we did, my panther stirred. She was so close to the surface. I could almost feel my skin rippling even as I saw her pacing back and forth in my mind.

"Finn, I need you to trust me now," he said softly. I nodded. I trusted him more after knowing him for only a few hours than I did most of those in my home clan. I certainly trusted him more than my former clan leader. "Shift. Show us what your animal is."

I knew better than to hesitate. Instead, I slipped out of the robe and dropped once more to hands and knees. The moment I eased my control, my panther was there. Pain, so different from what I'd suffered at the hands of the trackers, flowed over me. Muscles twisted and contracted, stretched and reformed. Bones altered. I threw my head back and a strangled cry filled the room. It was never a painless process to shift and forcing a shift is never fun. Doing so after being through what I'd suffered that afternoon only made it worse.

"Very good, my lady," Matt said, admiration in his voice as he reached out to stroke my head. "You can shift back."

God, he didn't ask for much, did he?

The shift back to human hurt worse than the shift to panther. I was so tired, almost too tired to shift. It didn't help that my panther, free for the first time in much too long, did not want to give up control. I needed to let her out for a good hunt soon. I'd feel better for it and the part of me that wasn't human would quit pressing for release.

Matt draped the robe about my shoulders and helped me to my feet. Then he seated me in the chair he'd occupied when I entered the room. I smiled in appreciation. I felt like I'd run three marathons back to back, without food or rest. All I wanted was to curl up and sleep for about a week. But that had to wait a bit longer.

"Thank you, Finn." Matt smiled at me in approval and then pulled a chair up next to mine. "Stefan was telling us what he found when he treated you."

"And?"

And did I really want to know?

Hell yeah, I wanted to know.

"The barbs broke off in your back," Stefan said, eyes grim. "A preliminary examination proved they'd been tainted with something. Judging from the way the wound in your side looked, so was the blade. If I had to guess, I'd say the barbs were never meant to stay in as long as they did. As for the blade, I don't know. All I know with any certainty is that's why you hurt so badly and why you hadn't started healing."

"I've never felt anything like it before. Do you know what was on them?"

"That I don't know. But I will. I've already sent them out for testing."

My concern must have shone on my face because Matt reached over to touch my hand, drawing my attention to him. "Stefan has a lab we use, a private one run by our kind. It helps keep nosy techs from looking too closely when one of us needs a blood test for whatever reason."

Well, that was good news and, after everything else that had happened today, I'd take any good news I could get.

"Finn, I want you to understand that you're safe here. I've already sent word to the rest of the clan to be on the lookout for the trackers. They're to report to me the moment those bastards are found."

"Thank you." It didn't seem enough, but it was all I could say.

"Two of our people went by your apartment. Unfortunately, the trackers made it there first. They trashed the place. Your roommate already made a police report."

I closed my eyes and fought for calm. At least Dana hadn't been hurt.

Had she?

"Dana?"

"She wasn't there when it happened."

Relieved, I dropped my head in my hands. I'd never have forgiven myself if anything happened to her, especially since it would have been my fault. I knew better than to risk a normal. But I'd hoped Jennings had finally given up looking for me. I'd been a fool and someone I cared about could have died because of it.

"She's really all right?" I looked up, praying he'd told the truth.

"She is. Your apartment, especially your room, was pretty much trashed."

That didn't surprise me. Not that it made it hurt any less. I didn't have much. I'd been living on the run too long to have many personal belongings. But there had been a few things, things of my parents, as well as a few photos. If those were gone. . . .

"In a day or two, I'll take you so you can see what can be salvaged. In the meantime, I have teams watching the place in case the trackers return. I promise we won't let anything happen to your roommate," Matt continued. "We'll discuss the best way to do that later. Right now, I'd like to introduce you to my inner circle. If you ever need anything and I'm not available, they'll help you."

"I'd like to ask a question first, Matt," a small brunette asked from where she sat cross-legged on the floor across from us.

"Sharon's my younger sister. Don't call her little unless you want a fight on your hands. She's proof that toughness can come in small packages." He grinned at his sister and, when she stuck her tongue out at him, I couldn't help it. I laughed. Their sibling interplay was just what I needed.

"Matt forgets that I can out-fight most everyone here, shifted or not." She paused and studied me, her head cocked to one side, just as her brother's had been earlier when he'd studied me sitting at the kitchen table. "He's told us how he saved you from the trackers and Uncle Stefan explained about the Taser barbs and knife they used on you. What we don't know is why you're in Fort Worth or why they're after you."

I looked at her brother and he gave a little shrug. "It wasn't my tale to tell."

And what would he think when—if—he ever learned the whole tale?

"I'll give you the short version. I grew up as part of the Northern California clan. My parents were the Alphas of first our pride and then the clan. When I was fifteen, they were killed. The new Alpha, Michael Jennings, didn't want the cops involved in what happened any more than was absolutely necessary. He said he was afraid that if they looked too closely, they'd learn about our kind. So, when the preliminary report of double suicide came out, he pressed the clan to accept it and let the normals close the book on the case.

"I knew better. I knew neither of my parents would have killed themselves. They were both healthy and believed our numbers too few to diminish them with unnecessary deaths. I tried pressing the issue. But I was just a kid to most of the other clan members, even to the members of my home pride.

"Then Jennings decided he needed to secure his place as Alpha. He tried to claim me as his mate. He didn't give a damn that I was still grieving, nor did he care that I had absolutely no desire to be his mate. He was *the* Alpha and, according to him, it was my duty to submit. He wouldn't listen when cooler heads in the clan reminded him I was not yet of legal age either by normal law or by clan law. All he cared about was the fact I was the only child of the previous clan leaders.

"I won't go into all the details right now." I couldn't. I wasn't ready to trust Matt and the others with everything that happened. "Let's just say it got bad enough that I packed a few things and ran. I figured he'd come after me and he did, or rather he sent trackers after me. They've come close over the years to capturing me, but never as close as today. If Matt hadn't turned up when he did, I'd be sedated, secured and on my way back to Northern California."

To a fate much worse than death, but I didn't want to think about that just then.

Sharon nodded, her expression hard. "You're an alpha. Why haven't you returned to claim leadership for yourself?"

I didn't answer right away. For one thing, I wasn't sure how to respond. Would any of them understand that I hadn't realized I was an alpha? I'd been on the run for so long, isolated from pack and pride all that time. Since leaving California, my main goal had been to steer clear of others of our kind. So I'd had no one to compare myself with. To me, I was still that young shapeshifter, only a few years into my shifting, who fled her clan.

To my surprise, Matt answered for me. "Shar, she's been running all this time, trying to stay off Jennings' radar. I'm betting she hasn't been around another of our kind in anything except passing since she left home." When he looked at me for confirmation, I nodded. "You should have seen the look on her face when I asked why a female alpha was on her own and not part of a pride and clan. She looked like I'd hit her with a two-by-four."

"He's right. Until that moment, I'd never even considered I might be an alpha. I've spent all these years doing my best to hide what I am. Guess I did such a good job that I hid it even from me. I still haven't wrapped my head around it."

And it was something I'd have to think about. If I really was an alpha, I could go back and challenge Jennings. Unfortunately, there was another disadvantage of being on my own so long besides not realizing how strong I was: I hadn't been able to shift regularly. Nor had I kept in fighting trim, especially not in my shifted form. If I were to show up and challenge that bastard now, I'd lose and then I'd be exactly where he wanted me, a member of his clan and subject to his whim.

"So, what are you going to do?" a slender man with thinning blond hair asked.

"Rico," Matt said, a hint of censure in his voice.

"Sorry. I'm Rico Garces." He blushed slightly.

I inclined my head slightly in response. "I'll be honest. I don't know what I'm going to do. In the past, when I felt the trackers getting close, I simply packed up and went on the run again. This is the first time in a very long while that they've gotten this close to me. Part of me wants to run as far and as fast as I can from here. But another part, the sane part, wants to accept your clan leader's offer of protection, at least until I know more, not only about how they found me but also what they did to make the Taser and knife hurt me like they did."

"I have one question," Stefan said softly from his place on the sofa to my right. "How did you happen to be there when all this was going down, Matt?"

That was something I'd like to know as well. I twisted slightly in my chair so I could watch him.

"Sheer luck. I was leaving the office and had just gotten to my car when I scented a shapeshifter I wasn't familiar with. It was followed almost instantly by fear and then anger. I figured we had a rogue in the area hunting a normal. The last thing I expected was to find a tracker, much less three of them, hunting a female alpha.

"Anyway, I went tearing through the garage, hoping I got there in time to prevent a slaughter. When I saw Finn here trying to get away, all I knew was I had to make sure those bastards didn't get their hands on her. It didn't dawn on me who she was, or what those bastards were, until we were well away from that parking garage."

"Thank God you were there," was all I could say.

"I'd say thank God you didn't hesitate when I told you to get into my car."

"So, what do we do now?" the last of his advisors wanted to know.

I'd nearly forgotten about him. He was almost as small as Stefan but, where the doctor appeared small and non-descript, he looked like he could go ten rounds with any of us and win. There was something about him, something dangerous. It was as if he barely had his animal form under control. I'd known people like that growing up. They'd often served as my parents' enforcers in pride and clan. They reminded me of the berserkers of legend. Always ready for a fight and, when angered, hard to control. But they had been loyal almost to a fault and they had been the first to leave the clan after Michael Jennings took over.

"Daniel Gillespie, my right hand," Matt supplied.

"Your enforcer, unless I miss my guess." Let them see I knew the dynamics of a strong clan.

"Yes," Gillespie confirmed. "I met your parents several times. You have the look of your mother."

I swallowed hard. "Thank you."

"But you do present a problem for the clan."

"That's enough, Danny!" Matt snapped.

"No. He's right. I do present a problem. If I stay here and accept your offer of protection, I put you in direct conflict with Jennings. We all know that."

"I'm already in direct conflict with him," Matt said simply. "He sent people into my territory without asking permission or giving me warning. If he wants trouble, he'll find it." He pushed out of his chair and paced the length of the room before coming back to stand next to me. "Damn it, he violated our territory. Worse, he's been hunting her, an alpha female, and lying to the other clans about why. I will not turn her over to him, nor will I force her to go on the run again."

"Matt, they're right to ask these questions. That's why you have them as your advisors." I waited until he nodded, some of the tension leaving his expression. "None of you have any reason to trust me. All I do is give you my word that I didn't mean to bring trouble to your clan. I never wanted trouble with Jennings. I simply didn't want to be forced to be his mate. That's just as true today as it was so long ago."

"As far as I'm concerned, you're one of us, Finn." Sharon got to her feet and moved to stand to my left, opposite her brother. "We've heard some of the stories coming from the Northern California clan and none of us have liked them. If Matt hadn't offered you shelter, I would have."

"As would I," Stefan said.

"Then it's settled." Matt looked at his sister and uncle, his expression reflecting a gratitude I shared. "Danny, make sure there's extra security around the house and at Finn's apartment. Use your contacts with the cops to keep an eye on the airports. I want to know where the trackers are. Hell, I want the trackers."

"Understood." Gillespie got to his feet and moved to stand before me. "Despite what you might think, I am glad you're here. Your parents were good to me back then. I was just starting college and they gave me a place I could go to if I needed it. I'm glad to have the chance to repay their kindness by helping their daughter now."

"Thank you. My folks were good people. I only hope I do them proud one day." Tears burned my eyes and I blinked them back.

"I'd say you already have, ma'am." He gave a nod and, a moment later, he was gone.

"Matt, let me know if you need anything," Garces said as he stood. "I'll touch base with my contacts and see if they can tell me anything."

"Thanks, Rico."

"You aren't getting rid of me that easily," Sharon commented once Garces and Stefan had left. "You're going to need some clothes, Finn. I'll pick some up for you."

"Thanks." Just then, that sounded better than almost anything. I really couldn't go around in a robe until Matt decided it was safe for me to go to my apartment.

"I'll be back in a couple of hours. Matt, make sure she gets some rest."

Rest? I wasn't sure I'd be able to rest until I knew for certain the trackers were far away from here.

CHAPTER FOUR

I was up before the birds, literally. Of course, that's not hard to do when you don't sleep. It didn't matter I was exhausted, both mentally and physically. Nor did it matter I knew I needed rest to allow my body to finish healing. Whatever the trackers had tainted their weapons with had slowed the natural healing process. There were still moments when I moved wrong and pain reminded me of what almost happened the day before. It also reminded me how much I had come to rely on the rapid healing shapeshifters enjoyed.

None of which helped improve my temper.

But that wasn't why I was up at this ungodly hour. Well, not entirely at least. I'd spent much of the night thinking about what had happened—and what could have happened had Matt not shown up when he did. I hadn't been exaggerating when I told Sharon that I'd have been sedated and secured—read bound and gagged—and on my way back to Northern California if the trackers had gotten their hands on me. The fact they'd risked the tainted weapons spoke volumes about how desperate Jennings had become.

That worried me because it didn't make any sense. Jennings should have secured his hold on the clan by now. So why did he feel like he still needed me? Surely, he'd already taken a mate, possibly even more than one. Clan leaders were expected to mate, to help propagate the clan. They didn't have to take a mate from within the clan, nor did they even have to mate with a shapeshifter. Our kind figured out long ago that we were the result of some sort of genetic mutation or recessive gene. We were born, not made. It wasn't like the movies where a bite or scratch from one of us would create a new shifter.

And that brought me back to Jennings. If he had taken a mate, why did he need me? Was he continuing the hunt because I'd hurt his pride when I ran? I'd known even then he was one to hold a grudge. But to hold it this long seemed impossible, even for him.

Of course, I had done more than hurt his pride. I'd used teeth and claws. I'd drawn more than a little blood to keep him off me that terrible day. Unless I missed my guess, he saw at least some of the scars I'd left him with every time he looked in the mirror. That might explain why he hadn't given up.

Of course, the explanation could be as simple as he'd figured out I was an alpha. If so, he'd be a fool if he didn't consider the possibility that I might come back and challenge him for the clan leadership. It didn't matter it made about as much sense as thinking I'd willingly return to be his mate. But if I hadn't known I was an alpha until Matt pointed it out, how could he? None of the previous trackers had gotten close enough to sense it. Hell, I'd done a very good job making sure no one like us ever got that close to me.

Now, as I stared out the bedroom window, watching the first rays of sun touching the sky, I was no closer to the answers than I had been since finding myself trapped in the parking garage. But I had a plan, or at least the first glimmer of one. Whether or not it worked depended on several things, not the least of which was Matt.

Matt.

Just the thought of him had my panther stirring. I couldn't deny the attraction I felt for the clan leader. Every time he came within ten feet of me last night, my pulse quickened and it had been all I could do to keep from reaching for him. It wasn't exactly that I wanted to throw him down on the floor and make love to him, although I'm not sure I'd have objected if he'd suggested it. There had been a need, that was the only way to describe it, to touch him, to be in contact with him. The fact my panther responded as well told me it was more than mere physical attraction. If that had been all, it wouldn't have bothered me on so many different levels, not all of them bad.

For the record, I am a normal, healthy young woman. Even though I've been on the run for years and have done my best not to form attachments, I haven't been celibate. I've been attracted to men before but never like this. Never had my panther responded to anyone on this level and that frightened me a little.

Okay, it frightened me a lot.

But it also helped me form a plan. Or the start of a plan. Hopefully one that would finally get Jennings to leave me alone.

But only if I managed to screw up enough courage to talk to Matt first.

One thing was sure. Nothing would be accomplished by staying hidden in the bedroom.

Ten minutes later, freshly showered and wrapped in the robe Stefan had given me the day before, I made my way to the kitchen. Early as it was, there could be no mistaking the aroma of freshly brewed coffee. Thank God. The world would look a whole lot better after I'd had at least a mug to kick-start my system.

Sharon sat at the table, hands wrapped around a mug. She looked about as perky as I felt. Dressed in a faded pair of black sweat pants and a tank top, hair mussed, there could be no doubt she was as much a night owl as I was. Most of our kind were. Mornings were an anathema we had to live with, but we didn't have to like them.

"Morning." I moved to the cabinets and opened one after another in search of a mug. Hell, I'd settle for a glass, even a bowl, anything that would hold coffee. Fortunately, I found a mug first.

"Morning." Sharon looked up, pushing back a lock of hair that had fallen across her brow. "You look better, tired but better."

"Thanks." I slid onto the chair opposite her. "I didn't expect to find you here this morning."

Smooth, Finn.

Sharon smiled. "Matt asked me to stay. He had an early morning conference call and wanted to meet with Danny beforehand."

Concern flared. "Has something else happened?"

"No. He's just covering all the bases. You'll learn that my big brother takes his duties as Alpha very seriously." She studied me as she took a sip of coffee. Then she reached out, her right hand pushing the left sleeve of my robe up past my elbow. "Finn?"

I didn't need her to voice her unspoken question. Not when she laid her hand, palm up, next to mine. There, on the inside of her forearm, was the tattoo of a mountain lion. Most people seeing it would only see a beautiful tattoo, something that truly rated the title "body art". But I saw the clan markings in the background. The totem and iconography marked her as a member of the Fort Worth pride and North Texas clan. Every member of the clan would have a tattoo with similar markings. It might not be as large, and it might not have the same animal, but the totem and iconography would be there, either on the forearm, bicep or shoulder.

"I left the clan before I received my markings. My parents hadn't encouraged me to take on my markings. They wanted me free to decide if I would stay with the clan when I reached my majority or go to another. After I ran away, there was no clan or pride I could claim."

Sharon's hand closed over mine. Sympathy reflected in her eyes. "Damn it, Finn, you've been alone too long."

I swallowed hard against the sudden lump in my throat. Maybe she was right. But I'd had no choice. Young as I'd been, I'd known I had to get away from Jennings. More than just my virginity rest on it. Fear and instinct sent me running from him just as instinct now had me considering turning to Sharon, her brother and the rest of their clan for help.

"Yeah." I couldn't say anything else. So I lifted my mug and sipped, hoping she'd let the subject drop, at least for a bit.

"Uncle Stefan will be over later to look at you," she said a few minutes later. "He wants to make sure you're healing now that the barbs are out and the knife wound cleansed."

"I am," I said before she could ask. "There's still some pain and the wounds haven't healed as much as they should have, but they are healing. But I would appreciate him taking a look."

"Matt said to tell you he'll be home by lunch."

I nodded, hoping she didn't notice the way my pulse quickened at the sound of her brother's name. Damn, this just wasn't normal.

"I hate to ask, but did you manage to find me some clothes? I don't feel right wearing nothing but this robe."

"God, I'm an idiot!"

I tried not to laugh as she smacked her forehead with the heel of her hand, just like the actors used to do in that old juice commercial.

"I've got some jeans and stuff for you. It's in my room. Let me have another cup of coffee and then I'll show you."

The next several hours were surprisingly busy. After more coffee and a breakfast I hadn't realized I was hungry for, Sharon and I worked side by side to clean the kitchen. Then, after assuring me she hadn't forgotten her promise, she set about putting together a large pot of stew. As she worked, she kept up a running commentary, not only about what she was doing but about local events, the clan, even her job as a teacher at a nearby high school.

Once the stew was on, she led me through the house to the bedroom she used whenever she stayed over. According to her, that happened on a regular basis. Matt was the epitome of the over-protective big brother. He didn't like her driving by herself when it was late, and he wouldn't let her drive if she'd been drinking. She'd threatened to move in with him after one such incident. He'd surprised her by asking when she wanted help closing out her apartment.

Listening to her, I was reminded again of all I'd lost with my parents' deaths. Family, friends, pride and clan. Jennings had torn it from me.

Damn him.

"God, I'm sorry!" Before I knew what she was about to do, Sharon threw her arms around me. "I'm such an idiot."

"No, you're not." I smiled down at her. I'd not had a best friend as an adult. Dana came close, but I'd kept her at a distance in an attempt to protect her. It wouldn't be difficult to let Sharon fill the job. "Let's just say the last day has made me think about a lot of things I've missed over the years."

She studied me for a moment and, apparently satisfied, nodded. Then she turned to the closet and pulled out an assortment of jeans, tee shirts, shirts and shorts for me to try on. Watching her, all I could do was shake my head. I'd asked for a change of clothes, something to hold me over until Matt decided it was safe for me to either return to my apartment or go shopping. Instead of a pair of jeans and a couple of tops, Sharon presented me with more clothes than I owned.

I blinked back tears before she could turn and see them. Damn it, I had to get control of myself.

"What'd you do? Blow your entire credit line?" I reached beyond her to finger a blouse that was, indeed, silk.

"Nah." She gave me a cheeky grin. "I blew my brother's. It's much more fun to spend his money."

I didn't know whether to laugh or sigh. Laughter won. She was right. It was more fun to spend someone else's money, especially if you had permission to. But it did put me even further in debt to Matt and that was a feeling I wasn't used to. I wasn't sure I liked it. Not that I had much choice just then.

In the end, I managed to convince Sharon that I didn't need all the clothes. I chose two pairs of jeans and a pair of shorts, along with several tanks and tees—and, yes, the silk shirt. The rest were to go back. She pouted a little, but I could see she approved. Interesting. Had this been a test to see what sort of person I was? If so, I approved. She had not only her brother's best interest but the best interest of the clan at heart.

I liked her more and more with each minute that passed.

Several hours later, I leaned against the bedroom door and sighed. It was only a little after noon and yet I felt like I'd been through a whirlwind. In a way, I had. Between getting a crash course in the clan and local pride from Sharon and being thoroughly examined by Stefan, I hadn't had time to do much more than breathe. Maybe it was better that way. It kept me from thinking too much about what happened the day before. It had also kept me from obsessing about what I was going to do about it.

And that seemed to have helped because my subconscious had reached a decision. Now all I had to do was screw up enough courage to discuss it with Matt.

But did I want to wait until we were alone to do it? Maybe I should. I had a feeling Sharon would agree with what I planned. Whether or not that was a good thing, I didn't know. It did make me feel better, however.

Mind made up, I drew a deep breath, held it for a slow count to five and then blew it out. If I was going to do this, I might as well get it over with.

I found Matt in the den. He sat in the over-stuffed chair from the night before. In his right hand, he held a battered paperback. Then, as if feeling my eyes on him, he looked up. A slow smile touched his lips and my pulse quickened. Damn, no man should have the ability to turn my knees to jelly just by looking at me.

"I thought you might be resting," he said as he put his book to one side.

"No." I shook my head and moved to sit on the couch. I needed some distance between us so I could think. Had I been away from our kind so long that just being in the presence of an alpha male turned me into a horny teenager?

"You look like you've got something on your mind."

I chewed my lower lip and then nodded. "I do. I hope you'll hear me out and not think I've lost my mind."

"Sounds serious." He leaned forward, elbows on knees and waited. "It is."

Where had my resolve gone? I'd started this. Now I needed to finish it. Instead, I wanted to slink back to my room and hide. God, when had I turned into a horny, scared teenager?

"Matt, I'll never be able to thank you for what you did yesterday." I held up my hand when he opened his mouth to interrupt. "Please, let me just say this. Then you can tell me to be on my way or you can call the men with the white coats to come for me." Neither would surprise me. What I was about to do was crazy.

I stood and took a step toward him. Then I dropped to my hands and knees. If I was going to do this, I'd do it right. I crawled to him, noting the way his eyes widened before narrowing in concern. But I didn't look down. Nor did I bow my head. My posture recognized him as an alpha but did not grant him dominance over me. It was the posture of equal to equal, at least among our people.

"Matt, you named me alpha. The others of your clan I've met confirmed it. You've graciously offered me sanctuary and protection. I appreciate it but that would open you to retribution—or worse— from Jennings, his clan and any allies they might have. I can't ask you to do that and receive nothing in return.

"As your sister reminded me this morning, I am not formally a member of any clan. I had not been marked as a member of the Northern California clan before I left, and I've not taken the markings of any other pride or clan since then." I pulled my tee shirt over my head and tossed it to one side. Clad in a sports bra and jeans, my lack of a clan tattoo couldn't be hidden.

Matt's expression tightened. At the same time, I heard a footfall behind me. Sharon's soft gasp followed almost instantly after it. But neither she nor Matt said anything. This was my show and I had to finish it.

"Clan leader, I come to you with a proposition. One you can freely refuse. If you do, I ask only that you give me forty-eight hours before you report my presence in your territory to Jennings." I paused again and watched as his hands tightened into fists on his knees. His cat was so close to the surface I could almost see it. My panther responded, and I knew he'd realize it. Best get this done quickly, before I lost control—or my nerve.

"I petition for acceptance as a member of your pride and of your clan. I offer myself to you as mate, female alpha to your male. I can't deny the fact your cat calls to mine. If you will have me, I will stand by you. I will protect the clan and the pride. I will be your right hand. My arm will be yours and my life willingly sacrificed for the good of our people."

Where the words came from, I don't know. They seemed right. Maybe I'd heard my mother say them to my father when I was a child. Or maybe it was something they had taught me, forgotten in the pain of their deaths. Whatever the explanation, all that mattered was Matt's response.

He said nothing. Instead, he dropped to his knees before me. His hands ripped open his shirt, buttons flying. As he tossed it to one side, I couldn't hold back my gasp. It is rare to find one of our kind out of shape. But he'd missed his calling. Designers would fall over themselves to have him modeling their clothes—especially if he'd do it shirtless.

He reached out and lifted me to my knees. His right hand cupped my cheek and then dropped to my shoulder. I held my breath —I think I held my breath—waiting.

"Finn, you're offering me something I dearly want to accept, but I don't want you to feel you're being forced into a position similar to the one you fled." He spoke softly, and I could tell how much the words cost him. He wanted to say yes. Was it possible he'd felt the same pull to me that I had to him?

Once again, I wished my parents hadn't been taken from me so soon. There was so much about our people and our ways I didn't know.

"Matt, I want this." I glanced over my shoulder. A slight smile touched my lips to see Sharon still in the doorway, turning purple because she didn't dare breathe. Seeing me watching her, she blew out her breath and gulped in another. "I understand if you don't, if you think this would be bad for your clan. I'll understand if there are conditions you want to put on our relationship. As long as they're reasonable, I'll agree."

I reached for his hands, holding them tightly. "I can't explain what I feel. I don't have the words and I don't understand it. All I can tell you is that I have wanted you since the moment my brain started working after I took that Taser jolt. Every time you've come close, my cat's responded and I've had to fight the impulse to reach for you. It's more than lust. It is as if some part of me recognized you and knows you are a part of me. I'm rambling, but I don't know how else to explain it."

He gave my hands a squeeze and spoke to his sister without ever taking his eyes from mine. "Shar, call CJ. Tell her to bring her kit and get over here just as soon as she can."

"CJ?" I repeated.

"Finn, I understand. I've felt it too." He freed one hand and once more reached out to cup my cheek. I leaned into it, nuzzling against his palm. If I'd been shifted, I'd have been purring. "I accept you as a member of pride and clan. You honor me by becoming my mate. I will stand with you and by you. Together we are stronger than apart." His lips lightly brushed mine. "We will be so good together."

We most certainly would.

"But CJ?" I repeated.

"The clan's tattoo artist." He grinned and pulled me into a bear hug. Then we stood, his arm around me. "Sharon, don't just stand there looking like someone hit you with a two-by-four. Call CJ. It's time our new alpha was properly marked.

"As for you, Finn, you need to decide what you want her to do and where." Now he held me at arm's length, studying me, a funny smile playing at the corners of his mouth. "We'll inform the inner circle tonight and go through the ritual with the clan this weekend. If you approve, of course."

I swallowed hard and then nodded. Even though it had been my idea, I hadn't expected him to agree so quickly. Still, if it meant we got to satisfy at least one of my appetites soon, I'd be more than happy to do almost anything.

"But I promise we won't be waiting until the weekend to seal the deal, so to speak," he whispered, as if he could read my thoughts.

Oh . . . my.

CHAPTER FIVE

W hich is how I came to be sitting at the kitchen table three hours later. I absently gnawed the top of my pencil as I studied the sketch before me. How could I explain to CJ—the purple-haired tattoo artist sitting next to me—much less Matt that I'd waited a lifetime for this image to become real? I'd seen it in my dreams since my first shift. Maybe something like this was normal for our kind. I'd never asked my parents about the dreams. Now it was too late. All I could do was hope these two understood.

At least CJ no longer looked at me with that patient "humor her" expression she'd worn when I first said I'd draw what I wanted her to do as my tattoo. I knew she thought she'd have to redo the image before making the stencil. I didn't even blame her. She didn't know me, so she didn't know one of my few real talents was art. Unfortunately, it's next to impossible to make a living as an artist, especially if you're on the run and likely to have to move without notice—or the chance to pack your belongings.

Even though part of me waited for the validation of my work that she could give, I was more worried about Matt's reaction. He'd recognize the markings on the totem in the background as those for his clan and pride. But there were others as well. Would he recognize them, and would he understand why it was so important for me to include them in the tattoo?

As if sensing my concern, his hands tightened on my shoulders where they had rested the entire time I sketched. A moment later, his lips brushed the top of my head. I waited, heart pounding, as he reached out to move the sketch so he could get a better look. His approval meant a great deal and I prayed he gave it—and soon.

"You are a woman of many talents, Finn," he said, admiration clear. "This is beautiful."

"Thanks. But at the risk of shattering any illusions you might have about me, this is my only real talent."

"Somehow I doubt that. I have a feeling you're selling yourself short." He pushed the sketch over to CJ. "I recognize our markings. I assume the dates are your parents' birthdays."

I nodded, emotion tightening my throat. God, even after all this time, I missed them so much.

"The other symbols on the totem, though, I'm not so sure about. I think I recognize the Oklahoma clan marking. I don't recognize the other." He didn't ask, but I could hear the unspoken question. "Nor do I see the mark of the Northern California clan."

I closed my eyes and drew a deep breath. I'd revealed more of myself to him in the last day than I had to anyone but my parents. So far, he'd been very supporting and understanding. Hopefully, that would continue.

"I'll never willingly bear the markings of the Northern California clan." If there was bitterness in my voice—and there was a lot of it—I didn't care. "The clan betrayed my parents and all our kind by not finding out what really happened the day they died. If they were killed by one of us, then their killer should face our judgment. If they were killed by a normal, we need to know why. It is possible our secret is no longer safe. You know what that could mean for all of us. Hell, Matt, if my parents really did kill themselves, there has to be a reason and we need to know that. There was no note and nothing in either of their histories to account for suicide actually happening.

"But there's another reason why I'll never bear the clan's marking. When Jennings tried to claim me as his mate, only a few members of the clan—my aunt and uncle and a half a dozen others—spoke against it. There were mumblings from others, but only they stood by me and said what he planned was wrong."

Tears burned my eyes as I remembered the scene. Jennings had denounced them as working against the best interest of the clan. He'd reminded the others that I'd be sixteen in a matter of months, close enough to my majority as far as he was concerned to be claimed. I was, he said, the daughter of the previous clan leaders, so I must understand the necessity of what he planned.

What I'd understood was that he took what he wanted without concern for the consequences. He felt his position as clan leader entitled him to do whatever he wanted, whether it violated our laws or not. As for violating the laws of the outside world, those obviously didn't exist in his mind.

When he banished Aunt Jane, Uncle Lou and the others from the clan, he'd shown he didn't care about anyone or anything except himself. It proved he would do whatever he wanted, whether it was good for pride and clan or not. And that, I knew, did not bode well for my future.

The night before they left, I'd listened in growing disbelief as Aunt Jane told me to run. I needed to get as far away from Jennings and the rest of the clan as possible and I needed to do it now, before Jennings realized what I planned. I couldn't go back to the house I'd shared with my parents. If there was anything there I wanted, Aunt Jane promised to make sure it found its way to me somehow, probably through friends and family in other clans. But I had to go underground. I couldn't go to anyone Jennings knew was associated with our family. She knew she was setting me on a lonely, difficult path but she feared it was the only way I'd survive.

I hadn't questioned her. How could I when she was telling me something I'd already figured out? So, over the next hour we established ways for me to contact my grandparents and others close to the family without giving away my location. Hopefully, it would be enough to keep me safely out of Jennings' hands. Then Aunt Jane hugged me, pressed a wad of cash into my hands and told me to go. If God was willing, I'd soon be able to come home, wherever that might be.

Neither of us expected that journey to last as many years as it had.

And I was home. I'd known it—well, my panther had—the moment I saw Matt. Now, if he understood . . . .

"Maybe I should excuse myself." CJ looked uncomfortable, kind of like a kid walking in on her parents in the middle of a very serious discussion.

"No, please. You're a member of Matt's pride as well as of the clan, so you need to know. Besides, I want you to witness something. That way you can confirm the validity of my claim of lineage should anyone question it."

"Finn?" Matt's concern was clear when I stood and moved to the counter, reaching for his cell phone.

"Matt, the totem represents my bloodline. My parents may have been clan leaders for the Northern California clan, but neither originated there. My father grew up in Wichita. His family has been in Kansas, mainly in the Dodge City and Wichita areas, since shortly after the Civil War. They originally came from Pennsylvania. Their ancestors came from Ireland and Germany for the most part.

"My mother was from Tulsa. Her family has been there for generations. Her maternal line includes survivors of the Trail of Tears. I have Cherokee and Seminole blood through her, as well as more Irish."

I could have named each of my relatives going back at least five generations. Most of our kind can. Because there are so few of us, relatively speaking, bloodlines often become important to make sure we aren't mating with someone too closely related. I didn't

name them though. I had something else in mind, something important if I really was going to be Matt's mate and a leader in pride
and clan.

I blew out a breath and steeled myself. This was the moment of
truth. Or at least one of them.

"Matt, I assume you know how to contact the head of the Oklahoma clan?" It really wasn't much of a question. Still, I waited until
he nodded. "Please call her. When you are sure you're talking to
Irene Walkinghorse, let me have the phone."

For a moment, he simply looked at me, a thousand questions
reflected in his eyes. Then he looked down at the cell phone I held
out to him. He took it and I waited as he programmed in a number.
Time slowed as we waited. How many times the other end of the call
rang before it was answered, I don't know. It felt like a lifetime. Then,
finally, he identified himself and confirmed he was, in fact, talking
with Irene Walkinghorse. He asked her to hold on a moment and
handed me the phone.

"It's me," I said simply. My grandmother gasped slightly before
regaining control. "Shenandoah." That was our code word I was safe.

"Fort Worth?" she asked simply.

"Yes. I need you to confirm my identity and bloodline to the clan
leader. He's offered me a place here and I want to accept. But I want
him to know exactly who I am before we make it official."

"Jennings?" She spat the name like an epitaph.

"Is part of the reason. I'll explain later, I promise. Please answer
any of Matt's questions and he has my permission to explain why he's
asking." I looked at him and he nodded, understanding easing his
concerned expression.

"All right."

I could tell we'd be having a long talk about all this, but it had to
wait. Something told me I needed to secure my position here as
quickly as possible. Once Jennings learned how close his trackers had
come to capturing me, he wouldn't give up. He hated losing and he'd
already proven he didn't care about the sanctity of clan territory.

That meant he'd do just about anything if he thought he could get me back.

I handed the cell phone back to Matt. Nerves on edge, stomach churning, I walked out of the kitchen. Unless I was badly mistaken, the call would take some time. He might be as drawn to me as I was to him, but he was still clan leader. He'd not forget his responsibilities simply because our cats wanted us together. That meant he'd quiz my grandmother as much as possible, confirming my bloodline, my early training and what little she could tell him about my years after fleeing California.

None of which would match her questions. Since I had no desire to listen in and I couldn't leave the house—no, I wouldn't leave the house. Matt would worry and there was no guarantee the trackers, or their human agents, weren't watching. So I returned to the guest bedroom and its adjoining half-bath. At the moment, nothing sounded better than standing under the shower and letting the hot water ease muscles suddenly tight with worry.

The water was beginning to cool when a slight draft warned me I was no longer alone. Someone was in the bathroom. Matt's scent reached me and a moment later the shower door opened. I didn't turn. I didn't even lift my head. Instead I let the water cascade down on me and waited, smiling slightly as hands found my shoulders and then made their way to my waist and pulled me close.

"You keep surprising me, Finn," he said softly. I moaned as his hands cupped my breasts. "If I had any doubts about our being mates —and I didn't—I most certainly don't now."

I didn't answer. I couldn't. Not with his hands playing with my breasts, his mouth moving to the crook of my neck. Part of me, one very small and quiet part, told me this wasn't me. I didn't have sex in the shower with a man I barely knew. I certainly didn't have shower sex when others were in the house. But the rest of me didn't care. Nothing mattered beyond what Matt was doing with his hands and mouth. I'd never felt so alive before.

He nipped and licked and sucked and all rational thought left me. I tried to turn. I wanted to face him, to touch him as he touched me. But I couldn't. He held me where I was. One hand cupped my right breast and the other found its way between my legs.

His fingers teased. His lips drove me wild. My hands braced against the tile, my head thrown back, my mouth open. The shower beat down on me and my heart beat in rhythm with it.

"Matt."

It was barely more than a whisper. He spun me to face him, his hands closing around my waist. My hands clasped behind his neck and my mouth found his. Finally. I'd needed this for what seemed like my whole life. Nothing existed before this moment and I'm not sure anything would after. I didn't care. Nothing else mattered except I was here, being loved by the man who was my mate, my other half.

"In me," I gasped, every nerve as alive as it had been the day he rescued me. Except this time, no Taser was involved. This was so different, so right. "I need you in me."

"Not yet."

He smiled, and I groaned as his finger plunged into me. I ground against his hand, desperate for release. But no. Not this way. I'd come for him gladly, but I wanted this first time to be ours—both of us giving the other satisfaction and release.

As if sensing my thoughts, not that coherent thought was possible just then, he withdrew his finger. My cat, so close to the surface now, protested. My hands dug into his shoulders and I nipped at his lower lip. His hands closed about my waist and we moved as one. He lifted. My legs wrapped about him. Finally.

Finally!

With the water beating down on us, we became one. Never had it been like this. I held him close, slowing the rhythm, trying to draw it out. This was too wonderful, too perfect to end quickly. But his need was as desperate as mine. I threw my head back and screamed, primal and triumphant.

Mine, all mine.

When conscious thought returned, I realized we were standing, sort of. What we were really doing was holding one another up against the far wall of the shower, cold water beating down on us. Our arms were wrapped around one another. In the back of my mind, my panther was purring in satisfaction. Well, if she thought the opening act was good, wait until she got a look at what I planned now.

Matt was about to learn he wasn't the only one who could get someone all hot and bothered.

"God, Finn, you're going to kill me," he groaned as I dropped to my knees in front of him.

I smiled and took him into my mouth, teasing with tongue and breath. His groan turned to a moan and I felt him stiffen. His hands fisted in my hair. I glanced up, pleased to see his head thrown back much as I imagined mine had been not that long ago, his mouth open. His chest rose and fell with quick breaths. I have to admit, there are a number of benefits to being a shapeshifter. Our ability to recover more rapidly than normals was definitely at the top of the list, especially now.

Grinning around his erection, I ran my tongue over the tip of his penis and then pulled away. Before he could protest, I guided him down to the shower floor. A moment later, I straddled him. Now it was my turn. I guided his hands to my waist and leaned in to kiss him. This was just the beginning, a promise of what our life together could be like.

"The water's cold," he complained later.

"Yeah."

Muscles cramped, I knew better than to try to stand. Instead, I sat up just enough to be able to reach the faucet handle. A quick twist and the water stopped pounding down on us. Then I pushed open the shower door and crawled out. Yes, crawled. Yes, my panther was laughing at me. I told her to shut up and, using the sink, carefully pulled myself to my feet.

"I take it you had a good talk with my grandmother," I said a few moments later as Matt handed me a towel.

"Let's just say she wants to talk to you very soon." He looked at me and grinned. "In fact, she'll be here tomorrow, along with at least one other from her clan, to witness our announcement to the pride. Unless I miss my guess, she'll stay through the weekend and the clan announcement."

I shook my head, not at all surprised. Well, I was surprised Matt would be presenting me to the pride so soon. I'd figured he'd do it at the same time he presented me to the clan.

"I'm a little surprised she isn't already on her way."

"Well—"

Matt grinned again as he stepped into his jeans. A fresh wave of lust washed over me and I pushed it back. There would be plenty of time for that later. I'd make sure of it. But right now, I needed to know exactly why he grinned like a loon and what, if anything, I needed to know about tomorrow night.

"She said she'd be on the road by early evening, but that we aren't to expect her until morning."

Excitement to see her and actually not worry about being discovered filled me. Then it was gone, just as quickly as it had come. If she came here, if Jennings knew about it . . .

"Matt!"

"Hush, Finn. It's all right." He pulled me close. His embrace was comforting, his hands gentle. "We talked about how this might tip Jennings off. But you have to trust us. There is a very legitimate reason for her to be coming here, especially after yesterday. You see, I sent word to the surrounding clan leaders. It seems I'm worried, and more than a bit angry, to learn someone sent trackers into my territory without permission. No, I don't know who they were after. But, worried that it might signal trouble for neighboring clans, I felt it necessary to let those clan leaders I have the closest relationships with know." He grinned, a hint of devilment reflected in his eyes. Then he turned serious. "Most of them told me to be careful not to overreact. But they promised to keep a look out and let me know if they have any trouble. I've let it be known that Irene

Walkinghorse, on the other hand, is as worried as I am about what happened and wants to meet to see if, together, we might not find some answers."

I looked up at him. Gone was the devilment from a moment before. In its place, confidence shone in his eyes. With it was a determination that reassured me. I smiled and relaxed. He was right. That was the sort of explanation that would satisfy almost anyone who might wonder why my grandmother suddenly decided to make a trip to Fort Worth. It might even satisfy Jennings. I didn't really think so, but I was willing to hope.

"And tomorrow?" Nerves knotted my stomach.

"You'll be introduced to the pride as my mate." His hand stroked my cheek and he bent to brush his lips against mine. "Don't look so worried. You've met my inner circle already. More than that, you've won over my sister. The rest will be a piece of cake."

"I hope so."

God, how I hoped so.

"Now, let's get you properly marked as a member of the pride and clan and as my mate. Then CJ can add to my markings. I want no one to doubt or question your place at my side."

Knowing he was right, I nodded. Finally, hopefully, I had found a home, one safe from the demons of my past.

Six hours later, I stared at my reflection, a bemused expression on my face. I had to admit it. CJ was more than good. She was a master tattooist. She'd taken my sketch and brought it to life. I twisted slightly so I could see the entire image on my upper arm and shoulder. It marked me as more than just a member of the Fort Worth pride and the North Texas clan. I marked me as Matt's mate.

And it was a work of art.

One that, at the moment, felt like a thousand, or maybe a million, ants were biting me. Not exactly painful, but annoying as hell. But it was worth it, especially when I remembered how Matt had asked CJ to add to his tattoo. A second panther—smaller, of course, as females of our kind tend to be, and with my green eyes—and my birth date had been carefully worked into his tattoo. She'd promised to add his birth date to my own tat after I'd healed up some.

When I stepped out of the bathroom, a grin touched my lips. Leaning against the far wall, doing her best to look nonchalant, was Sharon. Despite her expression, I saw the excitement in her eyes and scented it in the air. Well, I guess I couldn't blame her. I was just relieved she so obviously approved not only of me joining the pride and clan but of me becoming her brother's mate as well.

Without a word, she grabbed my hand and pulled me into the den. As she did, I heard Matt and CJ talking in the kitchen. Another voice joined theirs, soft but definitely male. Curious, I lifted my head and breathed deeply. Gillespie. Hopefully his presence didn't mean trouble had already found us.

"Don't worry, Finn. He's just reporting in," Sharon reassured me before I could ask. She drew me under the light and then moved so she could get a good look at my tattoo. "Damn, CJ was right. This is beautiful. I don't think I've ever seen her do better and she said that's because of your drawing."

A blush warmed my face. It's silly, but that drawing had been so much a part of me for so long that it meant a lot to know someone else appreciated it as much as I did.

"She tried asking Matt to see if you'd let her have the drawing—I think she offered to tattoo all your children and grandchildren for free—but he simply smiled and said no one got to keep it but the two of you."

If possible, my blush deepened.

"Now, before we join the others, let me welcome you not only to pride and clan, but to the family. I saw how Matt was drawn to you the moment I got here yesterday. More importantly, he felt stronger, more in control than ever before. Let me tell you, that's saying something." She grinned, her affection for her brother clear. "As his sister, I want to see him happy. As a member of his pride and clan, I'm glad he's finally found a mate worthy of him, one who is strong enough to keep him from doing anything foolish."

"Sharon." How could I tell her I felt the same way about Matt? It still seemed odd to me. Maybe because she hadn't been apart from our kind like I had, she understood, where it still felt like an odd dream to me—or one of those sappy movies where the heroine and hero fall in love the moment their eyes lock. Except what I felt for Matt wasn't love. At least I didn't think so. That might come later. What I felt was a kind of completion, of being whole for the first time in my life.

Hell, what did I know? This was all so new to me. Maybe it was love.

"Sharon," I said again. "I meant what I said earlier. I feel complete with your brother. I know we belong together. Does being with him, being part of the clan and being his mate, help protect me from Michael? It does, and I won't deny it. But that isn't what matters. Not now. All that does is that I help protect and nurture the pride and clan, that I do what I can to make Matt happy."

"Well," she began, her head cocked to one side, a slight smile tugging at her lips. "There is one other thing you need to do."

"What?" Suddenly, I wasn't sure I wanted to know.

"Be my friend and, at least sometimes, make common cause with me against my brother." Now she grinned gaily. "After all, we do have to keep him humble."

Laughing, I draped an arm across her shoulders. Damn but I'd forgotten what it was like not to be alone.

CHAPTER SIX

The chirping of birds woke me. I swear, if anyone ever needed proof God has a warped sense of humor, all they'd have to do is consider how sadistic it is to create something so happy to greet the morning and then let it sing and chirp and who knows what outside the bedroom window of someone like me. I buried my head deeper into the pillow, wishing with all I was worth for the birds to go away. Unfortunately, they'd accomplished their dastardly mission. I was awake.

As I rolled onto my side, an arm reached across my waist, pulling me back. For a moment, panic flared. My heart thudded and my breath caught. The first thought my sleep-fogged brain formed was that Jennings had finally found me. But that couldn't be right. If he had, I'd never have willingly gone to bed with him and, since I wasn't bound in any way and the only aches I felt most definitely hadn't come from a beating, the only explanation for me being in bed with anyone was that I'd wanted to be.

Matt.

Memory of how he'd almost shyly escorted me into his bedroom the night before returned. Gone was the confident man who'd joined me in the shower that afternoon. That was probably a good thing because, once alone in the house with him, I'd turned tongue-tied and unsure of myself. I wanted him as much as ever, maybe even more. But now, for the first time, it was real. My days of running, God willing, were gone and I was home.

"Don't get up," Matt murmured, his breath warm against my neck.

"I have to." My bladder reminded me I had things needing to be taken care of now that I was awake. Even so, I rolled over and rested my head against his chest. His heart beat slowly, reassuringly beneath my cheek. "Be right back." I pressed my lips to the line of his jaw.

As I slid out of bed, he sighed and threw an arm over his eyes. When he growled as the birds once more started their morning song, I chuckled softly. For some reason, it thrilled me to know he was no more of a morning person that I was.

When I emerged from the bathroom a few minutes later, a pang of guilt stabbed at me, followed quickly by frustration. The bed was empty, and Matt was nowhere to be seen. So much for spending the morning in bed. Still, I should have realized he couldn't lounge around all day. He had taken most of yesterday off so he could be with me. It only made sense that he had to make up for it today.

I found him in the kitchen, putting on the coffee. Dressed in only a pair of jeans, his hair sleep-tousled, he still managed to look as appealing as he had the night before. Desire flared. But, just then, I needed coffee more than I needed him. Still, he might be a great accompaniment to coffee.

Smiling, I moved across the cool tile floor until I stood behind him. He chuckled softly as I slid my arms around his waist and leaned into him.

"Thank you."

He carefully turned, not quite breaking my hold on him as he did. Then he cupped my chin in one hand and tilted my head up so I looked into his incredible blue eyes. I didn't try to look away as he bent to gently kiss me. Who gives a damn about morning breath when you have someone like Matt to wake up to?

"For what?" His thumb gently rubbed my cheek.

"Coffee." I grinned when he cocked an eyebrow. "And yesterday and last night and everything." Tongue-tied again, I swallowed. I had to explain. "Matt, you've offered me a home, one I feel safe in. You didn't have to, and you sure didn't have to agree to my offer to be your mate. I know that could put you at odds with some of the others in the clan." Funny, after talking with Sharon, and even Gillespie, last night, I didn't worry about the pride.

"I want you to understand I didn't make the offer lightly. I will do everything I can to help you be a stronger leader and to help keep pride and clan safe. I don't know any other way to say it except this: you saved me, and I will always thank you for that."

For several long moments he looked at me. Then he took my hand and led me to the table. The way he held a chair out for me reminded me of how my mother used to tell me gentlemen should behave. I swallowed hard against the lump in my throat as memory and reality collided. He left me sitting there long enough to pour us each a mug of coffee. Then he was back, sitting next to me.

"Finn, we need to talk." He ran a hand over the tabletop and it dawned on me he was nervous. "I know you think, at least on some level, that I believe you made your offer only so I'd protect you from Jennings. But you're wrong.

"I will admit, when I first offered you protection, it was because I couldn't stand by and let any of our kind be hunted as you were. Even without knowing why the trackers were after you, I knew what they were doing was wrong. They'd violated my territory which was bad enough. Worse, they'd used a Taser and blade that had somehow been adapted to cause the most pain possible. If that's not enough, whatever the taint, it also slowed your ability to heal, prolonging your agony."

I shuddered and pushed my coffee back. Even the smell of it turned my stomach as realization of what could have happened if

Matt hadn't shown up when he did returned. He must have realized what I was thinking because he shifted slightly in his chair. Then he reached for me, pulling me onto his lap and wrapping his arms protectively around me.

"But things changed as my anger cooled. That's when I realized there was something about you that called to me. I couldn't believe you didn't know you were an alpha. It didn't make any sense but I didn't care. The only thing that mattered was that you were here." He paused and I waited, barely daring to breathe.

"It didn't make any sense. I've never felt that way before and never had my cat reacted to another like that."

I had to see him, to look into his eyes as he spoke. Carefully, I shifted until I straddled him and we were eye-to-eye.

"After Stefan treated you and you'd passed out, I told him what I'd been feeling. He's pretty much filled in for my father the last eight years or so, ever since my folks moved to Ireland for Dad's job. Anyway, Stefan listened, a funny smile on his face. Then he poured me a whiskey and congratulated me, telling me I'd finally found my mate. That's when I remembered my dad telling me a long time ago that, if I was very lucky, I'd one day find my life mate. Too often we don't. And here, out of the blue, you appeared, and my world suddenly seemed complete."

My hand trembled as I reached out to touch his cheek. The stubble of his beard tickled my palm. Then a distant memory of my mother telling me much the same thing came. Could this really be happening?

"So, I guess you're saying I'm stuck with you." I grinned and then squealed in protest as his fingers found the ticklish spots at my ribs.

Before it could turn into full-fledged horseplay, the doorbell rang. I scrambled off Matt's lap, suddenly aware of the fact I wore nothing but the shirt he'd discarded the night before. Snatching my mug of coffee off the table, I hurried out of the kitchen. My life might have turned upside down—or right side up, depending on how you looked at it—but I wasn't ready to greet the world half-dressed. I'd leave that to Matt.

Five minutes later, dressed in jeans and a red tank top, my teeth and hair brushed, I made my way to the den. I'm not sure what I expected to find, but it certainly wasn't the sight that greeted me. Matt wasn't alone. A tall, thin man with long black hair pulled back in a braid stood near the door to the kitchen. To the casual observer, he might look relaxed. But I saw the tension in the way he stood, the alertness in his gaze.

Across the room, sitting in Matt's favorite chair, was a small, slender woman. Her salt and pepper hair was cut short and framed her angular face. The face had more wrinkles than the last time I'd seen her. But her green eyes were just as alert. What surprised me the most was the sense of power I felt. There was no question it emanated from her. Had it always been there and I just hadn't realized it? I certainly hadn't felt it the last time we'd been together.

God, had it really been five years since I'd last seen her? I swallowed hard, remembering that day. I'd been living in Boston, so sure Jennings would never find me there. After six weeks or so of always looking over my shoulder, I'd finally begun to hope I might actually be able to have a normal life—or at least as normal a life as one of our kind can. I'd even planned to go by the nearby community college to see about enrolling in some art classes.

I'd been a fool.

One morning I'd stopped by the coffee shop not a mile from my apartment. The barista greeted me with a smile. I inhaled the enticing aroma of freshly ground coffee beans and sighed in contentment. That was the best way to start the morning. Or it had been until I met Matt.

The world came to a screeching halt a few moments later when I turned from the counter, coffee cup in hand. Standing there, close enough to touch, was my grandmother. My cup slipped from fingers suddenly too numb to hold anything. The room spun around me. Fear washed over me. If she'd been able to find me, could Jennings be that far behind? Then, without a word, she reached out, steadying me before I could fall. A moment later, I found myself sitting at one of the small tables, watching as she slid onto the chair opposite me.

For more than an hour we talked. Or rather I talked. I asked questions and I despaired. Happenchance had brought us together. Just as easily it could have delivered me into Jennings' hands. A number of clan leaders were in town. I didn't know whether to laugh at the idea of a convention of shapeshifters or to cry because things could have gone so bad so easily.

When I left the coffee shop, I went straight to my apartment and packed up. Two hours later, I was on my way out of town. My life had once more been turned upside down and all because of Michael Jennings.

Now, seeing her sitting just a few feet away, all I could do was grin. Without conscious thought, I hurried across the room. I dropped to my knees in front of her and buried my face against her legs. Her hand gently stroked my hair. But she didn't rush me. She let the tears come. As sobs wracked me, she gently shifted positions so she could hold me. She whispered soft reassurances, a mixture of English, Irish and Cherokee, and I sobbed harder as memories of my mother doing the same thing washed over me.

"Finn?" Matt's worried voice broke through the pain and loneliness of all those years on the run. I choked back a sob and scrubbed my hands over my face.

"I'm okay." I sniffled, ruining any chance of him believing me. "It's just reaction." I reached for my grandmother's hand, clinging to it. Then, seeing how Matt still looked at me in concern, I reached for his hand with my free one. Anchored between the two of them, I felt my emotional equilibrium returning.

"You look good, child, if a bit splotchy."

There was just enough good-natured mockery in my grandmother's voice that I laughed.

"Thanks—I think." I gave Matt's hand a reassuring squeeze and let go. Hopefully, he'd understand. "I can't tell you how glad I am to see you, Grandma."

"And you, child." She dashed away her own tears. "You've grown in a number of ways since Boston."

"Oh?"

Yep, that's me: the great conversationalist.

"Yes, *oh*." She grinned, pride shining through. "When did you realize you're an alpha?"

"Honestly?"

She nodded.

"Day before yesterday when Matt asked why a female alpha was on her own and being hunted by trackers."

Grandma's sharp intake of breath spoke volumes as did the way her grip on my hand tightened.

"You've been alone far too long, child, and that is something Michael Jennings will pay for. But not today. Today is for us."

"You'll get no argument from me." I just hoped to be there, and taking part, the day Jennings finally atoned for all he had taken from me. "Right now, nothing matters but the fact you're here and it isn't to tell me to run again."

"If the look on your man's face is any clue, you'll never have to run again." Humor and approval colored her voice.

"My man?"

"Dear heart, even if he hadn't told me he wanted you as his mate, there could be no mistaking it. The moment you entered the room, his cat leapt so close to the surface I could see it." She smiled, and I relaxed a little. Unless I was greatly mistaken, she approved of this odd relationship Matt and I found ourselves in.

"Grandma, I can't explain it any other way than to say he completes me. I don't understand it. I don't have to. It's enough to know that it is right."

She nodded and motioned for me to help her up. I did and watched, holding my breath, as she moved to where Matt stood. He had to be at least five inches taller than she was but there was no question who controlled the room just then. Nor was I surprised when, as she reached up and pulled his head down so she could kiss his cheek, I whooped in relief. Then she turned to me and motioned me to her side.

"Your work?" she asked as she studied my tattoo.

I felt myself blushing, both because she remembered how much I'd love drawing when I was younger and because she recognized it as mine. Still, it was embarrassing how much blushing I'd done of that over the last few days.

"My drawing, yes."

"You honor our family, child. Thank you." Tears once more filled her eyes and I knew then that the years I'd been on the run had been as hard on her as they had been on me.

Michael Jennings had more to pay for than I'd realized.

"Have the two of you eaten?" Better not think about vengeance just then. Wasn't it enough to know I was safe now and reunited with my grandmother?

"She wouldn't eat until she'd seen for herself that you were all right."

I grinned, suddenly realizing who she'd brought with her. My mother's youngest brother, Adam. He'd been at college in England when my parents died. I'd been maybe ten the last time I'd seen him. But no one could ever forget his voice once they'd heard it. Mom had called him, "Singer," claiming he could soothe any situation just by talking.

"Uncle Adam." I dove into his open arms.

"You look so much like your mother." He whispered, and I felt a tear fall onto my cheek.

"Thank you." That was just about the nicest thing anyone had ever said to me. Mom had been beautiful. I'd never be that, but for him to say I looked like her meant a lot.

"I'll get breakfast started," Matt said softly.

"I'll help." I shook my head, grinning like a fool when he started to protest. "I want to help." Besides, it wasn't fair to expect him to cook for my relatives when it was obvious they'd shown up before he'd expected them. "Come. There's coffee brewed."

Pulling Uncle Adam after me, I reached for my grandmother's hand. Then we followed Matt into the kitchen. No doubt about it. The morning was certainly starting off with a bang.

"So," Grandma began two hours later. "You're calling yourself Finn now."

We were alone in the house. Matt and Uncle Adam had left after breakfast, Matt muttering something about wanting to make sure everything was ready for tonight. Uncle Adam, on the other hand, had promised he'd have Matt take him by my apartment. He said it was so they could get my things for me, but I wasn't fooled. He wanted to see if he could find anything there that might help identify the trackers. I'd wanted to protest. After all, I hadn't been there yet, and shouldn't I be the first to check to see what sort of damage they'd done? But then I remembered Mom telling me that her brother could not only charm anyone and anything with his wonderful voice, but he was also better than most trackers. So, if there was anything there to help us find those who'd been hunting me, he'd discover it.

Before they left, I'd called Dana. We'd spoken twice before. I'd done my best to reassure her I was all right. But I knew she'd been shaken by the break-in. When she talked about wanting to move, it gave me the opening I'd been hoping for. Matt promised to have one of the pride find an apartment she could afford on her own, one at least as good as what we'd been sharing. If the pride had to supplement her rent for a bit, so be it. He didn't want me worrying about my friend.

"Yeah." I closed my eyes and leaned my head against the back of my chair. We'd moved into the den after I'd put the dirty dishes in the dishwasher. "I learned pretty quickly after leaving California that I couldn't use my real name, at least not all of it. Even so, I always tried to use at least part of it. It's going to take time for me to be able to wrap my head around the fact I can once again be Meg Finley."

"And yet that is the name you gave Matt Kincade."

"I'd like to say it's because I knew in that moment we were destined to be mated, but I can't. I was hurting so badly from the Taser and knife wound—and that scared me more than you know. Then he told me how Jennings spread word around the different clans that I might be a danger to our kind. All my defenses dropped, and the truth came out before I could stop it."

She nodded, understanding reflected in her eyes. "I'm not criticizing, Finn." Now she smiled and the knot in my stomach started unwinding. "You've done well for yourself and our people. If anyone has failed, it is the rest of us for not standing up for you. The time has come for the clans to start working together. We can't continue to be autonomous. The danger everyday technology presents to our kind is too great."

"I agree." Especially since that technology was the only reason I could think of for Jennings suspecting I might be in Fort Worth. Either I'd been caught on some cell phone video posted to the internet or my fingerprints or DNA got flagged somehow. None of which I could have prevented. "I'm just glad I don't have to run any longer."

"You're sure? You're positive this is what you want and you're willing to take the risk of what Jennings will do when he has confirmation you've surfaced again?"

I opened my mouth to assure her it was exactly what I wanted. Then I closed it with a snap. Everything had happened so quickly that neither Matt nor I had really thought about the consequences of what we planned. For whatever reason, Jennings continued hunting me all these years. He'd violated territorial boundaries at least once and, unless I missed my guess, many times in his effort to find me. Who knew what other laws, both shapeshifter and normal, he'd violated?

And who knew what he'd do once he realized Matt had offered me sanctuary with his clan and had taken me as his mate?

But it was time to quit running. Even now, only two days after making the decision to stay, I felt better than I had in years. There was a sense of belonging I'd missed since learning of my parents' deaths. More than that, there were the beginnings of a sense of purpose at the very core of my being that hadn't been there before. I wasn't sure where it would lead, but I wanted to give it the chance to grow.

"I'll talk with Matt about it, make sure he understands the problems this could cause, but it is what I want." I stood and moved to sit next to her on the sofa. I hated the worry reflected in her eyes. More than that, I hated the fact I was the cause of it. How many of the wrinkles marking her face were there because of me? "Grandma, I won't say I'm not concerned. The thought of what Jennings might try next worries me. Hell, it scares the crap out of me after this last run-in with his trackers. But I'm tired of running. I'm tired of being cut off from my family. I've missed being with others of our kind. If that means facing Jennings at some point, I will." Even if the thought scared the hell out of me just then.

"You have grown up so much." She smiled and grasped my hands in hers. "You are always welcome in our pride and clan, Finn. You are one of us through blood and spirit."

Tears pricked at my eyes and I blinked them back. "I love you." I leaned in and kissed her cheek.

"Will you do me one favor, child?"

"Of course, Grandma. Anything."

"Shift for me. Let me see your other form."

Suddenly nervous, I could only nod. I reminded myself that she'd never seen me shift before. So it was only natural for her to want to now. Still, my heart beat a little faster as I stood and kicked off my shoes. It didn't take long to strip out of my clothes. To give myself a moment to calm my nerves, I carefully folded underwear, jeans and tank top and placed them on the sofa next to her. Then I stepped back and closed my eyes, reaching inward for my panther.

Forcing a shift isn't like what you see in Hollywood movies. We don't just start running and, between one step and the next, we change from human to animal. God, if only it was that easy. Instead, it's a twisting of muscles, a reshaping of bone. It doesn't obey the laws of physics as we know them, much less biology. It may take no more than a minute or so, but it is a lifetime of agony followed by a rush of sheer power and freedom.

Once shifted, we are not fully animal. Nor are we completely human. Some of us seem to retain more of our "humanity", that ability to think rationally and not be ruled by our baser animal instincts, than others. They are the ones who usually take on leadership roles within pack and pride. Those best able to control themselves, and others of our kind, become alphas.

"You are such a beautiful girl." My grandmother knelt next to my shifted form, her fingers scratching between my ears.

Shifted, I felt her power even more than I had as human. My belly dropped to the floor and I rested my head on my paws. It was the closest to bowing I could do. But I didn't roll over, exposing belly and throat in an act of submission. The panther-me wouldn't allow it. I was an alpha, and she was in my territory—or at least it would be my territory soon.

Her approval washed over me and I purred loudly in satisfaction. It had been so long since I'd had an alpha's approval. Too long. I'd forgotten how important it was to belong. But never again.

Never again would Michael Jennings drive me from what was rightfully mine.

"Such a beautiful girl," she repeated and moved so she lay next to me. I nuzzled her, tentatively licking her arm. "Rest now, child. Enjoy this moment of peace."

I nuzzled her once more and then rested my head back on my paws. She continued to stroke my head, my back, speaking softly. Purring happily, I felt my eyes grow heavy. I was home and I belonged. Nothing else mattered.

CHAPTER SEVEN

I stood in the doorway to the bedroom and my breath caught in my throat. Matt stood at the closet, his back to me. Barefoot, shirtless, he was everything I'd ever thought of as "mouth-watering." I felt his strength and power as if they were living things. Even though he had complete control over his cat, I sensed it just below the surface, just as I felt my own panther responding, wanting to claim it as I had already claimed Matt—mate to mate, equal to equal.

And yet I couldn't allow myself to accept it. Not yet. My grandmother had been right about that. We might be meant for one another, but there were others to consider. Matt held responsibilities not only to his pride but to all the packs and prides that made up the North Texas clan. As much as I might want to be with him—and it was difficult to understand how I was so sure we belonged with one another when we really didn't know anything about each other—I couldn't expect him to put everything he'd worked for at risk just for me and my desires.

"You're thinking awfully hard," he said, a smile in his voice.

He finished whatever he'd been doing in the closet and turned. As he did, he pulled on a shirt and buttoned it. Damn. Guess that meant no fun and games, which was probably for the best. We really did need to talk.

"Matt, are you sure about this? Really sure?"

The words, so simple to say and yet so hard to get out, were little more than a whisper. My right hand held onto the doorframe, anchoring me where I was. Intellectually, I knew there was a very real possibility that once he quit thinking only about how he'd found a mate that he'd decide the danger to those looking to him for leadership and protection was too great. If he did, I'd leave. The last thing I wanted was to bring Matt trouble. I'd go to the Tulsa pride. My grandmother and Uncle Adam had already made it clear I'd be welcome there. But, damn it, I was tired of running, of letting fear of Michael Jennings dictate my life.

"Having second thoughts?" he asked. He moved to sit on the bed and patted the mattress next to him, motioning for me to join him.

"No. Dear God, no!"

Now that I'd found him, I didn't want to lose him. He was my mate. Somehow, some way, we were bound to one another. I might not understand it, but I accepted it. Just as I accepted the fact I could live without him if I had to. It would hurt like hell and I'd never feel completely whole. But to protect him and those he cared for, I would do it if I had to.

At least until I figured out how we could be together without bringing down Jennings' wrath.

"Then what?" He shifted slightly on the mattress so our knees touched and his hands reached for mine.

"Matt, have you really thought about what might happen when Jennings realizes I've stopped running and you're protecting me?"

"Finn." He smiled and caressed my cheek with his left hand. "I've given it a great deal of thought. I'd be lying if I said I hadn't. I've discussed the possibilities with your uncle and your grandmother. I'll even admit that I'm concerned about what that bastard might do. He's already shown he doesn't respect the territories of other clans. Nor does he respect our laws. So yes, his reaction to the news that you are here and have agreed to be my mate is something I've thought about a great deal.

"That said, I do respect my pride and clan. I trust the clans in the surrounding territories. We have long worked together, forming an unofficial coalition of sorts. If Jennings tries to cause trouble, he will find he has far more than just the North Texas clan to deal with.

"Finn, I'm not just protecting you. I'd do that whether you were one of us or not. Jennings is the worst sort of man there is in my book. He tried to take advantage of you when you were grieving. What he did was straight out of the books describing classic sexual predator behavior. The way he has continued to hunt you, *to stalk* you all these years speaks of obsession and mental illness.

"But it is more than that and you know it."

I swallowed hard and nodded.

"And I know the arguments you want to make. We don't know one another. My pride, much less the clan, might not accept you. Then there are all the concerns about Jennings and what he might do. Right?"

Another nod.

"Finn, you are my mate. That will be all the pride needs to accept you. Remember, you've already been welcomed by Sharon and Stefan. Believe me, my sister would be the first to voice her concerns if she had any. Stefan might be a bit more circumspect, but he'd have already taken me aside to question my motives and make sure it wasn't just hormones making me take you as mate and offering you the protection of pride and clan.

"What both of them have said is something far different. They have offered to speak for you at the pride meeting. They want to champion you, if need be. That is all I need to know the pride will feel the same way and, where the pride goes, the clan will follow. Sweetheart, what you need to understand is that the leaders of the prides and packs in the clan have been after me for several years now to find a mate and I have—I found you."

I blew out a shaky breath. Relief mingled with concern, but the concern no longer paralyzed me. I drew strength from Matt's conviction that what we planned was right, not just for the two of us but for pride and clan as well. All I had to do was start believing it as well and quit thinking Jennings would show up at any moment to destroy this promise of happiness, the first I'd had in much too long.

"Matt, I've been on my own for so long. I'm afraid running has become too much a part of me–"

He shook his head and gently rested a finger against my lips, silencing me. "You have been alone too long. But no more. If you want it, this is your home. I won't force you to stay here. We'll find you a place of your own if that will make you feel better. But you don't have to run any longer. You have a pride and a clan and, if you'll have me, a mate." Now he grinned and pulled me close. "It won't always be easy. You're right. We don't know one another. We're both headstrong and opinionated. Hell, sweetheart, we're alphas. So, there will be times when we butt heads. But we are meant to be together and that's what we have to remember. For all I know, you'll leave your clothes all over the house and make me wear a French maid's costume when I clean up after you."

The image of him in a very short French maid's costume, complete with a tiny white apron and very high stiletto heels, sent me into peals of laughter. "Well," I said, trying and completely failing to sound serious. "If that's what it takes to get you to play dress-up."

"I can see I'm going to have my hands full with you." He grinned.

"More than you know."

"Promises, promises." He lightly kissed me and then leaned back. "So, no doubts?"

"Doubts, sure. But not enough to run again. Those days are over."

At least I hoped they were.

"Good."

He bounced off the bed and crossed to the closet. Curious, I watched as he leaned inside and rummaged around on the floor. Then he turned, a huge grin on his face and two large sacks in his hands.

I waited, wondering what he was up to. Excitement grew as he placed the sacks on the bed. When I reached for the one closest to me, he lightly swatted my hand. So, it was going to be that way, was it?

"Your uncle and I stopped by your apartment while we were out. I hate to say it, but Danny was being kind when he said the trackers searched it. I'm sorry, but they pretty much trashed it, especially your room."

"Dana?"

"We talked with her for a few minutes. She said to tell you she misses you and hopes to see you soon."

I nodded.

"And she was thrilled to get the lead on the new apartment. Said she hoped you didn't mind if she took it." Now he smiled slightly. "Adam told her not to worry, that your grandmother was getting you settled into a new place as we spoke."

"I wish I could do something to help her cover the damage to her things." It wasn't fair she'd have to pay for something that happened because of me.

"Finn, it's taken care of. You don't need to worry about it. Unfortunately, the trackers spared little of your belongings." Sympathy and anger colored his voice. My hands fisted at my sides. I didn't have much, but there were a few things that meant the world to me. They were my links to my parents and the life we'd had. If those were gone or destroyed–"It was bad, Finn, I won't lie to you. But we were able to salvage some things we thought you might want right away. I'll take you over tomorrow and you can collect anything else you want to try to save."

With what could only be described as a flourish, he began pulling items from the bag closest to him. My hands shook and tears burned my eyes as I reached for the first thing he produced. The small framed picture had been with me since before I'd run away. It was the only picture I still had of my parents. In it, they stood arm in arm, smiling broadly. Memories flooded back of that last vacation we'd taken together. It had been a year before they were killed. We'd been so happy then.

Anger flared as I ran a light finger over the cracked glass and chipped wood of the frame. At least the picture itself appeared to be undamaged. The frame could be repaired and the glass replaced. All that mattered was the picture had survived. Tears rolled down my cheeks as I clutched the frame against my chest and rocked back and forth.

Matt waited until I brushed away my tears. I didn't put the picture to one side. Instead, I placed it in my lap, not yet ready to let it go. Still, there was no denying the way my pulse quickened in expectation as he once again reached into the sack. Had he and Uncle Adam managed to save the other items that meant so much to me?

The next thing he produced was the battered copy of *Atlas Shrugged* that had been on my bedside table. At least that's where I'd last seen it. Like the picture, it had been with me since I'd left California. My father had given me the book, telling me to read it and understand that, for all its flaws, there was still a great deal of truth in what Rand had written.

Matt colored slightly as he then produced underwear. We both laughed when I snatched it from his hand. My cheeks burned as I quickly stuffed the bras and panties under the pillow behind me. It was so ridiculous. He'd seen me hurt and hurting. He'd seen me naked and had loved me long and well. And yet I blushed to have him handling my bras and panties.

Embarrassment disappeared the moment I saw what he held in his right hand. My mother's engagement ring lay nestled in his palm next to my father's pocket watch. Tears once more filled my eyes. These were the only things I had that had belonged to them. It would have killed me to have lost them.

"Thank you." It was barely a whisper, but it was all I could manage.

"Finn." He gently placed the ring and watch into my hands. An understanding smile touched his lips. "I want you to be comfortable here. This is your home now. That means you need to have your things here as much as I have mine. I promise, we'll go to your place tomorrow and bring back everything you want to save. Anything else you want or need, we'll go shopping for. But, for now, I thought these would be a good start."

The left side of my mouth quirked up in a half-smile. With the picture in my right hand, I stood and moved across the room to the dresser. When I glanced back at him, Matt simply nodded in approval. I set the frame on the far end of the dresser, carefully angling it so I'd be able to see it from the bed. Then Matt was there, sliding his arms around my waist and holding me close.

"Your parents?" I pointed to the framed photo of a man and woman resting on the other end of the dresser.

"Yes. I was already in college when Dad's job took them to Ireland, so I stayed here. Sharon moved back as soon as she could. And, before you ask, they'll approve of you." He pressed his lips to the top of my head. "We'll call them this weekend. I promise."

I nodded, suddenly worried they wouldn't approve.

"And, now that I can look at you and the photo of your mother, I have to admit that Adam was right. You do look like her."

"And you, Matt, are a flatterer. I'll never be as gorgeous as Mom was."

"We're going to have to agree to disagree about that, Finn." He gave me a hug and then led me back to the bed and the other sack. "There's some more from your apartment in here," he continued as we sat down on the edge of the mattress. "But there are also some other things. This first is from your uncle. He can tell you more about it later, but he said to tell you it had been your mother's and he knows she'd have wanted you to wear it tonight."

He produced a beautiful wristlet of woven leather from inside the sack. Approximately two inches wide, made up of three bands each of black and brown leather, the wristlet fastened with two clasps. In the center, where a watch might be, was the embossed head of a panther. I couldn't remember my mother wearing it, but that didn't mean she hadn't. It was enough that Uncle Adam said she had.

Matt reached for my left hand. I watched, a funny little smile on my lips, as he carefully fitted the wristlet in place. When he glanced up to see if it was comfortable, I nodded. Then, with a catch in my throat, looked from the wristlet to my new tattoo. They looked like they belonged together.

I belonged.

"This next is from me. You already wear the markings of my pride and clan. CJ will add the rest of it in a day or two." He paused and suddenly looked uncertain, maybe even a little nervous. Could he be worried I wouldn't like whatever it was? "When I introduce you to the pride tonight, I want them to see how proudly you wear our markings, just as I want them to see your strength."

I swear he turned beat red as he reached into the sack. A number of possible explanations came to mind and not one came close to reality. I whistled lowly as I reached for the leather vest, the softest leather I'd ever felt. The black leather laced up the sides with equally soft leather ties. To call it a mere vest was to do it a disservice, but to call it a bustier would be to cheapen it.

I held the vest before me and shook my head in wonder. It was cut in such a way my entire tattoo would be visible. Thank God I worked out regularly. It would be terribly embarrassing to wear such a beautiful—and revealing—vest and have chicken arms.

"Matt, I'll look like a dominatrix in these!" I laughed as he produced a pair of matching black leather pants.

"Well." He actually leered at me, humor twinkling in his eyes. "You can dominate me any time you want."

"Be careful what you wish for," I warned, grinning. "When do we need to leave?"

He checked his watch. "Sharon will be here in an hour and a half. Your grandmother and uncle shortly after that."

"Plenty of time then."

Matt gave an "oomph" of surprise as I twisted, swung a leg over him and straddled him. Hands against his chest, I pushed him back onto the mattress. He grinned and reached up, cupping my breasts. I bared my teeth and shook my head. Not this time. He wasn't going to distract me this time.

"Hands down," I ordered. I ducked my head and nipped at his lower lip. "Don't make me have to discipline you."

He grinned and dropped his hands. I guided them to the headboard, closing his fingers around the wooden posts. "Don't let go," I murmured against his mouth. My hands moved to his belt and he groaned softly.

"Finn, I want to touch you."

"Shh."

I kissed him and then reached up to yank off my tank top. Still straddling him, I fisted my hands in his shirt and pulled, sending buttons flying. I didn't care. I wanted skin against skin. I wanted to make him as insane with want as he had made me last night.

I wriggled out of my jeans and stretched out on top of him. His lips parted and his eyes shined. His grasp on the posts tightened and I knew he was fighting the impulse to let go.

"See something you like?" I teased as I shifted slightly so my right breast hung just out of reach of his mouth.

"Yes."

I shifted again, relishing the feel of his mouth as he sucked and licked and nibbled at my nipple. My hands slipped between us, working to undo his zipper. He groaned as his penis was suddenly free of his jeans. I gripped it, fingers teasing and taunting. When he opened his mouth, gasping, I shifted. My mouth closed on his and I kissed him deeply, losing myself in the moment.

Then my warped sense of humor took over. I trailed kisses down his throat to his chest, moving ever lower. He groaned again, muscles tensing as continued making my way down his body. His penis twitched and his eyes closed, desire hanging heavy in the air.

"This is my friend George." I pitched my voice lower, trying for the intonation of the cartoon from my childhood. "I will love him and lick him and kiss his little head." I deliberately misquoted the cartoon and then put action to the words.

"What?" Matt's eyes snapped open and his head popped up off the pillow. "Little? I'll show you little!"

He hands closed about my waist and he rolled. We both laughed like loons as I countered. Instead of me winding up beneath him, we rolled again. And then again. His sharp intake of breath came a split-second before we rolled off the bed. Fortunately, at least for me, he landed on bottom.

Not that he stayed there for long. His fingers found my ribs and tickled. Laughing, batting at the offending appendages, I let my guard down. I had a split-second's warning as I felt his muscles gathering beneath me. Then he quit tickling me and we rolled, but only once this time.

"I'll show you little," he repeated, spreading my legs.

"Yes," I whispered, pulling his head down. I ground my mouth against his as he plunged into me. "I want you, Matt. I want your scent on me. I want everyone to know we're together." Desire roughened my voice. My hands pulled him close, fingers digging into his shoulders. God, never had it been like this before.

"Then let's make sure no one can ever doubt it." He nibbled at my lower lip and I felt his smile as I moved against him, demanding more, always more.

Mine, all mine!

After a shower that, unfortunately, didn't include sex, I dressed in the leathers Matt had given me. I brushed my hair and then braided it. As I studied my reflection, I smiled slightly. I did look pretty damned kick ass between the leathers and tattoo. There was a determination reflected in my expression I hadn't seen in much too long. The butterflies in my stomach were only a mild distraction. Still, I wished Matt and Adam and thought to grab at least some lip gloss for me while they were out.

A soft rap at the door interrupted my thoughts. When I called out, I knew it would be Sharon who opened the door. What I didn't expect was the makeup bag she held in one hand or her surprised expression as she stepped inside. Before I knew what was happening, she dropped to her hands and knees, her forehead almost touching the tips of my boots.

"Sharon!" I laughed and reached down to lift her to her feet. "Save the dramatics for tonight."

"Dear God, Finn, what's going on?" She looked at me, eyes wide with disbelief.

"What do you mean? And please tell me there's makeup in that bag."

She blinked, shook her head and then smiled. Then she disappeared into the adjoining bath. I followed, watching as she went to work. I didn't doubt for a moment that she used the time it took to lay out the selection of foundation, powders, blushes, lip gloss and other makeup to gather her thoughts. Since I understood that sensation of being hit by a cosmic two-by-four, I let her work. She'd explain the rest of it when she was ready.

I just hoped she was ready soon.

"Shar?" I prompted finally. I sat on the commode, doing my best not to remind her—again—that I could put on my own makeup.

"As much as I do not want to think about my big brother having sex—that ranks right up there with thinking about our parents having sex—it's clear you guys put the afternoon to good use."

Well, that answered one question. The pride would certainly know we were together in every sense of the word.

"And I expected it," she continued. "What I didn't expect was to be hit with your power when I opened the door. Dear God, the control you must have been exercising all this time is more than I can imagine. All I can say is any shapeshifter who comes within half a mile of you tonight will know you're an alpha and very well matched for Matt."

As she spoke, she put aside the makeup brush she'd been using. For a moment, she studied me—well, she studied her work on me.

Then, with a satisfied nod, she pulled me to my feet and turned me to face the mirror hanging over the sink.

"Now," my grandmother said from the doorway. "You really do look like your mother."

I stared at my reflection and nodded, not quite believing my eyes. Sharon had worked some kind of arcane magic on my face. Without the makeup being noticeable, she'd highlighted my cheekbones and a smoky shadow brought the focus to my eyes. There was no mistaking my Indian heritage now, especially not with my braid, the leathers and the tattoo. Nor was there any denying the very strong resemblance I bore to my mother and grandmother.

"Wow."

"I take it you approve." Sharon gave me a cheeky grin.

"I do. Thank you."

I pulled her into a quick hug and then turned my attention to my grandmother. Embarrassment returned as I remembered what Sharon had said about being able to tell Matt and I had been together and I prayed my blush wasn't a deep as it felt. It was one thing having your mate's sister know you've just been loved very well. It was something very different to have your grandmother know it.

"I'll leave you two alone." Sharon slipped out of the bathroom, pausing only long enough to give a respectful nod to my grandmother.

"Finn, you're sure this is what you want?" Grandma asked as we walked into the bedroom. She sat on the edge of the bed and I sank onto the floor at her feet. I knew she was asking not only as my grandmother but as the closest thing to a pride leader I'd had in much too long.

"It is. Matt and I talked after you and Uncle Adam left. We both understand the possible consequences but feel the benefits not only to us but to pride and clan outweigh the danger."

"Good." She smiled in approval and reached out to lightly touch my cheek. "The wristlet your uncle gave you is one I gave your mother when she and your father joined as mates. That was three years before they were married. She told us then that she hoped her daughter would one day wear it when she formally joined with her mate.

"Your grandfather gave me this when we formally became mates. You would honor both of us if you accepted it and wore it tonight. It had been your great-grandmother's before it became mine. She had been shaman for her people, one of the few female shamans of the time."

She held a necklace in her hands. It was delicate and intricate and there was the strength of generations in it. Stones of malachite, coral, quartz and even petrified wood had been carved into animal shapes. Studying them, I swallowed hard. Those shapes represented the different animals those of our bloodlines shifted into. There were panthers and cougars, coyotes and wolves and even a bear. I bowed my head as my fingers closed over the necklace, too stunned to speak. Grandma was giving me our history and, in doing so, making sure no one could ever question my place in the bloodline.

"Thank you. I'm honored to wear this." I took her hands in mine and kissed them, recognizing her as an elder. Then I moved to sit on the mattress at her side and held her close, granddaughter to grand-mother. "You honor me and my mate by being here tonight and I am sorry for all the pain I've caused you these years I've been on the run."

"You didn't cause the pain, child. That falls squarely on Michael Jennings."

Before I could reply, there was a knock at the door and Matt asked if we were ready to leave.

Grinning, I stood and helped my grandmother to her feet. It was time to take back control of my life.

Take that, Jennings, and may you rot in Hell.

CHAPTER EIGHT

By the time Matt handed me out of the Mustang an hour later, I knew what I had to do. From now until we returned home, I had to live the role I'd accepted. I was his mate, the pride's female Alpha. I answered to no one save him and then only because I chose to. No one else in the pride or the clan outranked me.

Part of that included showing the proper respect to my grandmother, not only as an elder but as an allied clan leader. But we were both Alphas and she was in my territory. I was the host and she the guest. Somehow, I had a feeling she'd play her role better than I would mine.

Standing there, looking at the sprawling ranch-style house before us, I tried to remember how my mother acted at such gatherings. She'd always stood with my father as his equal. They'd consulted on all decisions concerning those they led and Dad's respect for Mom as an alpha, as the female Alpha, had always been clear. For her part, Mom had never tried to take the spotlight for herself. I knew it wasn't always like that among the other packs and prides, but I was damned if I'd accept anything less for myself.

Matt reached for my hand and gave it a reassuring squeeze.

When I looked up at him, he winked. Then his lips brushed against mine. It wasn't much, but it to let me know he realized how nervous I was and he wanted to reassure me.

"Stefan lives here with my Aunt Hannah. They converted the barn for us to use as a meeting place when I took over the clan," he said softly as we started down the gravel drive.

"Is your aunt one of us?"

"She is. They have three children. Two are shapeshifters." He held the door for me and motioned me inside.

I couldn't hold back my gasp of surprise. It might look like barn outside, but no one could ever mistake it for one once inside. The walls were lined with beautifully polished oak paneling. Brass fixtures reminiscent of old coach lights hung from the ceiling. What looked to be a full kitchen with eating area lined the far wall. We stood in what could only be described as a great room—one that could grace the pages of any of the top design magazines. I barely kept myself from dropping to my knees to run a hand over the beautiful hardwood floors.

Before I could comment, Stefan was there to greet me. He took my hands and smiled. That didn't fool me though. I saw how he looked me up and down, not missing a single detail. Then he nodded in approval.

"Finn, this is my wife, Hannah." He placed my right hand in his wife's left. As he did, I smiled. Blonde-haired and blue-eyed, there was no mistaking Hannah's Germanic ancestry. Nor was there any mistaking her strength. She was so close to being an alpha, I was surprised she hadn't taken that final step.

"Welcome to our home and family," she said, her soft voice betraying her German ties. The accent was faint, but there.

"Thank you" I smiled and held a hand out to Stefan. "Your husband might not have saved my life, but he treated my injuries and he eased my fears. I will always be in his debt for that."

"Just as we are in yours." When I looked at her in question, Hannah nodded to where Matt stood a few feet away talking to

Sharon, my grandmother and Uncle Adam. "I can see the change in him already. He's always been a good leader, but he lived only for it and for his job. There's a completeness to him now that comes from finding his mate."

"That's how he makes me feel," I said simply.

Before anything else could be said, the sounds of cars coming up the drive reached us. As Hannah and Stefan went greet the newcomers, I caught Matt's eye. He nodded and I stepped back. Now was the time to watch and wait.

"Relax," Sharon said softly from my side fifteen minutes later.

I leaned against the wall, taking advantage of the shadows cast by one of the stone pillars, and studied those gathered. More than two dozen men and women ranging from high schoolers to their grandparents were present. I had seen at least a dozen children and preteens as well. Then there were the adults I realized weren't shapeshifters who had retired to the house a few minutes earlier.

Matt moved among those gathered, smiling, talking. I felt Sharon's pride when her brother moved to the front of the room. Seeing how his pride members respected him, I couldn't blame her. It was clear Matt cared for each person present and they for him.

A touch of uncertainty knotted my stomach. How would they react when he announced he'd found a mate? That one announcement would completely change the dynamics of the pride. Not only was he bringing in a mate from outside the pride and clan, but he was bringing in one who had never formally been a member of any pride. There was bound to be concern and doubt. But would it be such that it could actually undermine Matt's position as Alpha?

"Easy, Finn." Sharon's voice was soft, reassuring. "Trust in Matt and in yourself."

I swallowed once and nodded. Trusting in Matt was easy. Trusting in myself was something else altogether.

"Is there anyone I need to be aware of?" In other words, were there any here who might have hoped to become Matt's mate and who would cause trouble because he'd chosen me over them?

"I don't think so. Almost everyone has been with the pride for years. There are a few who joined us over the last few years because their jobs brought them here, but no one's ever caused any real trouble."

I nodded and tried to relax, not an easy thing when my panther was so restless. No, that's not the right word. It was edgy and more than a bit pissy. It wanted to revel in being named Matt's mate, in taking its place as Alpha, but it sensed trouble. I wanted to put it all down to reaction. Between the run-in with the trackers, suddenly realizing not only that I was an alpha but that I'd found my life mate, and realizing I was no longer going to run, my emotional equilibrium was anything but steady. Even so, I couldn't completely ignore that sense of potential trouble ahead.

Damn it.

Before I could say anything else, Matt took his place at the front of the room. A smile, proud and possessive, touched his lips. He looked like a proud host, pleased his gathering was going so success-fully. Then that sense of power I'd felt from the moment my brain started working again after I'd been tasered rolled over everyone present. Matt didn't need the props so many other alphas seemed to favor—especially those in the bad Hollywood movies. He sat on a well-worn, over-stuffed chair. It wasn't on any sort of raised platform and in no way resembled a throne. But there could be no mistaking exactly who and what he was.

How very different the scene was from the last clan meeting I'd attended in California. It wasn't that there were fewer people here. It was the atmosphere. There had been such uneasiness and worry in that California meeting. Anger and frustration had matched it. Now that I was older and my own emotions no longer in turmoil, I realize just how volatile the situation had been that night. It wouldn't have taken much for the clan to have been torn apart as those who supported protecting me and preventing Jennings from solidifying his position of Alpha either left the clan or openly challenged him and his supporters.

Here the pride felt like they were a family. Sure, all families had the uncle they spoke of in whispers and the cousin who thought she was better than everyone else. But they'd stand by one another against all others. It had been that way when my parents led the pride. Even the clan, where disagreements and conflicts were more common because of the number of people—not to mention different animals once everyone was shifted—were involved, had been like that.

Still, I'd learned long ago appearances can be deceiving. The next few minutes would tell the tale.

"Thank you for coming," Matt began. He nodded in appreciation as Hannah brought him a mug of coffee. "I apologize for the last-minute notice, but several things have happened that we need to discuss." He sipped, and I wondered how many of those assumed he was gathering his thoughts and how many realized he was studying them, gauging their reactions.

"Several days ago, our territory was violated. Trackers hunted a lone shapeshifter through downtown during the middle of the day. They didn't care their actions could have revealed our existence to the normals. They hunted without informing me of their presence, much less their reason for being here. If that isn't bad enough, their clan leader has yet to contact me.

"Because of this violation of our territory and of shifter law, I contacted the clan leaders in the surrounding territories. They've had similar situations happen and aren't any happier about it than I am."

He paused again and climbed to his feet. His expression turned hard. Anger reflected in his eyes. And all I could think about was how sexy he looked. Damn, what happened to me? I've had more sex in the last two days than I've had in months and I thought about it even more.

"Know this, I will not allow our people to be endangered by anyone. If you know who these intruders are or where they might be, I want to know now."

"You're sure?"

I turned my attention to the speaker. If I had been surprised by his temerity in questioning Matt, the rest of the pride was appalled. A redhead in her early twenties hissed for the speaker to be quiet. Danny Gillespie, who stood almost directly opposite me, took a step toward the man and stopped only when Matt gave a quick shake of his head. But it was the way Sharon stiffened at my side and Uncle Adam moved even closer to my grandmother where they stood at the back of the gathering with Stefan and Hannah that had me tensing.

Before Matt could respond, the speaker stood. As he did, I frowned and fought the urge to bare my teeth in challenge. I've known too many like him over the years. Small of stature, they made up for their lack of height by excessive weight training and, all too often, chemical enhancements. My dad would've described him as "a brick shithouse and probably as dense." From the sly look on the man's face, I had a feeling Dad would've been right.

"No disrespect, Matt, but how can you be so sure?"

Well, I knew a great opening line when I heard one.

"He can be sure because he was there to save me from the trackers."

As I stepped forward, I released the control I'd held in place, letting everyone feel my panther. Gasps matched surprised expressions. Several of the women present automatically lowered their heads, their own cats responding to mine. I bit back the satisfied smile that tried to come. Time for that later.

"As Matt said, the trackers chased me through downtown, through the streets and into a parking garage. They didn't care it was daylight and there were people around—much less video cameras—to witness what happened. It wouldn't have mattered that none of us shifted if they'd managed to get their hands on me. The fact that someone would eventually turn a copy of some video of our chase over to the cops—or worse, post it on the internet—means questions would arise. Questions none of us want asked, much less answered."

As I spoke, a look of recognition crossed the man's face. He knew me, or at least knew who I was. But how? I'd never seen him before.

He wasn't the sort I'd have forgotten for the simple reason he made me uncomfortable. So how did he know me?

As we faced off, Matt stayed where he was. Even though part of me wanted him to stand with me, I knew why he didn't. He had yet to formally introduce me as a member of the pride, much less as his mate. The black leather jacket I wore hid my tattoo. Besides, he was letting me establish myself with the pride. If I proved to them not only that I had the strength to be an asset to the pride but that I also cared for the pride's well-being, the rest would be easy.

Of course, Matt wasn't leaving anything to chance either. A quick glance at the gathering proved that. Uncle Adam and my grandmother stood between the speaker and the door. Danny Gillespie boxed him in on one side, Sharon and I on the other. Whether he realized it or not, we had the speaker surrounded should he try anything foolish.

"And why would trackers be after you?" The man smirked and ran a hand over his close-cropped blonde hair. "And had you reported to presence to our Alpha?"

Oh my. He really did want to be smacked down and hard. My panther growled as it fought for release. My lips pulled back, baring my teeth. Only a fool would fail to recognize that for what it was—a warning that he was treading on very thin ice. Not that I expected him to realize it. He'd already proven himself to be a fool.

Out of the corner of my eye, I saw Uncle Adam take a step forward. My grandmother touched his arm and shook her head. I didn't need the enhanced hearing of my panther to know she'd told him to let me handle it. I just hoped I didn't blow it.

"And why should we believe anything you say when haven't even introduced yourself," he continued, pressing what he obviously saw as his advantage.

I laughed. I couldn't help it. And it was exactly the right reaction. The tension in the room evaporated. Disbelief and disapproval replaced it. Good. I could play on that.

"You mean like you've introduced yourself?" I grinned, mocking him. Well, he caught that if the way his face turned purple was any indication. "But to answer your question, my name is Meg Finley, granddaughter of Irene Walkinghorse, clan leader of the Oklahoma clan."

"And my mate," Matt said firmly as he moved my side. At his nod, I shrugged out of my jacket, revealing the tattoo marking me as a member of the pride and clan. "And you overstepped yourself, Thomas."

"And you endanger all of us if she is who she says," the smaller man countered. Those around him didn't attempt to silence him. Instead, they moved away, making it clear they were distancing themselves from him and his accusations. "It's well-known how she disrespected her Alpha and has been doing her best to destroy our kind."

This time I growled, giving voice to my panther's anger. How dare he! More importantly, where had he gotten his information—or misinformation? I couldn't believe Michael made what happened public knowledge. His ego wouldn't allow for that. I certainly hadn't gotten the impression from Matt or my grandmother that he'd told anyone outside the Northern California clan how I ran away instead of agreeing to become his mate. So, who was this man my mate called Thomas and how did he know about me?

And how did I put an end to his insolence?

At least that question was easily answered.

"Down!" I ordered.

Power rolled through me and I reveled in it. Disbelief drained the color from Thomas's face and he dropped to his knees. His muscles quivered and sweat pricked out on his forehead. I smelled his fear. Good. Let him learn I was no longer the scared girl who fled her home instead of being coerced into mating with an alpha forced on her. Let the others gathered here realize I was a worthy mate for their Alpha.

"Yes, I lived in Northern California. My parents were clan leaders at the time they were killed. As for disrespecting my Alpha, you have that very wrong."

Anger filled me as I remembered the horror of that last night in California. When I left Aunt Jane's and Uncle Lou's house, I meant to keep my word not to return to the home I'd grown up in, the house where my parents had supposedly killed themselves. But I didn't see the danger in going back just long enough to pack a few things, a few mementos of the life I was about to leave behind. What I hadn't planned on was finding Michael Jennings waiting there for me. He hadn't been dissuaded during the clan meeting when others had reminded him I was too young and hurting too much to be *claimed* just then. If anything, he was more determined than ever to make me his.

My stomach churned at the memory. I'd done my best to forget those few minutes he'd attempted to force me to submit. When I didn't immediately do as he said, he'd tried to force me by rolling his power over me. I can still see how shocked he'd been when I didn't instantly obey. I'd been so scared and angry, the implications of my refusal hadn't dawned on me.

"That Alpha didn't care I was underage, by our laws and by the laws of the normals. He didn't care I wasn't formally a member of the clan because my parents had been wise enough know I might not want to be part of the clan when I was an adult. They'd known my life might take me elsewhere. He didn't care that others of the clan warned him of the danger in his plan.

"I was fifteen. I was mourning the deaths of my parents, deaths Michael Jennings had done his best to insure weren't investigated by the authorities. When he couldn't force me to accept him as my mate before the clan, he tried to force himself on me that night. If my father hadn't trained me in hand-to-hand and insisted I train in the martial arts, that bastard would have raped me. He sure as hell tried and he probably still bears the scars from our fight—at least I hope he does." Bile rose in my throat. Matt's hand tightened around mine. I didn't dare look at him for fear of what I'd see. I should have told him what happened when we were alone not here, in the middle of the pride.

"But I have never worked against our kind. I may have come here and done my best to fly under the radar, but I still protected our people. I did it even though it meant the true circumstances surrounding my parents' deaths remained unknown. I did it to prevent war from breaking out among the factions within the Northern California clan. I did it by denying myself a life with my own kind for close to ten years."

Anger built. The pain of my nails lengthening and biting into my palms reminded me to maintain control. Tempting as it was to shift and deal with Thomas for his insults, I couldn't. I wouldn't. That had to be Matt's call. I wasn't yet the pride's, much less the clan's, female Alpha.

"Submit!" I barked it out when Thomas tried to stand. With a whimper, he fell to his stomach. Out of the corner of my eye, I saw Matt nod. Danny Gillespie moved to stand over the man.

"Ask yourself why Jennings has spent all this time hunting me, sending trackers into clan territories without permission. If he truly feared I was acting in a way to harm our kind, he'd have called in help from all the clans. Instead, he sent trackers into their territories without warning and without permission. He allowed them to act in ways that could lead to our discovery by the normals. Why, if he had nothing to hide?"

An angry murmur ran through those gathered as my words struck home. "Of more concern to me is how you came to have the so-called knowledge. You aren't one of Matt's advisors. If you were, I'd have already met you as I have them." At that, Stefan and Rico Garces moved to stand with Sharon behind Matt and me. "It has been clear from the moment Matt rescued me that he didn't know what happened after my parents' deaths. So how do you? How do you know something your clan leader does not?"

"I—I don't have to tell you anything," Thomas stammered.

"You really are a fool." I shook my head. Then I motioned for Danny to pull Thomas to his knees. It was now or never. "Your Alpha has named me his mate. I wear the symbols of pride and clan.

You've felt—and obeyed—me without either of us shifting. You have submitted to me." More murmurs, enough to let me know the others had felt my power as well.

Inspiration hit, and I turned to Matt. "How long as he been part of the pride?"

Sharon's quick intake of breath answered my question. He was one of those who had moved into the clan's territory over the last few years.

"He was accepted into the pride a year, maybe two, before I took over as Alpha," Matt answered.

"Where did he come from?"

"St. Louis," Sharon answered for her brother.

I quickly looked at those gathered. Seeing the spiked purple hair, I nodded in satisfaction. Good. Just the person I needed.

"CJ."

She stepped forward quickly. Even as she reached for my hand, she sank respectfully to her knees before Matt and me. The knot of tension in my stomach unwound a little as the others noted her actions and accepted what they meant.

"You did the tattooing marking me as part of clan and pride."

"I did." She stood and grinned as she faced the others. "Some of my best work, thanks to your drawing."

"Did you find any evidence I had ever been tattooed before?"

"No."

"Nor did I," Stefan said before I could ask. "I treated Finn after she was attacked by the trackers. They had knifed and tasered her. Both weapons were tainted with something that not only slowed her healing but also to cause more pain than they should have." There could be no mistaking his anger.

"Did you do the tattoo additions when he–" a nod to Thomas. —"joined the pride?"

"No." CJ gnawed her lower lip and I had a pretty good idea she was trying to recall every detail of when Thomas joined the pride. "If

I remember correctly—and I do—he said he had someone else he wanted to do his new markings."

"Check him. Tell me what you find."

For a moment CJ looked at me in question. Then she gave a quick nod. As she moved to where Thomas knelt, I prayed I was right. If not, then the few inroads I'd just made into gaining my place within the pride would be gone and Matt's position damaged.

God, don't let me be wrong.

No one moved. I'm not sure anyone even breathed. Before CJ could ask, Danny reached down and shoved Thomas' sleeve above his elbow. CJ nodded in appreciation and closely examined the tattoo on Thomas' forearm. With a frown, she ran a finger over it. As I waited, my heart pounded and my grip on Matt's hand tightened. Damn, I wish I felt more confident about what she'd find.

Hell, I wished none of this was necessary. Was Jennings always going to be there, preventing me from enjoying life?

"I'm not impressed with whoever did his ink." CJ's voice betrayed an anger that surprised me. "I can see where another tattoo, or at least part of one, has been lasered off. Whoever did his markings when he joined our pride wasn't very good at hiding the scar tissue. I need to check under better light to be completely sure, but I think I see what you suspected, Finn."

She turned her attention to Matt after taking one last look at the man's forearm. "I'd stake my life on him not originally being part of the St. Louis clan. I can see the outline of the symbols for the Northern California clan and one of their prides."

My stomach lurched. "The symbol?"

"An eagle."

I closed my eyes and breathed deeply, trying to still the fear growing in the pit of my stomach.

"Matt, you need to check with the St. Louis clan. See what they can tell you about him. If I'm wrong, it's just a coincidence that he's here. But if CJ is right about his markings, he was part of Michael Jennings' pride before moving to St. Louis."

"Wasn't Jennings a member of your home pride?" Stefan asked.

"No. That was one of the reasons there were concerns about him taking over. He was young, and he'd just assumed leadership of the Eureka pride. My parents didn't approve of some of the changes he'd instituted, but they were killed before they could do anything about it."

"Sharon, make the call. Danny, take him up to the house. I'll deal with him later." Matt's anger radiated off of him. Thank God it wasn't directed at me.

"Irene, I apologize to you and Adam," Matt continued, leading me to stand before my grandmother. "I had not expected trouble tonight."

"Every clan has at least one like him. Hopefully, no real harm has been done." My grandmother smiled and reached out to touch my cheek. "Your parents would be proud, child. You handled him and the situation well."

"Thank you." I hoped she was right.

My grandmother then turned to face those watching us. "I accept your pride leader's claim on my granddaughter and hers on him. Do you?"

As one, they all dropped to hands and knees. To my relief, I sensed nothing but acceptance from them. I'd most definitely had enough surprises for one night.

CHAPTER NINE

"Finn, wake up."

A warm hand slid down my bare back. I burrowed my head deeper into the pillow and groaned. I didn't want to wake up. It was too early, and we'd been up way too late the night before. All I wanted was to be left alone to sleep.

"Come on, Finn. Wake up."

The offending hand lightly swatted my equally bare ass. I pulled the pillow over my head. Maybe if I ignored him long enough, he'd give up and go away.

"Don't make me tickle you."

The humor and threat in his voice had me flopping onto my back, the sheet tangling around my legs. My eyes opened a slit before I squeezed them shut. Not only was it too early, but it was too bright. Light shone in my eyes, beating against my eyelids.

"It's too early," I replied, throwing an arm across my eyes. It might have blocked the light, but the memory remained. Worse, he chuckled, damn him. He was enjoying this.

"You have a choice—coffee." Steam teased my nose and the tantalizing aroma had me almost—almost—relenting and opening my eyes again. "Or tickles." That wonderful smell moved away, and fingers lightly ran down my ribs, sending shivers through me.

"You wouldn't dare!" My eyes flew open. "You're dressed!" It came out sounding like an accusation.

"I usually get dressed when I get out of bed." He was laughing at me, the bastard. It wasn't my fault that I'm not a morning person.

"Too many clothes." I reached up, loosening his tie.

He laughed and shook his head even as he reached up to straighten his tie. Then he bent and kissed me. He tasted of mint and coffee and it reminded me that something had crawled in my mouth overnight and died. Sighing, I kicked at the sheet and sat up.

"Don't go anywhere," I said as I hurried toward the bathroom. "And don't drink that coffee!"

Wise man that he is, Matt was waiting for me when I returned a few minutes later. His eyes followed me as I moved to the closet. I grinned as he shook his head when I slipped into one of his shirts instead of a robe. A moment later, I stepped into a pair of panties. That was as close to dressed as I could manage without coffee, lots and lots of coffee.

"I still say you have too many clothes on." I took the mug from him and sipped, careful not to burn my mouth.

"I wish I didn't have to." His hands cupped my butt and pulled me close. Another kiss, this one deep enough to curl my toes. Well, that certainly woke me up. "Unfortunately, I need to run into the office for a couple of hours."

I looked up, searching his expression for any sign something might be wrong. "I thought you were taking today off."

"I have a meeting I can't postpone. But I'll be back as soon as it's over." He smiled and brushed his lips against mine. "Danny's going to stop by later. He needs your date of birth, Social Security number, that sort of thing."

"Why?"

As if sensing my sudden flare of suspicion, Matt tilted my head so I looked in him the eye. "Finn, Danny works for the DA's Office. He needs the information to make sure Jennings hasn't put your name into the system. We don't need the cops showing up, thinking we kidnapped you or, worse, that you committed some sort of crime."

Outrage sparked. God, he was right. That was exactly something I could see Jennings doing. He'd already proven he'd stop at nothing to get me back. Why else continue to hunt me for so long? Since I had absolutely no desire to return to the Northern California clan, much less to him, anything I could do to throw roadblocks in his way, I'd do.

"I'll give him anything he wants."

Matt smiled in approval and gently cupped my cheek with one hand. "Finn, I know how hard this must be for you. I'm asking you to trust not only me but others with your life. You honor me and them by doing so. It goes beyond accepting me as your mate and I swear you will never regret it."

"Matt."

God, he was too good to be true. Level-headed and understanding, at least so far. Last night, when we finally returned home, he'd been so gentle with me. It didn't take a rocket scientist to realize it was because of what I'd revealed about that last night in California. When I first tried talking to him about it, he'd been quick to tell me I didn't have to. What he hadn't understood was that I did. I needed him to know that what we had was different, in so many ways, from what happened that long ago night. I didn't feel coerced to be with him. Far from it. I wanted to be with him, not that I didn't still have more than my fair share of demons.

"I'm not going lie. It's a struggle not to run right now. I almost did last night when I realized Meehan had a connection to Jennings. Then you were there, standing with me and for me, even after I told everyone what happened that terrible night. Sharon, Stefan and even Danny were all there as well. Then there were my grandmother and Uncle Adam. I have a life here and I'll be damned if I let that bastard Jennings take it from me."

"Always with you and for you, even when you're a slug-a-bed." His fingers found my ribs for one quick tickle before he moved out of range, grinning. "When I get home, we'll run by your apartment and then go shopping. Sharon will be here after school to help get ready for tonight."

Tonight. I wasn't sure I was ready for that. Tonight, I'd be meeting the leaders of the other packs and prides that made up the clan. Matt would introduce me as his mate and then we'd begin what could only be called a war counsel. I knew, even if Matt didn't, that the line had been drawn in the sand. When Jennings violated other clans' territories, when he allowed his trackers to taint their weapons, he crossed the line. Sooner or later we, all our kind, had to step in. He couldn't be allowed to continue operating in ways guaranteed to reveal our existence before we were ready.

"What about food for tonight?" I remembered Mom and Dad telling me meetings were always more fruitful when food was served because everyone relaxed and quit posturing. "I guess this is where I confess I'm not much of a cook."

"No!" He clasped a hand to his heart, a horrified expression on his face. "My mate must be a gourmet chef."

"Bastard." I laughed and threw a pillow at him. He caught it and grinned. "But seriously, Matt, we should feed them."

"We will. Fortunately for both of us, my sister not only loves to cook but she's very good at it. She always cooks for these meetings."

Yet another reason to like her. Maybe she'd be able to teach me how to boil water without burning it.

"And, as much as I hate to say it, I need to run." He reached for his jacket where it rested across the foot of the bed. "There's more coffee in the kitchen and your grandmother's up." A kiss, deep enough to be a promise of loving to come, and a hug. "Don't go outside unless someone's with you. We still don't know where the trackers are."

I wanted to argue, but he was right. I had no desire to risk falling in their hands, not now that I'd finally found a home.

"I'll be good," I promised. "Go on. You don't want to be late."

Two hours later, I sat on my heels and pushed my hair back from my forehead. Until that moment, I'd never thought about how exhausting it could be to shapeshift. It was just something I did. Of course, I didn't usually shift back and forth and back and forth. Now all I wanted to food and then sleep. My grandmother, on the other hand, had other ideas. She seemed determined to make up for any training I'd missed by running away and hiding all these years. I was grateful, really I was, but did she need to try to do it all in one sitting?

Grandma knelt opposite me. I might be exhausted, but she looked remarkably fresh. Of course, she was fully clothed and hadn't been shifting on demand. More than that, she hadn't been forced to hold the shift, mid-way between human and panther. That had been the hardest, but it was something I needed to master. The run-in with the trackers had shown me that much. If I'd been mid-shift, I would have moved faster, my senses would have been keener. More importantly, the partial shift wouldn't have been noticeable to anyone but one of our kind. No one else would know I was anything but a "normal" human.

"Excellent, Finn." Grandma smiled in approval and handed me a bottle of water. "You've done well on your own, much better than I'd hoped."

"I don't know." My shoulders lifted in a shrug. "Mostly I just tried to control the need to shift and to do everything I could to hide who and what I am." Now that I thought about it, that probably explained not only why I hadn't realized I was an alpha but also why others of our kind hadn't realized I was nearby. That was something else I needed to think about.

"I know your mother taught you our family history."

I nodded. It was important that every shapeshifter know their bloodline and what animals their relatives changed into. Yes, animals. While we usually tended to mate—or marry—only those who shifted to the same animal as we did or who didn't shift all, that wasn't always the case. There were also the rare ones of our kind who could shift into more than one type of animal. These shapeshifters were the basis for the skinwalker legends. Our family boasted at least three skinwalkers but, to the best of my knowledge, there hadn't been one in recent generations.

"So, you know what I have to ask," she continued.

"I do and, no, I've never shifted into anything except my panther."

"I can't deny I'm disappointed. I will also admit to wondering if part of the reason Jennings kept after you all this time is because he suspects you might be a skinwalker."

Now that I thought about it, I was a little disappointed as well. I'd been so focused over the years on trying to keep one step ahead of Jennings that I hadn't given much thought to my family history. But now I could. I could let my guard down and I could let myself relax—and let my panther have more freedom than ever before. That meant I could finally think about it. Interesting as it might be to shift into different animals, I was already different. I didn't need anything else adding to it.

Then the second part of Grandma's comment hit me. Could Jennings believe I was a skinwalker? It did add another layer to his obsession. A male alpha who could count as his mate a female who not only was an alpha but was also a skinwalker would command the respect of his own clan as well as that of the other clans and their leaders. Given the chance, Jennings would do all he could to spin that respect into even more power for himself.

I shuddered and wrapped my arms around myself. Thinking about what Jennings might do if he got his hands on me and realized I was an alpha was bad enough. If he decided I was a skinwalker . . . I didn't want to consider what he'd do. Would he try to force me to shift? What would he do when I didn't shift into anything but my panther?

Fear churned deep in my stomach and I swallowed against the bile rising in my throat. I couldn't think about that. I refused to run again. Jennings had cost me too much already. No more. I'd found my mate and I'd found a home. I wouldn't let Jennings take that away from me. If he wanted a fight, by God he'd get one.

But I needed something to have a real chance at finally taking control of my life—knowledge. I needed to know everything that had happened, not only with regard to the Northern California clan, but with all our kind since I ran away. That was something my grandmother could help me with. I had no qualms picking her brain for anything and everything that could help me, help us, defeat Jennings once and for all.

"Finn, can we talk?"

I looked at Danny Gillespie in surprise. He and Matt had been in the den with my grandmother the last I knew. I'd opted to "help" Sharon with dinner, although I'm pretty sure she'd call it something else, especially after I managed to catch a paper towel on fire.

"Sure." I dried my hands, hoping my nerves didn't show. I still hadn't quite figured him out. I knew he was part of Matt's inner circle in the pride, not only a valued advisor but also a close friend. But I'd been on my own for so long. It was hard to trust anyone. Matt was different because of our connection. Sharon and Stefan had become the closest things to real friends I'd had since leaving California. But Danny was still something of an unknown.

"What's up?" I asked as we stepped onto the back porch.

Danny leaned against the railing and studied his feet. I waited, standing by the back door. The sounds of Sharon working in the kitchen mixed with the sounds of crickets singing somewhere in the dark. An afternoon rain had cooled the day off some, not enough to be chilly, but enough that the temperature was comfortable. None of which mattered as I waited for Danny to explain why he wanted to talk.

"Finn, I ran you through the system, including all the different aliases you've used since leaving California." My heart beat faster and my fists clenched behind my back. "Jennings did file a missing persons report when you ran away. At the time, he told the police he was the executor of your parents' estates and your legal guardian."

"What? No way." My parents sat me down on my thirteenth birthday and explained how they'd arranged for Aunt Jane and Uncle Lou to look after me if anything happened to them. Nothing, absolutely nothing, would have convinced them to name Jennings to that role. "Aunt Jane and Uncle Lou were my guardians. My folks told me that much before they died. It was also how Aunt Jane said they could keep me safe after Jennings attacked me."

"Which is what the police found out during the course of their investigation. It seems your parents' attorney wasted little time in getting that information to them. Then the detectives went back to ask Jennings about it, he said he made the claim because he thought they wouldn't pay attention otherwise."

"And?"

"They left the report open. They figured there was more to the story and that maybe you had good reason to run as far from Jennings as you could. There was a supplemental report filed later, after they'd tracked down your aunt and uncle. They said you'd gone to live with friends across the country in order to put the trauma of your parents' deaths behind you and that, as your guardians, they approved. When pressed by the cops for your location, they refused, saying they were worried about Jennings trying to get in touch with you and they alluded to concerns about his intentions where you're concerned."

I moved to the edge of the porch and stared into the distance. Thank God the cops realized something was off about Jennings. "I guess I should be grateful I didn't have to worry about the cops finding me all this time."

Danny nodded. "I called a friend out there we can trust. He'll make sure the flags on your name are removed."

Relief so great I almost sagged under it filled me. "Thank you." I turned back to look at him.

"No need." He smiled, the first real smile I'd seen from him. It transformed him from a serious, almost scary man into one with more than a touch of the imp in him. I liked the change.

"I also contacted your cell phone provider. They'll let me know if there's any activity on your phone. Unfortunately, your laptop won't be as easy. The uniforms will check with the local pawn shops, but I don't want you to get your hopes up."

I sighed and frowned. Then, seeing him watching me in concern, I smiled. He'd done more, much more than I dared hope for and in a very short period of time. "Thanks, Danny. I mean it."

"I just wish I had better news for you."

"Don't. You've given me information I didn't have and you're helping give me back my life. You have nothing to apologize for."

"Matt told me the same thing. He also said that's what you'd say." Now he grinned. "It's hard to realize you two have only known each other a few days. You're so good together.

"Finn, I wasn't lying the other night when I said I'd met your parents. I was a student at UCLA and your mother was a guest lecturer in one of my classes. She was the first female alpha I'd ever met. It was all I could do not to fall on my knees right there in the middle of her talk. She must've realized it because she asked me to stay behind when class ended.

"You remind me of her in so many ways. I feel much the same when I'm near you that I did with her. It's the same with your grandmother. Then, when you're with Matt, there's a completeness and power that is all I need to know you two belong together." He paused and gave a rueful laugh. "I guess what I'm trying to say is I'm glad you're one of us and I'm here if you ever need anything."

He extended his hand and I took it. I had a feeling he didn't easily let his guard down. Glad he was that good of a friend to Matt and hoping this was the beginning of a friendship between the two of us, I pulled him into a quick hug. "You just keep looking after Matt," I whispered, mouth close to his ear.

"I will," he promised. "And I'll look after you as well."

"Thanks." I stepped back, figuring we were through but the look on his face stopped me. "What?"

He didn't answer immediately and my stomach did a slow flip.

"I asked my friend for another favor, Finn. He's going to send me copies of what they have on your parents' death."

His words hit me almost like a blow as waves of conflicting emotions rolled over me. Why would he want to see the reports? Did he think I had something to do with what happened? What if Jennings found out? What good would looking at the reports do now, after so long?

"Finn, it's okay." Now he moved to me, his hands reaching out to steady me. "We can trust Eddie not to tell anyone that I'm looking into the case. There's no way Jennings will find out I've asked for the files. I promise."

"But why? Why look at the reports?"

"Because I did know your parents. Not well, but well enough to know that you're right. There's no way either one of them would have committed suicide, much less both of them. They loved one another too much and, more than that, they wouldn't do anything to leave you at Jennings's mercy. Because of that, I want to see if the cops missed anything. More importantly, I want to know if there was anything besides wanting to keep our existence secret behind Jennings pushing everyone to accept the suicide ruling."

For a moment I looked at him, disbelief filling me. Finally, someone wanted to know what happened as badly as I did. Then the implications of what he said hit and my stomach pitched. Jennings had been the one to push us into not questioning the initial ruling that my parents had killed themselves. Just like he pushed to be named Alpha before the clan had a chance to grieve. He'd been there, strong and determined, to take charge and everyone agreed because they'd been too stunned to do anything else.

Oh God, what if he killed my parents?

That possibility had always been there in the back my mind, but I never allowed myself to voice it. Now that I had, fear rolled over me. I knew what sort of man Jennings was. He'd tried to rape me and only the fact Dad taught me how to defend myself had saved me. If Jennings was capable of that, I had no doubt he was capable of wanting my parents dead. But had he killed them? If he had, what would he do to me now, should he manage to lay his hands on me?

My stomach lurched again, and I pulled free of Danny's supporting grasp. I stumbled down the three steps to the backyard. My feet moved across the grass like they were slogging through six inches of mud. Stomach heaving, I dropped my knees.

"Finn!" Matt's voice, full of worry, sounded through my retching. "Danny, what the hell happened?" Then he was next to me, his hands pulling my hair back, his voice soothing. There was a murmur. Danny? I couldn't be sure. All I heard was the pounding of my pulse and the retching as I emptied my stomach there in the middle of the backyard.

"Easy, Finn. I've got you." Matt gathered me in his arms and carefully stood. "Danny, call Stefan and ask him to come over."

"No." I shook my head. He could have put me down but just then it felt good—it felt safe—to have him hold me close. "It was just reaction. I'm all right."

"The hell you are. What did he say to upset you so badly?"

"Not his fault." I punched his shoulder to make him look at me instead of glaring at his friend. "Matt, I mean it. It's not his fault."

"Then what happened?" He carefully set me on my feet and looked me square in the eye.

"He did what should've been done years ago. He did what I should have. He asked for copies of the reports into my parents' deaths." I gave Danny a weak but grateful smile. "That made me accept what I've suspected all along—that my parents were murdered and that Michael Jennings may have been responsible. That made me remember how he'd tried to rape me and to wonder what he'd do now if he managed to catch me." I tried to smile but settled for a slight shrug. "Call it reaction. But don't blame Danny. I'm grateful he's concerned enough to want to see if the cops missed something."

"You're sure you're okay?"

"Feeling a bit rocky and very foolish is all." And in dire need of mouthwash.

"All right." Matt slipped an arm around my waist, protective and a bit possessive. Unsteady as I still felt, I didn't mind the possessiveness just then. "Danny, I want to know what you find out."

"I'll let you know as soon as I've seen the files." He stepped forward until he stood in front of me. He smiled slightly, understanding reflected in his eyes, as he reached for my hands. "Finn, I'm sorry I brought your fears and suspicions back like this. But I didn't want to go behind your back. More than that, I wanted you to understand exactly what sort of danger you might still be in. I swear Jennings will never lay a hand on you. I'll kill him before he can. If it turns out that your parents were murdered, their deaths will be avenged—either by our law or by the laws of the normals."

"Thank you." I squeezed his hands. "I'm glad you're Matt's right hand and his friend. Promise me you will always protect him."

"I will, just as I'll protect you." Danny let my hands go and stepped back. "Matt, she needs to replace her cell phone and laptop. We haven't been able to find them."

"We took care of the cell phone this afternoon. If she hadn't been so damned hard-headed about not wanting me to buy her a replacement laptop, we'd have dealt with that as well." He grinned down at me. He'd been frustrated because I wouldn't let him buy me what he wanted, but he needed to understand I wasn't going to rely on him for everything.

"Finn?" Danny looked at me in question, not understanding any more than Matt had.

"Men." I rolled my eyes and grinned. "Matt wanted to buy me a top of the line laptop. I don't need anything like that."

"If you're going to do your art, you do," Matt countered.

Danny had the good sense not to laugh, but amusement danced in his eyes. "I see this is something you two need to discuss. All I'll say is that your laptop does need to be replaced."

The sounds of the car door opening and closing prevented either Matt or me from commenting, which was probably for the best. We'd hash out that particular issue later.

"Danny, go see who that is," Matt said. "We'll be along shortly."

Danny nodded and hurried inside.

"Are you sure you're okay?" Matt wanted to know.

"I'm fine. I promise. It really was only reaction." I leaned into him, drawing strength from him. "You'd better go greet your guests. I'll be there as soon as I wash my face and rinse my mouth."

Hopefully, by then I'd feel a lot more emotionally stable.

He gave me one last look, searching my face to see if I was hiding anything from him. Then he lightly kissed me. "Our guests," he corrected. "You need to get used to the fact you're no longer alone, Finn. I'm here for you and so are all the others."

"I'm trying. Just be patient with me. It's been a long time since I had anyone but myself to consider or rely upon."

"All the time you need." He gave me a hug and then, with his arm around my waist, led me inside.

Matt smiled and walked to my side when I entered the den a few minutes later. Seeing the worry reflected in his eyes, I nodded, hoping he understood. I was all right—now. Maybe for the first time since my parents' deaths, I was all right, or as close to it as possible given the circumstances.

I glanced around, doing my best to appear casual as I did. The room was crowded. Additional chairs had been brought in to handle everyone. It didn't surprise me to find more men than women there. Our kind is all too often patriarchal. One reason is that female alphas are rare. Because of that, they tend to be protected, cherished even. If they were the only leader of pride or pack, they could be challenged and injured or killed trying to maintain their position as the Alpha.

For another reason, we tend to follow societal norms. That meant males usually took on the leadership and combat roles. Yes, combat. We don't fight others of our kind as often as we used to, but we remember the old wars. We also remember that we are the vast minority of people living on this Earth. Discovery of our existence by the normals could lead to our extinction and, like any living, thinking being, we have no wish to die.

"I've been explaining why I asked them to join us tonight," Matt said as he led me to his favorite chair. He waited as I sat and then he carefully settled on the chair's right arm. "This is Meg Finley, my mate. Finn, these are the leaders of the eight other prides and packs that make up our clan." He went on to introduce everyone, taking care to name not only their pride but their animal as well.

"Welcome to the clan, Finn." A man with the darkest skin I'd ever seen said. There was a hint of the Caribbean in his voice, just enough to let me know he'd spent much of his life here.

"Thank you."

How easy it was to face these people, much easier than it had been to face the pride last night.

"Have any of you discovered anything about the trackers?" Matt asked. As he did, Sharon and Danny entered, carrying trays of food and drink.

"Nothing solid." I identified the speaker as John Martinez, leader of one of the packs. "A couple of my people heard of someone looking for information about you and a woman who might be staying with you."

"It has to be them." The second speaker was one of three women present. Matt had identified her as Tamara Jungst, also a pack member and mate to Martinez. "Word of Finn's joining the pride as your mate has already spread through the clan."

"And?" My heart beat a little faster as I waited for her answer.

"We're glad he found someone finally, ma'am." Brian Jacobson, pride leader and cougar, said with a grin. "Matt, we all felt Finn's power when we entered the house. If that wasn't enough, we can feel the way you two complement one another. This is right for you and that means it's right for all of us."

"Thanks." I meant it. "But back to the trackers. Do your people know where we should be looking for them?"

"Right now, no. But they know to contact me as soon as they have a lead on those sons of bitches." Tamara gave me a nod that left no doubts she'd do her best to do exactly as she promised.

"Why don't you just let Jennings know that he can no longer stalk her without repercussions?" Colin O'Malley, pack leader from close to the Oklahoma border, asked.

"Much as I'd like to do just that, I can't." Matt answered. His right hand fisted at his side, an indication he was doing his best to keep his frustration in check. "There's no doubt the men who tried to take Finn were trackers. It's obvious Jennings sent them, but we have no direct proof of it—yet. That's the main reason we need to find them. I want to prove Jennings was behind the attack. Then he can be dealt with—not just for trying to harm Finn but for putting all our people in danger."

"And if we can't find the trackers?"

"Then we figure something else out."

"There is something we can do to flush them out." And possibly Jennings himself. Neither prospect made me feel better, but I'd do almost anything to quit living in fear. When the others looked at me in question, I continued. "Send word to the other clan leaders that I will formally be presented as Matt's mate and the clan's female Alpha this weekend."

"Finn!" Matt's hand gripped mine so tightly I wondered if my bones might break.

"Matt, it's the sort of slap in the face Jennings can't ignore. He'll order the trackers to take me before the ceremony can happen."

"It's a good idea," Danny said, albeit reluctantly, from across the room. "And it gives us control over the situation. But not this weekend. We need time to plan."

Matt frowned. He didn't like it. Hell, I didn't like it. But if putting a great big target on my back, at least metaphorically speaking, gave us a chance to trap the trackers, it was worth it. Besides, I knew Matt and the others would protect me. Not only was I their female Alpha, but none of them approved of their territory being violated. Jennings might be untouchable, at least for now, the trackers weren't. They needed to be stopped before they caused even more trouble.

Besides, once we had them, we would have Jennings.

"How long?" Martinez asked, looking from Danny to Matt and me.

"I'd prefer a minimum of a month, but two weeks will do it." When I started to protest, he shook his head, stopping me. "Finn, you've spent years doing your best to hide what you are. You need the time to sharpen your connection with your panther and to learn exactly what it means to be an Alpha. But there's more. I know we can protect you, but we have to be prepared for the unexpected. If the trackers or Jennings somehow manage to get past our defenses, you need to be able to protect yourself, shifted or not."

"He's right," Tamara said. "What can I do to help?"

No one said anything for a moment.

"Let's get a general plan put together tonight. We'll meet again tomorrow and fine tune some of it, especially Finn's self-defense training," Danny said.

Tamara nodded.

"Matt?" I didn't want to wait that long to formally be announced as his mate. If I was honest with myself, I worried he'd realize he'd been wrong to ask me to stay and to take me as his mate.

He pulled me close. "We have the other pride and pack leaders here. Your grandmother and uncle are here. If no one objects, we will take care of the formalities tonight. The ceremony can be held later." As he spoke, he glanced around the room, all but daring anyone from objecting. "If that's what you want." When he looked down at me, I saw his uncertainty.

"I do."

"All right. I'll agree to Danny's suggestion. Understand that I will not allow Finn to be placed in danger. We will take all necessary precautions to protect her."

"I'm not going argue." I smiled up at him, hoping he understood I trusted him and the rest of the clan to keep me safe.

"Then here's what we'll do. Danny, I leave the security arrangements to you and Tamara. I want one of you to brief us tomorrow afternoon. Finn, you will do whatever they say when it comes to self-defense."

"Understood."

"In the meantime, if any of you hear anything about the trackers or Jennings, let me know." Matt paused when Sharon appeared from the kitchen. "Dinner's ready. Let's not think about trackers or what they might do for the next few minutes."

More than happy to do just that, I let Matt help me to my feet. The look he gave me spoke volumes. We'd be having a *discussion* once the others left. Well, maybe it was time he learned I had a temper and wasn't going to let him wrap me in tissue paper.

CHAPTER TEN

"**D**amn it, Finn. Have you lost your fucking mind?"

I guess I ought to be glad Matt waited until everyone except my grandmother, Danny and Sharon left before exploding, but I wasn't in the mood to put up with his temper. I understood why he was angry. I'd sprung the idea of my being the bait to draw out the trackers without warning. I'd denied him the opportunity to consider my plan, much less voice his reservations, without undermining me in front of the pack and pride leaders. He knew better than to do that, especially since he wanted their approval of me as his mate. So, he'd kept silent—hell, he'd probably bitten through his tongue—until now.

Well, too bad. The last few days had proven one thing if nothing else. I was tired of running. I was tired of looking over my shoulder, always afraid of who or what might jump out of the next shadow. It was time to take my life back and this was the best way I knew to do it. At least it was the first step in doing so. Until we managed to deal with Jennings, I'd never be truly free. But first things first. Find the trackers and tie them to Jennings. Then we'd figure out how to take him down so he'd never again bother me.

"No, I haven't lost my mind." I did my best to keep my temper under control. Matt might be my mate and we might share a bed, but he was still a stranger. I didn't know how he'd react to a direct confrontation, so I needed to be careful about what I said and how I said it. "Matt, I'm sorry. I should have discussed this with you before bringing it up with the others, but it just came out. I hadn't thought about it before then." That much, at least, was the truth.

I wanted to go to him, but I didn't. He needed to think about what I said and what it meant. At least I'd want to if our positions were reversed and I hoped he'd give me that time. I also hoped he took the time to think and not just react.

"Maybe we should leave," Danny said softly, almost hesitantly.

He and Sharon stood near the front door, looking like they desperately wanted to escape. Not that I blamed them. But, like it or not, I needed them there. If Matt calmed down enough to think about what we could do to draw the trackers out, they needed to be included in the planning, just as my grandmother did.

My grandmother. She had remained silent during the meeting, speaking only when asked for her opinion. Not that it fooled me. The moment I suggested drawing out the trackers and, by extension, Jennings, she'd frowned. In the back of my mind, my panther flattened her ears and mewled in protest. She didn't like upsetting my grandmother any more than I did. Now, whether we were ready or not, we needed to face her and Matt.

"No. Stay." Matt dragged a hand through his hair and then shook his head. Anger no longer clouded his expression but his frustration was still clear to see. Well, that was a step forward—I hoped. "I'm not going to say I like the idea, Finn, because I don't. Nor do I like the fact you basically ambushed me with it. Don't ever do that again." The warning was clear.

"Matt, I am sorry." Slowly, giving him time to stop me, I moved to where he stood and reached for his hands. Then I waited until he looked down at me. I wanted him to see I meant every word I said. If we couldn't get past this, I might as well move on now, while I still could. "Matt, you are my mate and I am yours. I swore my life and my arm to you, the pride and the clan. But we don't know one another yet. That's going to take time and it means we will both make missteps along the way. It doesn't help that I've been on my own for so long. I've forgotten what it's like to have to take another person, and their feelings, into account when planning what I'm going to do next.

"That said, I did tell the truth when I said the idea just came to me. Yes, I could have waited to say anything until we'd had time to talk about it. If I had, I'd have shown that I trust you and respect your role as clan leader. For that, I'm sorry I didn't wait."

God, I hope he understood.

"Matt, if I'd waited, what would have happened?"

For a moment, he didn't answer. Instead, he looked at our joined hands. As he did, my heart thudded in my chest. I swallowed hard, wondering how long he'd make me wait before saying anything.

"We would have moved before we're ready. Before you're ready." Suddenly, he pulled me close, cradling me against his chest. "You had the right idea and Danny had the best way to execute it so we don't put you in any more danger than necessary." He tilted my face up and brushed his lips against mine. "And you wouldn't formally be my mate and the clan's female Alpha now. That gives you protection and power you wouldn't have otherwise."

"Matt." I freed one hand from his and rested it against his chest. His heart beat steadily as he looked down at me. "You were so pissed at me."

He chuckled softly and didn't deny it.

"Why did you go ahead and ask the other pack and pride leaders to confirm me as your mate?"

I didn't want to ask, but I needed to know his answer.

Instead of answering, he led me to a chair and seated me. Then he reached out with his right leg and hooked the footstool. I watched as he dragged it in front of my chair before he lowered to sit on it. His position wasn't lost on me. For the first time since I dove in his car to get away from the trackers, he placed himself lower than me—well, the first time except when I'd been on top of him during sex. But then he'd been on top of me pretty much as often as I'd been on top of him.

"Finn, I did it because you are my mate. You are the strong female Alpha our pride and our clan needs. You proved that by voicing an opinion you knew I wouldn't agree with, at least not at first. I might not always appreciate that strength, but it is something that will help make me a better clan leader and help make our clan stronger." He once again reached for my hands and turned them over so our fingers could twine.

"But you have to understand something. As my mate and as the clan's female Alpha, I will do everything I can to protect you. That means you aren't always going to like what I do or say."

I smiled and inclined my head. I understood. But did he understand it went both ways?

He smiled and released my right hand before standing. He kept his hold on my left hand as he turned to face the others. "Danny, I want extra security here until this is over."

"I'm already on it. Tamara will be by tomorrow with a crew to update your security system. I'll make sure there are eyes on you both, electronic and real, all the time."

"Danny," Matt growled.

I fought my smile. Clearly, my mate appreciated being watched constantly about as much as I did.

To my surprise, my grandmother responded before Danny could. "Matt, think. Jennings has already proven he'll do almost anything to get my granddaughter. Do you really think he'd balk at hurting you, or maybe Sharon, in an attempt to force you to turn Finn over?"

Matt growled again. His panther was so close to the surface, I saw it ripple across his face. He dared Jennings to be so foolish. Unfortunately, he didn't know Jennings and didn't understand exactly how far the man would go to get what he wanted.

What surprised me, however, was the second growl to fill the room. Danny still stood near the door. Lips pulled back, teeth bared, he'd shoved Sharon behind him, as if to protect her from some unseen attack. Interesting. I hadn't picked up on that aspect of their relation-ship and, judging from the look on his face, I had no doubt Matt remained clueless to it.

"Then that means Sharon needs security as well."

"Matt!"

"It's that or you stay here with Finn until this is over."

"I don't care if you like it, Sharon. I'm not going to risk either of you. If that means the two of you stay here, out of sight until we spring the trap, so be it."

I narrowed my eyes. If he thought I'd stayed locked away in the house until this was over, he had another thing coming. From the way my panther paced back and forth in my head, I knew she shared my feelings.

As if sensing my thoughts, Matt looked at me and sighed. "We will discuss this more tomorrow, after Danny and Tamara have pulled together their recommendations. Until then, Finn, I'm asking you to stay inside."

I nodded once. He had asked, after all.

"Just remember we can't risk the trackers leaving our territory before we tie them to Jennings," I reminded him.

"Agreed. But we can't have them moving on you until we're prepared." He pinned me with a firm look and I nodded again.

Then, seeing he still needed to be convinced, I searched for the right words to reassure him. "Matt, I'm not going to lie. I'm terrified of what the trackers will do if they get their hands on me." And that was putting it mildly. I moved to stare out the window. Then I stepped away, closing the blinds against any prying eyes that might be hiding in the shadows. When I turned to face the others, I made up my mind. I needed to reassure them, especially Matt and Grandma, that I wasn't going to do anything foolish. "I've always known the day would come when I'd have to face Jennings. But it was never real until the trackers cornered me in the parking garage. Matt, if you hadn't been there." I broke off as the fear I'd felt before his car came to a screeching halt next to me returned. "The fact the trackers didn't seem to care if they revealed our existence to the rest of the world is bad enough. Worse, I know Jennings told them to do whatever it took to bring me back to the clan. That, combined with his other violations of our codes, simply proves he is as close to going renegade as possible without being cast out by the other clans."

Hopefully, that would soon change.

"All of that should be enough to make the other clan Alphas to take a hard look at everything he's done since taking over the Northern California clan. Add in what they did with the weapons that bastard used on me when they tried to take me and Jennings is edging close to a death sentence. My question to each of you is if you —if *we*—are ready to take the next step."

Matt opened his mouth to answer. Before he could say anything, my grandmother laid a gentle hand on his arm and shook her head. Then she motioned for us to be seated. This might be Matt's home, but she was our elder. We respected her as such and also as an Alpha powerful enough to wipe the floor with all of us, no matter what her age.

"Before we answer, how far are you willing, Finn?" Grandma asked.

Sharon gasped, and Matt once again started to say something. Ignoring them, Grandma waited. Her eyes locked on mine and I was transported back to my childhood. I'd been unable to hide anything from her then and I doubted I could now. Not that I wanted to.

"There's no simple answer, Grandma." I glanced down at my hands and the ring I now wore, my mother's engagement ring. "I want to know the truth behind my parents' deaths. Danny's already looking into it for me." I looked at the man and nodded, hoping he understood how much I appreciated it.

"If we find out Jennings had anything to do with what happened to them, or that he knew and helped cover it up, I want his head." His head, his dick, and every other part of him. I wanted him to hurt as I'd hurt. Then I wanted him dead and buried, erased from existence and memory.

"If we can tie him to the trackers, I want him to answer to the other clan leaders. His actions have risked all of us and he needs to be held accountable."

As I spoke, Matt moved to stand behind my chair, His hands rested on my shoulders, anchoring me and reminding me I was no longer alone. I reached up and rested my right hand on his. After so many years on my own, I relished having someone at my side, someone to watch my back. Most of all, I knew he, as well as Sharon and Danny, intended to do everything they could to keep me safe and make those responsible for hurting me pay. That knowledge was a gift I'd never forget.

"Are you willing to accept the consequences, not only for yourself but for your new pride and clan?"

This time, I didn't answer right away. I knew the answer. I'd considered those consequences from the moment I decided to offer myself to Matt as female alpha to his male. If this backfired, we would all pay. The pride and clan would survive but I face the very real possibility that we wouldn't. I'd pay that price and gladly to end this with Jennings, but I couldn't ask Matt to.

"For me, yes. I won't risk clan, pride or my mate." I didn't dare look at Matt. Not that I needed to. I felt his anger at my comment.

"And my mate forgets that I can speak for myself," he ground out. "I accept the risk for myself and for the clan." He moved to stand in front of me. "Finn, if we don't stop him, he will bring about all our deaths. Not just yours and mine, not even just our clan but all our kind. You know that."

"Matt's right." Sharon moved to her brother's side. "Finn, I hate like hell what that bastard did to you. The fact my big brother here thinks I might be a pawn in whatever game he's playing only makes it worse. I say we take the fight straight to him, but on our terms, not his."

"Agreed." My grandmother gave a decisive nod.

"So, what do we do?" I looked at Matt and read the answer in his eyes. "I can't disappear between now and the clan meeting. If I do, we risk the trackers giving up and leaving. If that happens, we've accomplished nothing and I'll still be looking over my shoulder, waiting for Jennings to send someone else after me."

"Finn's right," Grandma said. "She can't just disappear between now and when you present her formally as your mate."

"I won't have her put in danger." Matt pulled me to my feet and drew me against him, as if by doing so, he could protect me from Jennings and anyone else who might want to harm me.

"Matt." I reached up and gently cupped his cheek with one hand. "I'll be careful. I promise. Believe me, the last thing I want is for Jennings to get his hands on me. But you know we're right about this."

I waited, hoping he understood and agreed.

"God, I want to hide you away from that bastard, maybe send you to my parents in Ireland until this is over." He leaned down and rested his forehead against mine. "But that doesn't mean I have to like it." He lifted his head and looked across the room to where Danny and Sharon sat watching us. "Danny, I'm trusting you and Tamara to keep her safe. Finn, you aren't to step outside unless one of us is with you, at least not until they have security set."

"Agreed." I relaxed, glad he wasn't going to fight us on this. Even so, I had a feeling I'd hear an earful once we were alone.

"There's one more thing, Finn."

I narrowed my eyes and looked at my mate suspiciously.

"What?" I drew the word out until it was three syllables long.

"Don't spring any more surprises on me for a while. Promise."

"I'll try."

Relief washed over me as he smiled and shook his head, a soft chuckle escaping his lips. One crisis averted, at least for the moment.

"I think we could all use a drink," Grandma said, and Sharon disappeared into the kitchen, Danny on her heels. "Shall we?" she asked and nodded in the direction they'd gone.

"You go ahead. We'll be right there," Matt replied. He waited until we were alone before continuing. "Finn, you're right about us not knowing one another. That means we both need to work hard or all we'll have between us is sex and I want more. I want my mate to be more than just someone I sleep with. I guess I should have told you that before, but I'm telling you now."

Relief filled me. I hadn't really thought about it, but he'd just said exactly what I'd been hoping for. I wanted what my parents had, and my grandparents. I wanted a partner as well as a lover.

"Good." I pulled his head down and kissed him. "I want the same thing."

He grinned. "Very good." Another kiss. "Let's go join the others and see what we can figure out."

By the time we entered the kitchen, Sharon—probably with help from Danny—had set out bottles of merlot, Irish whiskey, single malt and glasses. An assortment of crackers, chips, cheeses and dips had also been laid out. Seeing how she kept herself busy at the sink, rinsing dishes from dinner and putting them in the dishwasher, I knew she was worried. Not that I blamed her.

"Shar," Matt began. I placed my hand on his arm and shook my head. I needed to do this.

"Sharon, we're okay." It was simple to say and, thankfully, something I believed—at least for now. "And I—we—want your help, yours and Danny's and Grandma's."

She turned off the water and wiped her hands. It seemed to take a long time and I guessed she was gathering her thoughts. I'd learned over the last few days exactly how much alike she and her brother happened to be. It wouldn't surprise me at all to have her volunteer to hold me down while he tried to pound some sense into me. When she turned and I saw the approval reflected in her eyes, I almost sagged with relief.

"Sit. Neither of you ate much earlier." She motioned Matt and me to the table and waited until we'd complied.

"Finn, please tell me you aren't going to make a habit of dropping bombshells without warning," Danny said as he took his place at the table.

"I'll try not to." I waited as Sharon and my grandmother joined us. The next few minutes were spent pouring drinks, filling plates and eating. "So, do you all think I'm crazy?"

"No comment," Danny said with a grin. "That's one of those questions like 'do you still beat your wife?' There's no way to answer without getting in even more trouble."

"Coward." Matt grinned and tossed his napkin across the table at his friend. "Except I don't think you're crazy, Finn. I know you are."

"Maybe not crazy, but not cautious either." My grandmother leaned back, studying both Matt and me.

"I think I like your response best, Grandma." I reached over and gave her hand a squeeze. "I have another question. Assuming Tamara's people are right, how did the trackers know I'm staying here with Matt?"

"You caught that, huh?" Matt frowned.

"I don't understand. Why wouldn't they know she's here?" Sharon asked.

"The only time they saw us together is when Matt rescued me. I doubt they got a good look at him. Especially since he sent one flying over the car as he braked next to me. That means they either accessed the security video or they got his license plate and ran it."

"And that plate is registered to a holding company," he took up. "There's no way they'd figure out this quickly that I was behind the wheel."

"Then someone in the pride or clan told the trackers." Danny's voice was hard.

"Not necessarily," Grandma put in. "They could simply assume that, after being injured and so nearly captured, she'd come to Matt for protection. It's what most of us would do if we were in her position."

"But the possibility that someone told them exists and we have to consider it."

There could be no mistaking Matt's concern or his anger at such a betrayal. Unfortunately, he was right. Even so, I leaned toward Grandma's explanation. It made more sense, especially when you considered the timeframe involved. Then there was the simple fact Matt was a strong and caring clan leader. Only a fool would do anything to betray him and risk not only Matt's anger but that of the rest of the clan.

"Matt, we can make a pretty good guess about the source if we find out when Tamara's people started getting wind of the trackers." Sharon, thank goodness, had managed to keep control of her anger. Hopefully, her brother could follow her example.

Matt looked at her, his brow furrowed. Then he nodded. A moment later, he produced his cell phone. We waited as he programmed in a number. It wasn't long before he asked one simple question: when had word come in that the trackers thought he might be harboring someone? Not about to move, barely daring to breathe, I waited for him to end the call. I think I even prayed about what his response would be.

"Well?" I asked when I couldn't take the waiting any longer.

"It seems your grandmother may be right. Tamara first heard about someone looking for me and the woman I might be harboring two days ago. That's before we let the pride know you were here, much less that you are my mate."

"That means the trackers either recognized you or they simply assumed Finn had done what most of us would do in a similar situation," Grandma commented.

"At least both explanations are better than the alternative." Sharon reached over and poured me another drink before refilling her brother's glass.

"But that doesn't make planning our next move any easier," Matt grumbled.

I sipped and thought. Tonight seemed to be my night for making snap decisions. I wasn't sure I liked that. Maybe it was simply because I'd gone so long without making any major decisions except when to run and where to stop for a few days or weeks. If I'd been lucky, I'd manage to stay in one place for a few months. Until I'd come to Fort Worth, I'd never been anywhere more than four or five months. I hadn't dared stay too long and risk discovery by either the local clan or by Michael and his trackers.

"How badly do we want to force Jennings' hand?" The question was out of my mouth before I could stop it.

"What do you mean?" Matt's voice might have been calm, but his expression darkened toward thunderous again.

"We can try to capture the trackers and use them against Jennings or we can go direct to the source." My heart thudded as I said it. I couldn't believe what I was about to suggest.

"Finn?" Sharon's concern filled her voice.

"I think I know what you're about to say, but talk us through it, child." My grandmother, bless her, wasn't having the knee-jerk reaction I felt building in the others.

I smiled at her in appreciation and tried to gather my thoughts. "If we play this conservatively, we're still at Jennings' mercy, in a manner of speaking. The longer I stay out of reach, the more likely it is the trackers will pack up and leave town. Even they have to realize the longer they're here, the more likely we are to find them. That means the smart thing for them to do is leave town and come back later, when my guard's down. If that happens, I could be hurt—or worse—before the rest of you could intervene."

I waited, giving them time to consider and accept what I said.

"What are you suggesting?" Matt reached over and turned my face so I looked at him.

"Let's throw Jennings completely off-balance. The last thing he'd expect is a call from me. Imagine how he'd react to me telling him I'm not running any longer. I've found my home and my mate. If he continues trying to harm me—and the actions of his trackers prove his intent to harm or worse—my mate and I will take our grievances with him to the other clans. Does he really want the other clan leaders sitting in judgment of him? He'll know he can risk that no more than he can risk me telling them how he tried to rape me."

There. I'd said it. Now all I could do was wait.

"It's a good plan." Danny shook his head before Matt could interrupt. "But not one we put into play just yet." Now he pinned me with a firm look. "My duty to the pride and to the clan is to keep both you and Matt safe, Finn. If we act now and Jennings manages to get his hands on you, I'd have failed. That means we play this smart. You and Sharon, and even Matt and your grandmother, will keep close to the house until Tamara and I have set up security. It also means you are going to work-out with both Tam and me. We need to see what you can do and what we need to teach you that can help keep you alive."

I wanted to argue, but he was right. I wasn't the only one involved now. Jennings wouldn't hesitate to target Matt, or even my grandmother, once he knew they'd helped me. I couldn't let that happen. I wouldn't let that happen.

"All right. I'll be good."

For now.

CHAPTER ELEVEN

For the better part of a week, I kept my word. I didn't leave the house without Matt, Danny or Tamara being with me. Even when it was "just the two of us", we weren't really alone. Tamara made sure we had eyes on us at all times. It didn't matter where we were. Even at home, between the new security system and the guards they'd set on us, I doubt a fly could approach the house without them knowing.

As much as I hated being on such a short leash, it beat the alternative. We still didn't have a location on the trackers. Matt and the others worried they'd left the area. I knew better. Jennings wanted me, and he didn't care what it took to get me. If he knew I'd taken Matt as my mate, he'd stop at nothing to "reclaim" me. That was enough to keep me from screaming in frustration or worse—slipping the guards and searching for the trackers on my own.

Even so, I felt the proverbial noose tightening. The question was whether it was tightening around my neck or the necks of the trackers or, better yet, Jennings.

Each morning began the same. Tamara arrived at the house before eight. God, why did she have to be a morning person? It was bad enough she came before I had enough coffee to function properly. But did she have to enjoy it so much?

She and Matt converted the garage into a gym. Various torture devices—pieces of exercise equipment—seemed to arrive overnight. Each morning began with weights and then a run on the treadmill. Then we'd move inside to the basement. It, too, had been converted. Furniture had been moved out or against the wall. Mats covered the floor. When I asked, Matt explained he wanted to make sure no one could sneak up on us while Tamara and I worked on our hand-to-hand.

"Better."

Tamara bent and extended her hand. I grabbed it and let her help me to my feet. Then I reached up and pushed the hair back from my face. I'd lost count of how many times she'd put me on my back that morning. Damn it, I was out of practice.

"Much better." Tamara tossed me a bottle of water and nodded for me to sit.

I didn't need any further encouragement. I dropped to the mat, leaning against the wall. With a twist of the wrist, I removed the lid from the water and tossed it to the side. For a moment, I considered upending the bottle over my head. Then I decided drinking it was better. I'd get a shower soon enough.

"Really?" I tossed the now empty bottle into the trashcan near the door.

"Really." She grinned, as if realizing I didn't know what she meant. "Finn, do you remember what you told me the first time I showed up here to work with you?"

I frowned and shook my head.

"You said you had a feeling I'd wipe the floor with you. You admitted you hadn't kept up with your training because you didn't want to do anything to call attention to yourself. You didn't go to gyms because you might run into one of our kind who would ask questions you didn't want to answer. You didn't come to one of us to work with you—and I agree with your reasoning." She paused, waiting until I nodded.

"You were right. You were and are rusty. But your 'rusty' is better than a lot of people's normal. What you need to do now is quit holding back. You're keeping too tight of a rein on your panther. That's something you need to stop, especially if you get into a fight with one of our kind. Let her help you. Draw on her strength, her instinct and her reflexes."

I opened my mouth to protest and then snapped it shut. As I did, my panther kneaded my consciousness, agreeing with everything Tamara said. At the same time, I remembered Dad telling me much the same thing during one of our training sessions. I'd trusted him and did as he said. Now I needed to trust Tamara and trust myself. But it was hard, so very hard. I'd done everything possible to hide who and what I was for so long, I wasn't sure I could drop those defenses.

And, if I couldn't, it might get me killed.

"Finn, look at me."

I glanced up. Tamara knelt in front of me, so close our knees almost touched. Her expression serious, I swallowed hard, wondering what she had to say.

"I am not criticizing. Trust me, you'll know when I don't like something you do." She grinned, and I chuckled softly. "Honestly, I'm surprised you've managed to keep your skills as sharp as you have. Yes, you need to work some more with weapons. But that will come. I promise."

I grimaced slightly at the memory of our last trip to the range. To say I was rusty was putting it mildly. Not that it surprised me. I'd never wanted to rely on a gun or knife for protection. After leaving California, I moved around too often to carrying a gun. The last thing I wanted was to be picked up for unlawfully carrying concealed. As for carrying a knife, if the fight was close enough for a blade, it was close enough for claws.

"In the meantime, I want you working with your grandmother. I know she's been helping you get closer to your panther. That's important, especially for an alpha. I'm going to talk with her about helping you learn to tap into your cat's reflexes and the like. If this goes down the way I think it will, you're going to need that advantage. We all will."

I swallowed hard and nodded. Before I could respond, a soft tap sounded at the door. Almost instantly, my panther pushed against my control. She recognized the scent coming from beyond the door. Trusting her, I opened my senses and inhaled. A slight smile lifted the corners of my mouth. Tamara saw and patted my knee in approval. She knew without asking what happened. I nodded in reply even as my panther preened under her approval.

"You both need to eat and then it will be time for our lesson, Finn," Grandma said as she stepped inside. "Matt called a few minutes ago to say he's going to try to join us before we're done but he's not guaranteeing anything. He has a meeting after lunch and he's not sure how long it will run."

I nodded and pushed to my feet. Lessons with my grandmother were, if possible, more intense and certainly exhausting than anything Danny and Tamara put me through. Occasionally, Sharon joined us. The real surprise had been Matt. He joined us whenever he could. My mate, and it still felt strange to say it, took instruction from Grandma with a grace and appreciation that warmed my heart. Part of me knew he did it to help keep me focused. But that wasn't the only reason. He did it because he respected my grandmother, not only because of our relationship but because of her strength as an alpha. Besides, by training together, we became a stronger, more cohesive team. The pride and clan could only benefit from that.

Tamara glanced at her watch. "Finn, remember what I said."

"I will."

"Then I'll see you later. I need to get to work." As she walked past my grandmother, she asked if they could talk privately for a moment. Grandma nodded and followed her out of the basement, leaving me time to gather my thoughts and grab a quick shower, something I badly needed after our workout.

Three hours later, I lay flat on my back in the middle of the basement. Tamara might not have been beating me black and blue, but I felt like it. Instead, my grandmother had been putting me through my paces. While I showered earlier, Tamara told her I needed to learn to trust my panther. Grandma took her comments to heart. After having me shift back and forth several times, she told me to stand in the middle of the basement's main room.

For what seemed like an eternity, she studied me. She walked around me, never saying a word, just looking. When she finally stopped in front of me again, she smiled slightly. Oops. I knew that smile just as I knew that twinkle in her eyes. She had something up her sleeve.

"Do you think you're faster than me?" she asked simply.

I had a sinking feeling that was like asking if I still beat my mate. No matter what I said, it would be the wrong answer.

"I think you are about to make a point."

She chuckled and shook her head. "Answer my question. Do you think you're faster than me?"

I looked at her. She wore a pair of jeans and a short sleeved, cotton blouse. Worn cowboy boots completed the outfit. Her salt and pepper hair framed her face and her green eyes seemed to bore into my soul as she waited for my answer. To the casual observer, she looked like a woman in her sixties, still vibrant and full of energy. Even so, a normal would never think twice when faced with the question she'd posed to me.

So why was I hesitating?

Because I knew better. Our kind lived longer than normals. I had a feeling she could still beat my butt, given the chance. So, what was she up to?

"In our human forms?"

She nodded.

"Will you let me get away with a qualified yes?"

She grinned, showing her teeth and shook her head. Her eyes danced with amusement. That was the only warning I got. One moment, she stood before me, grinning pretty much like a cat does just before it pounces. The next, I hit the floor, hard. My breath exploded in a *whoosh* and I swear stars danced before my eyes. My grandmother, damn her, simply chuckled and reached down to help me to my feet.

Or so I thought. I had a moment's warning from my panther before I hit the wall, face first. I hissed in a breath as I pivoted to my right, alert for another attack. When I swiped my hand under my nose, it came back bloody. So that's the way it was going to be, was it?

I straightened. One corner of my mouth lifted in a smirk. Two could fight that way. She'd made her point and now I'd counter.

I hoped.

Okay, cat, let's see what we can do together.

Almost instantly, I felt the difference. I'd called on the enhanced senses of my panther before. But this—this was so much more. Everything seemed sharper, clearer. An energy similar to what I felt during a shift filled me. Now all I had to do was figure out how to control it, much like the way Grandma was teaching me to control my shifts.

"What the hell?"

Matt's voice echoed off the walls of the basement. Distracted, I started to turn toward him. Almost instantly, my jaguar exerted control. My left arm lifted, bending at the elbow, to protect my head. At the same time, I pivoted to the right, bending at the waist. Air rushed past me as my grandmother's hand reached, and missed, its target. But the damage had been done. Her booted foot connected with my thigh. Pain flashed, followed by a numbness that ran the length of my leg. That knee buckled and I went down, catching myself with one hand while used the other to counter whatever her next move might be.

Not that a follow-up move came. Grandma stepped back and blew out a breath. Then she reached down and helped me to my feet. Balancing on my right leg, I pushed the hair out of my eyes. Then I grinned before wincing slightly. Between my work-out with Tamara and then my grandmother pushing me, forcing me to rely on my panther to keep from having my head handed to me, I hurt pretty much everywhere. I'd heal but, for the moment, I'd pay for not keeping in fighting trim.

"Never let yourself be distracted in a fight, child," Grandma said as she slipped a supporting arm around my waist. "You're lucky I wasn't trying to really hurt you."

I nodded. That was a lesson Dad drilled into me, painfully, when he first taught me to fight. Apparently, it was also one I'd forgotten. I wouldn't make that mistake again.

"Would someone kindly tell me what the hell is going on?"

Matt stood in the doorway. Hands fisted at his sides, expression dark with concern, he waited. In my head, my panther bared her teeth, not quite a challenge but a clear indication of her displeasure at being questioned. Before I could reassure her, or answer Matt's question, my grandmother did.

"Tamara pointed out something she'd noticed working with Finn, something she felt I could help with." She led me across the room to where Matt stood.

"Oh?" He still sounded skeptical, but he relaxed some and pulled me close.

"Oh." Grandma gave him a cheeky grin and I ducked my head, hiding my smile, as he blushed slightly. "She's spent so much time hiding who and what she is, she forgot she can call on her panther for help without actually shifting. Let's just say I was driving the point home again."

"Finn!" He looked down at me, both appalled and horrified at my lapse.

I shook my head and frowned. How could I make him understand?

By telling the truth.

Whether that was my subconscious or my panther, I didn't know. It didn't matter. The advice was sound and I planned to follow it. I'd like to do it after showering and maybe getting something to eat but I had a feeling sooner would be better.

"Grandma's right, Matt." I winced slightly as the feeling started returning to my leg. "Let's go upstairs and I'll explain. Then I think we need to talk about what comes next."

I stepped into the bedroom, a towel wrapped around me. As I did, I smiled slightly. Matt sat on the foot of the bed. His hands dangled between his legs, his eyes watched as I crossed to the dresser. He didn't say anything. He didn't need to. I felt his concern just as surely as I felt every bump and bruise from my workouts with Tamara and Grandma.

"Finn, are you all right?" he asked as I stepped into a pair of panties. Then he was there to fasten my bra for me.

"I am." Or I would be by morning. "You aren't to be upset with anyone except me and my hard head. They did what needed to be done." I turned and looked him in the eye, holding his gaze until he nodded.

"I know. Your grandmother explained and then I talked with Tam. If I'm upset with anyone, it's me for not realizing what you were doing." He stepped back and watched as I pulled on a black tee shirt and pair of jeans.

"Don't." I lifted a hand and cupped his cheek. "You didn't know. Hell, babe, I didn't know." And that bothered me more than I wanted to admit. If Tamara and my grandmother hadn't realized what I'd been doing, it could have been disastrous.

"They really put you through the wringer." He gently touched my swollen and discolored eye. When he did, he winced slightly.

"Most of it's from Grandma. She pushed me, forcing me to call on my panther. That's something Tamara hadn't managed to do." Even though Tamara and I fought without pads, she didn't wear cowboy boots and use them as very effective weapons the way my grandmother did. It was call on my panther or take an even worse beating. Since I wasn't into pain, I reached out for any help my panther could give. "I think she's trying to make up for all the years I've been on my own and not training the way I should have been."

He nodded, his expression still grim. "You've been alone much too long, Finn."

I nodded. The last week had driven that lesson home.

"But no more." Hands gentle, he pulled me close. I slipped my arms around his waist and rested my head against his chest. As I did, I smiled slightly my panther's purr of satisfaction rumbling in my head. "You're home now. You have a pride and a clan at your back and a mate who will not let anything else happen to you."

I lightly kissed the line of his jaw and said a quick prayer. He'd given me an opening. Now if he listened before he reacted. . . .

"Tam told me her people finally got a line on the trackers yesterday. Not enough to get a location but enough to confirm they're still in the area."

I tried to sound casual, not that it fooled Matt. He stiffened and his hands tightened their grip on my waist.

"And?" he all but growled. His eyes narrowed and his expression left no doubt he suspected he wouldn't like what I had to say.

"I asked Danny, Sharon and Tam to join us for dinner tonight." When he simply arched one brow at me, I chuckled. "All right. I asked Danny and Tam to join us for dinner and I asked Sharon if she'd help Grandma cook." I really did need to learn to be a better cook. But that had to wait.

"Finn." He relaxed and stepped back. "This is your house, at least I hope you consider it to be. That means you can ask whomever you want over." Now he cocked his head to one side and narrowed his eyes. "But there's more."

I nodded. "There is and I'm trying not to spring it on you, at least not in front of others."

"Which I appreciate. So tell me."

Three hours later, we sat around the dining room table. Dirty dishes had been cleared from the table. Coffee and tea cups refilled. Everyone turned down Sharon's offer of wine or something harder. It was as if they knew they needed to keep a clear head.

Either that or they figured they'd need a stiff drink after I laid out my plan.

"Danny, how hard would it be to find out if someone turned on or used my old cell phone?" I asked as Sharon and Grandma returned to the table.

"Not very. Why?"

I glanced at Matt. He didn't look particularly happy, but he nodded. I clasped his hand where it rested on the tabletop and gave it a quick squeeze.

"It's time to take control of the situation." I waited, wondering if anyone would figure out what I had in mind. "Okay, let me be a bit more specific. If I were to place a call to Jennings, would there be any way to see if he called my old cellphone afterwards?"

"Smart." Danny grinned and I relaxed some. "Block your number when you call and see if he calls your old cell phone after you hang up. I like it." He glanced at Matt and shrugged. "Sorry, but it is a good plan."

Matt's only response was to nod. I'm not sure he could do anything else. He might understand and even approve on some level, but he didn't like me painting an even bigger target on my back.

"If this works, it will put another nail in his coffin." I looked straight into Matt's eyes, willing him to hear and accept. "The only way he'd have that number is if the trackers recovered my phone and then gave it to him. No one else with the Northern California clan would have it."

"And if he does try to call, we can locate the phone and the trackers."

"Yep." I watched Matt, praying he agreed.

"How long do you need to get things set up?" Matt asked.

Danny grinned again as he pulled out his phone. We waited as he programmed in a number. He had a quick conversation with someone I assumed was a judge, promising to get a written copy of the oral search warrant he was requesting emailed to the judge within the hour. Then he ended the call. "Give me an hour. I need to make sure the paperwork is in order and the judge signs it. Then I'll send it to the carrier. It's more of a CYA in case this happens to go to trial. My contact has already assured me he'd let me know if the phone is activated and where it pings back to."

"Trial?" My voice didn't break—quite—but my concern was obvious. We couldn't take this to trial. Didn't he understand that?

"Finn." He waited until I looked at him. "Breathe. I swear, this is merely a tool to get us the information quicker than we could otherwise. Tam could have someone hack into the phone company but neither of us wanted to risk that. This way, we have a warrant. The judge thinks we are investigating a case of domestic violence. Once we have the information we're after, I'll bury this so far no one will ever find it." He waited, watching my closely. "I swear it. No trial and no paper trail."

"We trust you, Danny," Matt said and I added my agreement.

"Why don't we plan what Finn is going to say to Jennings while he takes care of the warrant?" Grandma suggested, her approval clear.

"All right." Matt didn't sound convinced, but at least he wasn't fighting me on this.

"I do have one other suggestion." Now she leaned forward, looking very much like the predator her shifted form could be. "While Danny is getting everything in place, set up a conference call with several other clan leaders, those we both agree will back us if we have to take this to the other clans. Have them listen in as Finn makes her call. Between that and the recording I'm sure Danny will insist upon—" She smiled as he nodded — "there will be no way Jennings can deny what happened."

"Sounds like a plan." Matt gave me a look that told me he wasn't happy but that he trusted me to know what was best in this situation.

Then, as Danny excused himself to go work on his search warrant, he leaned back. "Let's get to work."

An hour and a half later, we once again gathered around the kitchen table. Resting on the table in front of me was a legal pad with my notes about what I was and wasn't to say. Matt had been firm that I wasn't to go off-script this time and I was inclined to agree. I was taking a risk, a huge one, by contacting Jennings. But it was something I had to do, not just for myself but for Matt as well. As long as Jennings felt he had a claim on me, he'd stop at nothing to get me back. I couldn't—and wouldn't—let his obsession cause Matt harm.

That meant the time had come to finally stand up to him. Hopefully, this would all be over very soon.

"Ready?" I asked, looking at each of my companions in turn.

"Are you?" Matt's concern was clear.

"Yeah." I reached for my new cell phone. As I did, Matt's hand closed over mine. I nodded and let him program the phone so my number wouldn't be displayed when the call was made. Then he nodded to Danny who, using his own cell phone, set up the conference call we'd discussed. Once the others had answered and agreed to listen in, he placed his phone in the center of the table and nodded that he was ready.

I'll admit, I'd been surprised to discover that my grandmother had Jennings' number. Before I'd been able to ask about it, she explained how she'd kept in touch with him since I'd run away. Part of the reason was to see if he had heard anything about me—not that she'd ever expected him to tell her if he had. But another part was to keep track of him. Even though I hadn't told her what happened that last night in California, she'd guessed. Between what Aunt Jane and Uncle Lou told her about that terrible clan meeting when Michael had tried to "claim" me and the way he'd continued to hunt for me after so many years, she knew there was much more to the story than she'd been told. As a result, she wanted him to know that she was keeping an eye on him.

Now Matt programmed in the number and placed the cell phone

next to Danny's on the tabletop. As he did, Danny turned on his digital recorder. Then, with Matt's arm around my shoulders, reassuring and supportive, I waited, wondering if I'd actually be able to carry this through.

"Hello?"

His voice was soft, almost cautious. Maybe it was because he thought the call to be from some telemarketer. Or maybe he'd figured out this was what we'd do since his trackers had failed. God, why had I agreed to do this?

"Hello, Michael." Despite my fear, despite the sudden dryness of my mouth, my voice sounded remarkably calm.

"Who is this?"

The sound of his voice sent me reeling back to that night in my parents' house. I could feel his hands on me, could smell his breath. God, I'd been so scared. I couldn't do this. Why had I thought I could?

Matt's hand closed over mine. At the same time, Grandma moved to stand behind me, her hands resting on my shoulder. They anchored me, reminding me I was no longer alone. I had a life, one that included family long-denied and a mate. Both of which I'd fight for.

Jennings was about to discover first blood would be mine in this renewed war of ours, at least figuratively speaking.

"Think about it for a moment. You'll figure it out. After all, you've spent enough time trying to find me."

For a moment, only silence came from the other end of the call.

"Meg." He almost spat out my name, not exactly the reaction you'd expect from someone supposed to be worried about your well-being.

"Got it in one." I relaxed a little. Maybe this would work. "I have to say, Jennings, you've got some very sloppy trackers. They missed the other day, something no tracker trained by a strong Alpha should have done. Although I will say the *little surprise* you told them to do with their weapons wasn't much fun."

He growled before regaining control. "I wouldn't have authorized such unorthodox measures if you'd just come home. This is where you belong."

Bingo! He not only admitted he sent the trackers after me but that he'd authorized the tainting of their weapons. Score one for the good guys.

"That's where you're wrong." I let a hint of confidence color my voice. Jennings needed to understand I would run from him any longer. "I am home. This is where I belong."

"I don't think so," he countered. "Not unless you're waiting outside my door and I happen to know you aren't."

"Nor will I ever be, unless it is to challenge you for leadership of the pride and clan." Matt's grip on my hand tightened in warning. I was going off-script. I knew it, but this was something I needed to say. "But you don't have to worry--yet. I have no desire to return to California. I've my own pride and clan now—and my own mate. I proudly wear the markings of my new clan and have pledged myself not only to my mate but to the clan."

"You're my mate, Meg, and you'd be wise to remember it!" Jennings snapped.

Even though more than a thousand miles separated us, I could almost feel his control slipping. "Sorry, Jennings, but you're deluding yourself, not that it surprises me. You've yet to admit you were wrong to try to claim me when I was only fifteen. Or that you were wrong to try to rape me. Hell, you haven't admitted any of the ways you've wronged me, my family or your pride and clan."

I inhaled, held it and then exhaled. I needed to keep my temper in check, but it was hard. So very hard. "However, your punishment for that is more than fitting, at least in my eyes. You and you alone caused me to leave the only home I'd known. Your trackers forced me to move time and again in an attempt to keep from falling into their hands. That led me here, to my new pride and clan and into the arms of my mate.

My panther reared up in my mind, roaring in challenge. I gave her a mental pat. Part of me agreed. I'd like nothing more than to make Jennings pay for what he'd done to us. But not yet. There were still too many questions unanswered. So I'd push and hope Jennings would do something foolish.

"Here's what is going to happen, you bastard. You're going to call off the trackers. Then you will formally apologize to my mate and all the other clan leaders whose territory you violated in your obsession to find me. You will admit that you have no claim on me or mine and you will no longer try to do anything—and I do mean anything—to force me to return to California."

He laughed, but it was a hollow laugh, more for effect than anything else. I'd rattled him and everyone listening in knew it.

"If what you said was true, your clan leader would be speaking to me, not you."

I shook my head at Matt when he opened his mouth to respond. It was time to drive my point home.

"You fool." I put as much scorn as I could into my voice. "My mate is my clan leader. I'm an Alpha, like my mother and grandmother before me. I've been accepted not only by his pride but by the other pride and pack leaders as such. As for you, well, you're beneath Matthew's contempt and I wouldn't ask him to waste any of his time on you.

"But know this, Jennings. Matt isn't weak, and he doesn't take intrusions into our territory lightly. If we catch your trackers, they will be punished. We'll make sure they name you as the reason they are here. I will stand by Matt's side as we present evidence against you to the other clan leaders. I will tell them how you were willing to violate our laws to secure your place as the new clan leader in the wake of my parents' murders."

His gasp of surprise at that last was audible. I looked up and saw Grandma's eyes burn with the need for vengeance, a need I shared. His reaction was enough for both of us to know he'd had a hand in what happened so long ago. By God, if I ever found proof of it, I'd see him dead by my hand.

"I don't want the Northern California clan. I have no intention of ever returning there. However, if you don't leave us alone, I will return, and I will call you out. Do you want to risk that?"

"You bitch!"

"Jennings, Jennings, Jennings." I shook my head, not that he could see it. "I expected a better response than that." Humor mixed with contempt. That was the surest way to irritate him even further. "Now call off your trackers and get them the hell out of my territory. This is your one and only warning."

"You don't scare me, Meg. You aren't the female Alpha of the clan yet. I'd have heard if that happened."

Interesting. So he did have someone in the clan working for him, or at least someone who didn't know how to keep their mouth shut. From the way Matt's grip on my hand tightened painfully, my mate realized it as well. But that was something we'd worry about later. Now I needed to play my final card, so to speak.

"You're behind the times, Michael. It's a done deal, or it will be once my markings are finished. Then they will be witnessed and approved by the appropriate pride and pack leaders and blessed by my grandmother. Don't be any bigger of a fool than you've already been. You have seventy-two hours to issue your formal apology and admission or we will take this to the other clan leaders."

I nodded and Matt reached out to end the call. Then he wrapped his arms around me and pulled me onto his lap. I buried my face in the crook of his neck, breathing deeply and trying to slow my pounding heart. Hopefully none of my nerves had showed during the call. Now that it was over, reaction set in. My teeth chattered, heart thudded and it was all I could do to breathe. I'd done more than draw a line in the sand where Jennings was concerned. I'd all but challenged him and that could prove deadly, possibly for both of us.

"You were wonderful!" Sharon said as she threw her arms about both her brother and me. As she did, I heard Danny tell the other clan leaders that Matt would be in touch soon. "I bet that son of a bitch was pissing in his pants."

"Sharon!"

"She's right, dear heart. You were wonderful. More than that, you played him perfectly. He all but admitted everything you said. He certainly didn't deny any of it and that most definitely will not win him any supporters among the clan leaders." Grandma poured me a drink and pushed it across the table to me.

"And you were right about something else, Finn. Someone just called your old cell phone." Danny listened to whoever was on the other end of his call. "I'll be back. They're working on getting a fix on the phone's location. My money's on Jennings panicking and calling the trackers. If they still have it, we'll have them." He slipped his cell phone into his pocket and stood. "I'll be in touch." With that he was gone.

"We'll give you two some time alone." My grandmother gave Sharon a significant look. A moment later, they left the kitchen, closing the door behind them.

"Are you all right?" Matt asked in concern.

"Yeah. Just hold me a bit longer. Please."

"As long as you want."

CHAPTER TWELVE

"Finn, are you sure you're okay?"

Matt sat next to me on the sofa and turned so our knees touched. His eyes were dark with concern. Instead of answering, I snuggled against his chest. His arms went around me, comforting and reassuring.

Across the room, the clock chimed eleven. Sharon was in the kitchen, doing lesson plans for the next week. More than an hour had passed since my grandmother had retired to the guest room I'd occupied my first night here. She'd said she had some calls to make. I didn't need to be a rocket scientist to know the first call she'd made once alone had been to Uncle Adam. There were arrangements he needed to make in light of my conversation with Jennings. No doubt Uncle Adam would bring as many members of their clan with him as possible when he returned for the weekend. That didn't bother me one bit. Far from it, in fact. I had a feeling we'd need all the allies we could get before this was over.

Nor would it surprise me if Grandma didn't call the clan leaders who had listened in on my short conversation with Jennings. She'd kept her emotions under control, both during the call and after, but there was no denying her anger. No, anger wasn't strong enough a word for what Grandma felt. She'd been furious. Before going to bed, she admitted she'd shared my suspicions about Jennings and his involvement in my parents' deaths. If she thought talking with the other clan leaders would help us stop Jennings from coming after me as well as bring him to justice for my parents' deaths, more power to her.

But that didn't answer Matt's question.

"I'm not sure." It was the best I could do. When he shifted me on his lap so he could look at my face, I knew I needed to explain. "Matt, I know it was my idea to talk to Jennings. Hell, I even know I needed to talk to him if I'm ever to move on with my life. But hearing his voice after so long, hearing him all but admit not only that he'd sent the trackers after me and had given them carte blanche on doing whatever it took to bring me back but that he'd been behind my parents' deaths, it was almost more than I could take."

I gently pushed out of his embrace. He watched as I stood and moved across the room. For a long moment, I stared out into the darkness of the front yard. "I'm not going to lie to you, Matt. I'm scared. I'm scared of what that bastard will do next. I all but called him out. He knows that I'm here, with you, and the last thing I want is for him to take his anger with me out on you or anyone else."

"Finn." Tenderness and understanding filled his voice. He moved to where I stood and gently turned me to face him. "Michael Jennings is a coward. He won't come after any of us. If he does, we'll be ready for him. I promise."

I wanted to believe him, but it was hard. I knew Jennings wouldn't just give up. He'd proven that time and time again.

"This is a new beginning for you," Matt continued, reaching for my hands. "You don't have to run and hide. You can be Meg Finley again if you want. Hell, you can be anything you want, anyone you want."

I prayed what he said was true, but I couldn't bring myself to believe it, not yet. As for being Meg again, I wasn't sure I'd ever be able to go back to that girl I'd once been. Too much had happened since I left California. I was Finn. But maybe I could let myself remember what it had been like to be Meg.

"Matt, I want to believe you." I looked down at our linked hands. "God, how I want to believe you. But I'm damaged goods. Even now, knowing you'll do everything possible to protect me and make Jennings pay for what he's done, I want to run. That impulse got stronger when I heard his voice. For the first time in years, he knows exactly where I am. My fight-or-flight instinct is definitely set to flight, at least where he's concerned." Misery filled me, and I couldn't bring myself to look up at him. I didn't want to see the disappointment—or worse, the disapproval—that might be reflected in his expression.

"Finn." He pulled me close and cradled me against his chest. His lips pressed against the top of my head, a benediction of sorts. "I understand. You've spent so much of your life running from that bastard. To finally confront him, even over the phone, must have opened all the old wounds. Anyone with an ounce of sanity would be tempted to run, especially since it is pretty damned clear he had a hand in your parents' deaths. The fact that you're still here tells me you're strong and more than ready to take back your life."

I drew a deep, shuddering breath and wrapped my arms around his waist. I wasn't sure he was right, but I was willing to let him try to convince me.

"You've already taken the first steps to doing just that. You agreed to be my mate, to stand with me in and for the pride and clan. You've taken on our markings and have been accepted by our pride.

"But it's more than that and you'd know it if you'd just cut yourself a break. You've spent close to a week with your grandmother. You're reconnecting with parts of your past that had been forbidden to you for too long. If that's not enough to convince you, remember that you're the one who suggested calling Jennings and facing him down, so to speak. I have nothing but respect for what you've done to survive and what you are doing now."

"But—"

"Shh." He held me far enough away from him that he could look into my eyes. "Finn, there's more. You aren't thinking of Jennings the same way you used to."

My brow furrowed, and I looked at him in question.

"Finn, think about it. What have you felt when you've thought about that bastard the last few hours?"

He waited, watching me. For a moment, I wasn't sure I knew what he meant. Then it dawned on me. I might still be scared but I was taking a stand. I wouldn't let Jennings drive me from my home, not a second time. More than that, I wanted him to pay for his crimes against not only myself and my parents but all our kind. A part of me still wanted to run and hide, but I wouldn't. Not now and not ever again.

"Thank you."

"For what?" Now his brow furrowed much as mine has a few moments earlier.

"For being you. For helping me in that parking garage. For not tossing me out when you discovered that helping me would put you in direct conflict with another clan leader. For caring enough to talk sense to me when I most need it."

"Finn." He smiled and shook his head. "You have nothing to thank me for. I'm just a Texas boy who firmly believes that no man has the right to tell a woman who she belongs to. I hate bullies and will be more than glad to knock Jennings down a peg or ten for how he's treated you. I'm in awe of the woman you've managed to become despite all the obstacles he's thrown into your path."

Before this mutual admiration society could get any more sickly sweet, Matt's cell phone rang. I tensed, waiting as he dug into his pocket for it. It seemed like ages since we'd last heard from Danny and I couldn't help wondering if the trackers had managed to give his people the slip. Dear God, if we'd lost them before we actually found them, this nightmare wouldn't be over. Even if he'd found them, there was no guarantee they'd implicate Jennings. But we had a better chance closing the noose around him with them than without.

Unfortunately for my rising level of anxiety, Matt's responses were short, usually mono-syllabic. He'd listen, expression intent, and then nod and say "yes" or "no". Then, finally, he seemed to relax. He gave me a quick wink before turning his attention back to the call.

"Danny, no confrontations unless as a last resort. Keep an eye on them. See if you can get a trace on their phones. And don't lose them. Make sure you and the others have all exits covered. If they try to leave, stop them and let me know. Otherwise, call me in the morning and give me an update." He listened for a moment and then rang off, sliding the cell phone back into his pocket.

"What?" He could have at least angled the phone so I could have listened in.

"We have them." Now he grinned and gave me a rib cracking hug. "They're holed up in a motel out in Irving. Far enough away to give credibility to a claim they are just passing through but close enough to be able to keep an eye on you. Danny, Tamara and some others they hand-picked are keeping an eye on their room and vehicle."

"He's sure?" Relief filled me. If they knew where the trackers were, there was a chance our plan might actually work. I still wasn't quite ready to believe it, but at least things were looking up.

"He's sure." Another hug, this one not so strong and then he smiled down at me, understanding reflected in his eyes. "You've had a long, trying week, Finn. Why don't you go get some rest now?" His hand gently brushed a lock of hair back from my brow.

"I am tired."

That was putting it mildly. Learning we finally knew where the trackers were, I felt exhausted. It was as if all the years of being on my guard finally took their toll. My knees threatened to buckle and my eyelids drooped. I shook myself and forced the exhaustion back. It wouldn't last long, but I couldn't give in. Not yet.

"Finn."

Matt looked past me in the direction of the bedroom. As he did, I realized he was uncertain. Worried, I reached up and cupped his cheek with my hand. If confronting Jennings wound up hurting what had started building between Matt and me. . . .

"Finn, you've been through so much, especially the last few days. You're finally starting to believe that you're free. I meant it when I said that means you're finally able to choose what you want from life."

Now he was the one to move away. Worry was replaced with a mixture of disbelief, humor and respect. He was trying to be gallant. At least that's what I thought he was leading up to. God, he really was too good to be true.

"I will never push you, especially not when I look at you and you look so damned fragile," he continued.

Fragile?

No one had ever described me like that. I really must look like I was at the end of my rope. One more thing to blame Jennings for. Damn him.

"You are my mate. We both know that. But I will never force myself on you. I won't demand you share my bed unless it is something you want. You alone have the right to decide who you sleep with and when. I want you to know I'm nothing like Jennings and will never, ever treat you as he has."

I didn't know whether to laugh or cry. Sincerity radiated from him. But so did concern and anxiety. He needed me to understand he'd never force me to be with him just as badly as I needed him to believe in me. I wasn't sure how to make him understand he didn't have to worry. He was my mate and I knew he'd never betray me. To do so would be like ripping out his own heart.

"Matt." I moved to him, sliding my arms around his waist and resting my head against his chest. For a moment, I just stood there, breathing in the scent of him, listening to the steady beat of his heart.

"Finn, I mean it. If you want to share my bed and just cuddle, that's what we'll do. If you want to sleep alone, we'll do that. It is your call. You are my mate, my partner—not my property and certainly not my chattel."

"I want to be with you, Matt." It was so simple to say, especially when you meant it. "But I'll be honest. I am tired and emotionally drained after today. Hell, after the last week. Right now, nothing sounds better than just going to bed and cuddling."

"Then that's what we'll do." He stepped back and reached for my hand. "Come on. We both could use some rest. I have a feeling tomorrow will be as busy, if not more so, than today was."

Hopefully, there's be no unexpected surprises.

CHAPTER THIRTEEN

"Ready for a day out?" Tamara stood on the front porch and grinned.

"More than." For more reasons than she knew.

I closed the door behind me and followed Tamara down the walk to where her car sat in the driveway. To anyone watching, we looked like two young women heading out for a late breakfast or maybe some shopping. Tamara, in her short denim skirt, red tee and sandals resembled a college student taking a break from her studies. I wore a pair of jeans and a tee shirt. Despite the urge to stop and look around, I didn't. Instead, I took a moment to admire Tam's vintage Triumph. The 1973 black TR6 all but gleamed in the morning sun. I ran a light hand over the fender, fully understanding her pride in the car.

"Did you rebuild it?" I asked as I slid inside.

"My dad did. I bought it from him a couple of years ago." She slid in behind the steering wheel and started the engine. "I was lucky. He gave me a good price and it had the original factory installed AC. That's a must down here in the summer."

I nodded and, recognizing a signal when I saw it, rolled up my window. Tamara turned in her seat to check behind us as she backed down the drive. As we drove away, she glanced at me and winked. So far, so good.

"Well?" I asked as we left the neighborhood.

"Nothing so far, but my gut tells me we won't have long to wait." She checked the mirror before glancing across at me. "In the glovebox is a Bluetooth earpiece. It will keep you tied in with the rest of us. Not that I plan to let you out of my sight until I get your back home."

"Thanks." I retrieved it and slipped it into my left ear. "What now?"

"Now we play catch-me-if-you-can."

Even though she didn't look at me, I saw her smile. She was actually looking forward to this. Of course, so was I in a way. If the trackers took the bait, we'd have them, assuming everything went according to plan. I had no doubt Matt, not to mention Tamara and Danny, would and could get the information we needed to finally removed Jennings from my life.

God, I hoped so.

Almost forty five minutes later, Tamara pulled to a stop in front of a single story brick building. Across the street, one of the inevitable strip malls boasting a convenience store, dry cleaners, barber shop and more bustled with business. Unlike the strip mall, Tamara's car was the only one parked in front of the single-story building. But we weren't alone. Lights shone through the front window and I saw the shadow of someone moving about inside.

Apparently, I wasn't the only one, judging from the low growl that came from the other side of the car.

"She wasn't supposed to be here." Frustration roughened Tamara's voice and her hand's tightened their grip on the steering wheel. I had a feeling that, at the moment, she envisioned them wrapped around CJ's neck. "Damned stubborn woman."

With that, she slammed out of the car. Before I touched the door handle, she snarled for me to stay where I was. I bristled and my panther bared her teeth. We were the Alpha. How dare she tell us what to do. This was our fight, not hers alone.

Except that was my cat talking. For the moment, this was Tamara's fight and it didn't include the tracers. This was between she and CJ, although I had to give it to the young woman. I'd learned over the last few days that it took a lot of guts to stand up to the clan's security expert.

"What the fuck are you doing here?" Tamara hissed as the front door swung open.

CJ stood framed in the doorway. Her short hair was now black with deep blue highlights that reminded me of a raven's wing as the sun caught it. Dressed in jeans and a black tee shirt with her shop's logo on it, she simply arched one brow and then smiled. As she did, she waved for me to come inside.

"Morning, Tam, Finn."

I'll be damned, but she sounded as if she'd not only been expecting us but looked forward to our arrival. She either had a death wish, because there was no doubt what Tamara thought about her little change in our plans, or she knew something we didn't.

"CJ." Tamara reached for her arm.

"Inside and now."

In that moment, CJ sounded very much like Tamara and I bit my lower lip to keep from laughing. The tattooist might not be an alpha but she had a spine. More than that, she didn't look like she planned on backing down. Since I didn't like being out in the open and not knowing how close the trackers might be, I slid out of the car and crossed to where she stood.

"C'mon, Tam. I'm curious to see what CJ has in store for us today."

"That makes two of us," the woman muttered in ill-temper.

Without another word, Tamara motioned for me to get inside. I wasted no time doing so. Not only because of the trackers but the look on her face spoke volumes. She was pissed. Clearly, she liked surprises no more than Matt did, at least not this sort of a surprise.

Not that I blamed her. The last thing I wanted was for CJ to be caught in the middle of anything that might happen.

"All right, CJ, what the fuck do you think you're doing?" Tamara demanded the moment the door closed behind us.

"I think I'm covering your ass, Tam, yours and the clan leader's."

Oh my.

I leaned against the glass counter that displayed tee shirts and other merchandise. No doubt about it. I didn't want to get in the middle of this. CJ had a point to make. The only question was if she'd be able to before Tamara decided to pound her into the ground.

"What does that mean?" Tam's voice softened, and I swallowed hard. I knew that tone. She used it whenever I had the temerity to tell her I thought I'd learned her lesson for the day—usually just before she threw me against a wall or to the floor.

"It means the two of you, as well as Danny and anyone else who had a hand in this scheme of yours, didn't think it through. I don't mind you using my shop. Hell, it's a good idea to use it. I'm known among the clans already for doing most of our ink and my reputation is good enough a number from out-clan come to me to do their tats. It makes sense I'd do Finn's new markings."

"And?" Tamara drawled.

At least she no longer looked ready to pound CJ to dust.

"Don't you think Jennings and his trackers would know that?" She waited, staring Tamara down. "Think for a moment. From what you told me last night when we set this up, Finn told that bastard she was getting inked. Unless he's a complete fool, and I doubt that he is or he wouldn't still be clan leader, the first thing he'd do is find out where. That would be here. Then he'd do his research and, if he did, he'd know I am always here half an hour—or more—before my first client of the day. I certainly wouldn't leave my clan's new female Alpha sitting in the parking lot while I got my morning coffee."

Tamara opened her mouth and then shut it with an all but audible snap. "Damn it, I hate when you're right." She glared at CJ a moment before she grinned and shook her head. "Okay, so how do you suggest we play this?"

I relaxed and waited. My contact with CJ so far had been limited to when she did my initial inking and at the pride meeting. I liked her, more than I had most anyone in a long time. But she hadn't struck me as a particularly strong shifter. Watching her deal with Tamara, I knew I needed to reassess my first impressions. CJ might not be an alpha, but she had a very good head on her shoulders and Tamara obviously respected her and her opinions—even when she wanted to pound her into a red stain on the floor.

"We do what we want the trackers to think we're doing. I'll work on Finn's tat and you'll keep us company." Now CJ grinned and mischief danced in her eyes. "Or you can leave and explain to Matt how you changed the plan without talking with him about it."

Oh, she was good. She had no problem changing the plan—and for the better, in my opinion—nor did she have any problem tweaking Tamara. I had a feeling CJ could be a very good friend if I gave her half a chance.

And I planned to do that and more.

"The trackers?" I didn't want to risk anything happening to her or her shop.

"I'm trusting Tam here, as well as the others, to make sure they don't cause any problems. She knows I'll come tattoo something awful on her forehead while she sleeps if she lets those bastards mess up my shop." She gave Tamara a cheeky grin, suddenly looking much younger than I knew she had to be. "Now come on back. I've got cameras on the parking lot and front area. We'll know if anyone gets close to the building. Plus, I have a feeling Tam here, not to mention Matt and Danny, have eyes on us."

Looking like she didn't know whether to laugh or curse, Tamara nodded.

"Then, if you don't have any other objections, let's get to work." She walked to the front door and flipped the sign to over to "open", as if inviting the trackers inside. Interesting. "Tam, there's a pot of fresh coffee in the kitchen if you want some. As for you, Finn, get out of that shirt and let's get started."

With that, she indicated a padded table at the far end of the front room and, without checked to see if I complied, she started laying out her tools. When she glanced back a moment later and saw me still standing there, fully clothed, she pointed to my tee shirt and motioned for me to lose it. She was obviously serious about working on my tat.

How the hell could she be so calm when she knew the trackers might burst in at any moment?

Two hours later, I lay face down on the padded table. My shoulder and upper back felt like I'd been stung by a million—or more—ants. The buzzing of CJ's tools mixed with the very interesting eclectic mix of music playing in the background. A young man who looked more like a college student majoring in finance than a tattoo aficionado manned the front counter, answering the phones, setting appointments and talking with clients who came in hoping to have CJ work on them that morning.

All very normal, at least I assumed so, for a standard day at the shop.

Tamara, on the other hand, looked anything but comfortable. When CJ first started working on me, she'd paled slightly. From the way CJ teased her, offering to add to Tam's ink when she finished with mine, I guessed the security specialist hated needles. That guess was confirmed when CJ stepped over to her, tattoo machine in hand. Tamara actually shrank against the back of her chair. All the color drained from her face. Then, hearing my laugh, she pinned me with a look that threatened dire consequences if I ever mentioned what I just saw.

"You are evil, CJ, and I love it," I commented softly as Tamara said she needed another cup of coffee. "Now, care to tell me what you're actually doing back there. I didn't think you had that much left to do on my tat."

"The clan leader showed me the other sketch you did after your first tat. He said you were going to talk to me about adding it to what I'd already done. Plus, he and your grandmother had a small addition they wanted made." She wiped my shoulder blade and stepped back, examining her work. "If you can hang in, I can finish this up. Assuming we don't have any interruptions. I have maybe another three hours left on this part of it."

Before I could respond, CJ laid the palm of one hand to the small of my back. A light touch but enough to warn me. Doing my best to appear casual, I turned my head, pillowing it on my arms, so I could see the tablet she'd set up next to the table. For there, I could watch the security camera feeds showing the shop's front door and parking lot.

"Tam, company," she said softly, without lifting her head from where she continued to work on my tat.

A buzzer sounded as the front door opened. Fighting the urge to sit up and turn toward them, I watched the display. Three men, all clad in jeans and dark tee shirts, stepped inside. One, who looked like a fighter, remained by the door. Eyes alert, he scanned the small waiting area, apparently paying little attention to the two bikers waiting for CJ to finish so she could work on them. The other two approached the counter.

"Ray, can you get me some more antiseptic ointment?" CJ asked before the men could say anything.

"Sure thing, boss." The young man stood and started out from behind the counter. "Got a couple of possible customers here. Can you take care of them?"

"Sure. You lie there, Finn. I'll be right back."

To the casual eye, the hand she placed once again at the small of my back might have seemed gentle but there'd been strength to it. I had no doubt she expected me to remain exactly as she left me. I might be the alpha but this was her shop and she had a role to play. Besides, I had a feeling she'd give me hell if I didn't do as she wanted.

"Morning, guys. Are you here for some ink?"

My eyes widened in surprise, and it was a good thing my face was turned away from the men. There was a confidence to CJ, a cockiness, I hadn't seen before. As the men stammered for an answer, my panther pushed harder for release. We shouldn't be lying there, prey to their predator. Without thinking, I started to roll onto my side. I liked this sense of helplessness no more than my cat did.

"Lie still," CJ snapped, putting a bit more strength behind the hand at my waist. "We're not finished yet."

I bared my teeth and fought the urge to growl. Instead, I once again turned my head and angled it so I had a clear view of the three men. As I did, I heard the door leading to the back of the shop open. Tamara's scent once again filled the room and I relaxed. Now the odds were in our favor. The three trackers had walked into our trap. They simply didn't know it—yet.

Not that it was easy to lay there as if nothing untoward was about to happen. I recognized the three. I'd seen them that day in the parking garage. But there had been other times as well, times when I'd spot one or more of them in the crowd or on the street as I went about my life. How long had they been following me?

"Easy," Tamara whispered as she stepped up next to the table where I lay.

"Clear the shop," the lead tracker said. As he did, the one by the door flipped the sign over to "closed".

The two "bikers" got to their feet but made no attempt to leave. Instead, almost in unison, they rolled their shoulders and then cracked their knuckles, their message clear. You don't mess with CJ or her shop.

"Now you wouldn't be thinking about causing CJ here any trouble, would you, son?" one of the bikers asked.

I didn't laugh, but it was a close thing. Two of the trackers looked like they could handle themselves in a fight but they were nothing compared to the "bikers". Those two weren't the beer-bellied, gray-haired Harley riding bikers you see so often. Far from it. They wore jeans and tee shirts that stretched tightly across very well-defined chests. Biceps and triceps strained the arms of their shirts. They were bikers and fighters and looked as if they'd like nothing more than to mix it up with the trackers.

"You really don't want to be part of this," the first tracker said. "We've business here and you don't want to be part of it."

"And what would that business be?" CJ asked.

"Nothing that concerns you."

He glanced in my direction and gave a jerk of his head. The younger of the three took a step toward me only to come up against one of the bikers. Things were about to get interesting.

"I'll tell you this one more time, get out. Our business isn't with you and you don't want it to be." The tracker's right hand moved closer to his pocket, the threat clear.

"I really wouldn't do that if I were you." CJ's voice sounded cold as ice. But it was the sound of her racking a very deadly looking shotgun that stopped everyone in their tracks. "Now, I'd prefer not having a mess in my shop. Blood and other body parts are hell to clean up. However, don't let that fool you. I'll gladly bring in a service to clean the mess if that's what it takes to protect my Alpha."

She nodded to the bikers who quickly and efficiently searched and disarmed the three. As they did, I sat up and swung my legs over the edge of the table. I'd been sitting—well, lying—around long enough.

"And don't get any funny ideas, gentlemen. And I am using that term loosely. I'm a crack shot and, at this close range, if I don't manage to kill you, I guarantee you won't be getting up any time soon. You sure as hell won't be adding your sperm to the gene pool again. So get down on your knees and put your hands on your heads."

I glanced over at Tamara who only shrugged. Obviously, she was as surprised by this side of CJ as I was. Then, as if shaking off her disbelief, Tam motioned for me to stay where I was. Once I nodded in understanding, she stepped away from the table, just in time to see one of the bikers taking the tracker by the door down to the floor.

"Finn!" Matt burst through the door, Danny and several others just behind him. "Secure them!" he snapped even as he crossed the shop to where I stood.

"I'm all right," I assured him as he held me close for a moment before stepping back to make sure I told the truth. "CJ, I think you can lose the shotgun now." I grinned as she carefully set the shotgun on the counter.

"When those bastards are out of my shop." She kept her hands on the shotgun, her eyes never leaving the trackers as they were secured and then escorted outside to three waiting SUVs.

"If you've got this, Matt, I'd like Tam to come with us and get those three safely secured elsewhere," Danny said.

"Go." Matt nodded to Tamara and stopped her long enough to thank her for keeping me safe.

"That was all CJ," the security specialist said with a grin. "Seems she takes a dim view of anyone messing with her shop or her clients."

"Damned straight." CJ gave us a cheeky grin before returning the shotgun to its place behind the counter. "Brett, Rocky, thanks. Come back next week for some free ink."

"No need, CJ. Glad to help," the taller biker said. He turned to Matt and nodded once before looking at me. "Ma'am, glad to help. CJ knows where to find us if you ever need us for anthing." With that, he and his companion left the shop.

"They're loners from the area. Loyal to the clan but they prefer to be on their own," CJ said before I could ask.

"I'll make sure they know how much we appreciate their help," Matt promised when I glanced at him. "Now, are you all right?"

"I am."

In fact, I was better than I had been in a very long time. We had the trackers in custody. Sooner or later, they would give us the evidence we needed to tie them to Jennings. Then, finally, we'd be able to take our case against Jennings to the other clan leaders. For the first time since leaving California, I believed the nightmare was ending.

At least I hoped so.

"Then get back up on the table so I can finish your tattoo."

"CJ!" I didn't know whether to laugh or grab Matt and beg him to take me home. Surely, she wasn't serious.

"Finn, I'll understand if you want to wait." She leaned against the counter. "It's been a tough day for you. I have a feeling you hate being the one to sit—or lie—there and do nothing while everyone else takes action. But those bastards are out of the way now and I think the best way to drive the point home to what's-his-name—Jennings?—is to finish your tat and then to proudly display it at the clan meeting this weekend."

Well, she had me there. Besides, I wanted to see what she'd been working on the last few hours and I'd rather see the finished product. Matt looked at me and I nodded. This was one more way to prove to myself, to him and to everyone else that this was my home and I wasn't going to let anyone take it away from me.

"All right." He bent and lightly brushed his lips against mine. "Call me when you're ready and I'll pick you up. I need to run into the office."

"Those bastards?" I didn't need to explain who I meant.

"Danny or Tam will let me know if they learn anything from them."

"Go, Matt." CJ all but shooed him toward the door. "And don't worry about Finn. I'll drive her home when we're finished."

CHAPTER FOURTEEN

"Are you sure you're up for this?" Matt asked as he parked his car at the back of a rundown motel almost an hour away from his house.

A little more than three hours had passed since he left me at CJ's shop. In that time, she'd finished my tattoo and drove me home. Matt arrived shortly after I did. With Sharon and my grandmother wanting—demanding would be more accurate—to know everything that happened, the five of us settled down at the kitchen table to talk.

Only to be interrupted by a call from Danny. When the call ended a few minutes later, Matt slid his cell phone into his pocket and stood. As he extended a hand and helped me to my feet, he promised to explain everything later. All he could tell us just then was we needed to go. Nothing, he assured everyone, was wrong. In fact, things were very right.

"I am." I rested a hand on his thigh, waiting until he looked at me. "My place is here, with you, Matt. You are my mate. Together, we are the clan Alphas." Even if it still felt strange saying it, much less believing it. "More than that, I need to be here."

For more reasons than I could explain, probably even to myself.

"All right. But if you want to leave at any time, just tell me."

He switched off the engine. For several moments we sat there, studying the scene before us. Danny had been right. The unit the trackers rented was not only as far from the office as possible, but was on the backside of the building, out of sight of the road. The only vehicles in sight were a black panel van with Texas plates and a small sticker on the bumper identifying it as a rental, an ancient white Impala that looked like it hadn't been moved in at least a month and a silver Toyota I recognized as Danny's.

"Well, they certainly made our job easier," Matt commented.

I nodded. I'd stayed at motels like this before. You could rent a room by the day, week or month. They were popular with workers who moved from job to job. But, glancing around, seeing the general state of disrepair of the motel, I doubted that I'd ever have willingly stayed here. I do have a few standards and not sleeping with cockroaches, or worse, was high on the list. But I knew why the trackers had chosen it, or at least I had a pretty good idea. This was the sort of place where no one would ask questions about why they were coming and going at odd times or why three men were staying in the same room. Of course, those same folks who wouldn't ask those questions wouldn't ask why we were now there and that was very, very good.

Still, we didn't waste any time getting out of the car and hurrying across the parking lot, just in case someone did decide to become curious.

We found Danny standing just inside the room. He was busy taking pictures and documenting everything. As we waited for him to finish, I looked around, more than a little surprised by how well-ordered the room was. The beds were made but there were signs of someone sitting or lying on top of the covers. Across the room from the front door was what could euphemistically be called a dressing room. Basically, it consisted of a mini-alcove with a yellowing countertop and a single sink. From where I stood, I saw the requisite coffeemaker and what looked like three shaving kits. Nothing, at least so far, to indicate the three weren't anything more than businessmen here for work.

Curious, I moved to the levered closet doors just inside the room. Hopefully, the closet held something to tie the three to Jennings.

"Finn, wait."

There was enough command in Danny's voice to have me turn to him in question. Before I could say anything, he tossed me a pair of what looked like surgical gloves. I caught them and looked at him in question.

"Glove up."

"Why?" Surely, he didn't want to put the trackers through the justice system.

"No, I haven't lost my mind and decided to arrest those bastards." Now he grinned. Clearly my thoughts had been written on my expression. "But I have taken a few precautions to protect us just in case. I got a search warrant—all nicely sealed so prying eyes can't get to it—for this room and the van. That way, if anyone staying here does suddenly grow a conscience and calls the local cops, we have reason to be here, doing what we're doing. But that also means we have to look like we are following standard procedure."

I had to give it to him. I wouldn't have thought of that. Of course, all I wanted was to tear the room apart. I wanted—no, I needed—to find something tangible linking the three to Jennings.

"Good thinking." Matt took a pair of gloves and pulled them on. Then he moved to my side, his expression concerned. "You okay?" he asked softly.

"Yeah." Well, not really. I was on the verge of starting to tear the room apart and I would if we didn't find something and soon. "Tell us what you want us to do, Danny." Maybe if he did, I could concentrate on a particular task and not lose it.

"Check the closet, Finn. Look everywhere, inside pockets, shoes, bags, whatever you find. Just be careful. There's no telling what those bastards might have stuffed away in them."

I nodded and opened the closet doors. There wasn't much there for three men. A couple of pairs of running shoes, two backpacks on the shelf above the clothing rod. A single garment bag hung from the rod. Much as I wanted to rip into the backpacks, I started at the bottom, telling myself to take my time and not miss anything.

The shoes were a bust and the garment bag not much more. There was nothing in it other than a few receipts dating back three weeks and clothes I'd rather not touch judging from the rancid odor that hit me as soon as I unzipped the bag. At least we now had confirmation the trackers had been in the area for three weeks. That was more than we'd known a few minutes ago. But it also sent a chill through me. Maybe I had gotten as sloppy as I feared. Not that it mattered now. I had a home, a mate and a pride and clan to back me. Jennings would not win.

Finally, I lifted the backpacks, one at a time, from the top shelf and carried them to the nearest bed. As I did, Matt joined me. When I glanced over, he gave a quick shake of his head to let me know he hadn't found anything useful. Hopefully, I was about to change that.

Carefully, I unzipped the front pocket of the first backpack. Other than a couple of pens and more receipts, it didn't contain anything of interest. But the inside pocket, oh inside it was a completely different matter.

My heart beat faster and I resisted, barely, the urge to shout for joy at the first thing I pulled out. We had them. We actually had them, and they would give us Jennings. I didn't doubt it for a minute. Not with this. Not when we had, in their own handwriting, notes about how they found me, followed me and planned to kidnap me to take me back to California. The idiots. It was all there in black and white—well, blue and white—but it was there. This was the leverage we needed to get them to roll over on Jennings.

And that only assumed that evidence needed to sign his death warrant wasn't present on the laptop still inside the backpack.

"Looks like we hit the mother lode," Danny commented as he appeared from the bathroom and looked at the contents of the backpacks that were now carefully laid out on the bed. Two laptops, several notepads, a disposable cell phone, photos of me. "Finn, do you recognize this?" He tilted the wastepaper basket he held so I could see inside. Damn, it just got even better.

"That was my cell phone." With emphasis on "was". The face of the phone was cracked and broken, as if someone had tried to grind it to dust under his heel. Too bad, at least for them, that they hadn't tossed it in the trash far from here or hadn't taken it with them when they decided to grab me.

"We need to know if there's anything on the laptops that will help us," Matt said, voice tight. Worried, I looked up. Expression grim, mouth tight, his right hand fisted at his side, to say he was angry was putting it mildly. The trackers ought to be glad they weren't anywhere near Matt just then. I had a feeling he'd have killed them, or come close to it, otherwise.

"I can do that. I might not have many talents, but computers and I talk the same language," I said. "But not here."

"Agreed." He nodded once and then seemed to shake himself, as if trying to shake off his anger. "What about the van?" He turned to Danny and I waited, wondering if we'd have to search it as well.

"I've already taken a look. They didn't keep much in it. Seems they had most of their stuff in the duffel bags we took from them when we moved in. Tamara has those at the safe house."

"All right." Now Matt gave me a grim smile before reaching for my hand. "Let's pack up the stuff we're interested in and get it back to the house. We can go over it in more detail there."

Not about to argue, I started reloading the backpacks. I'd feel better once we were well away from the motel. I'd feel even better after a shower to wash off the filth of the place. Hell, I might even burn my clothes because I was half-convinced they were already infested with bedbugs and who knew what else. At the very least, they'd be going into the washer for a heavy-duty cycle before I'd consider putting them back on.

"**F**inn."

I finished wrapping the towel around me and looked up. Matt stood just inside the bathroom. That didn't surprise me but the worry reflected in his eyes did. Had something happened while I showered?

And did I really want to know?

"Matt, what is it?" I stepped forward, stopping when we stood almost toe-to-toe.

Instead of answering, he pulled me close and leaned down, resting his forehead against mine for a few moments. Then he stepped back and reached for my hands.

"Please don't take this wrong, but I have to ask."

My stomach did a slow roll. Something had happened. Was he about to ask me to leave not only his bed but his territory?

Barely daring to breathe, I nodded for him to continue.

"Back at the motel, you said you could get into those bastard's laptops. Be honest with me. Can you?"

For a moment, I looked at him, wavering between anger at being doubted and worry because of the doubt. Then it dawned on me. Matt didn't know anything except the little I'd told him about what I'd been doing to support myself in the time I'd been on the run. I'd even said my only real talent was my art. Which, in my mind, was true. My art was a talent and one I was proud of, even if I knew it would never pay enough to support me.

Computers, well, I guess you could say I had a talent where they were concerned as well. It might not be the same, but there wasn't much I couldn't do with one. Unless the trackers were a lot smarter about security than their motel room led me to believe, I'd easily crack any security they might have on the laptops. But first, I needed to reassure Matt I hadn't been blowing smoke out my ass when I said it.

"Come here." I led him to the bed and sat down, waiting until he dropped onto the mattress at my side. "Matt, there's so much about one another we don't know. So here's the short version where I'm concerned. I haven't been to college but I've done my best not to be forced to rely solely on my high school education. I learned back then that I enjoyed working with computers. I was pretty damned good at it.

"Once I ran away, I learned quickly that I needed to be able to demonstrate more than a passing knowledge of them if I wanted a job that would pay anything close to a living wage. I didn't want to work sales or something similar that could bring me into contact with others of our kind. I needed work where I knew who I'd be seeing on a regular basis."

When his brow furrowed, I knew he was thinking about my last job for the messenger service. That had been the exception, done when my previous job had been phased out. It had been meant to be temporary which, in a way, it had been. I'd not be returning to it now. I didn't have to. Now I could find a job I wanted, without fear of running into others of our kind.

"I made sure I took what classes I could, sometimes at community college, sometimes online. But I learned and I got better, much better, at it. Unless those bastards have topline security on their machines, I can break it without much trouble. Even with topline security, I'll be able to break it. It will take time, but it can be done." I paused, giving him time to consider what I said. "I'm not being cocky, Matt, at least not too much." Here I gave a smile and he seemed to relax a little. "I promise I won't do anything to compromise the data."

"Finn, it's not that I doubt you," he began.

"Matt, it's okay. You have more than just my feelings to worry about." I patted his leg and decided what I needed to do next. "Let's see if I can reassure you."

To prove I knew what I was doing, I gave Matt a crash course on how easy it is for most people with even a little technological savvy to hack someone's accounts. Too many people leave reminders for themselves on their computers about what their passwords are. They tend use the same password for everything. They don't erase their cookies or browsing histories. In other words, they make it very easy for folks who might not have their best interests at heart to exploit them.

Which was exactly what I hoped to do now.

Because I knew how easy it was to manipulate data, I wanted to make sure no one could accuse us of doing just that. So I asked Matt to make sure the keyboard and screen of each laptop was covered by a video camera. I wanted every stroke I entered recorded. I wanted every image that appeared on the screen to be seen. There was no way I would let Jennings claim we set him up.

I just hoped it was enough.

It had to be enough.

"Ready?" Matt asked half an hour later as he handed me a bottle of water.

"Yeah." At least I hoped so. "Where's my grandmother?"

"She is finishing up a call to your uncle. Said she'd join us just as soon as she can."

"Then let's get started."

I moved to take my place at the table and waited as Matt checked the focus and aim of the camera behind me. He lightly patted my left shoulder, my signal that he was ready. Then he moved to sit next to me. We'd decided that was the best way to insure no one thought he was manipulating the camera, stopping and starting it, as I worked.

I reached out, hoping my hands didn't shake as nerves suddenly flared, and opened the first laptop. As I did, I took a moment to study it. While it wasn't new—I'd guess it was at least a year old—it didn't look like it had gotten much use. The letters on the keyboard were still clear. There wasn't much wear and tear on them or on the touch pad. What that meant was anyone's guess. The owner could have used it only for e-mail or could simply be a Luddite who hated computers and used it only when necessary. Frankly, I didn't care as long as there was something on it that linked the trackers to Jennings.

There was no sense in putting off the inevitable. I pushed the power button and waited. The familiar whirring of the hard drive starting was music to my ears. Just as the logo that popped up a few moments later was a welcome sight. So far so good. Now to see if there was a log-on screen. That was the first test.

"Idiots," I muttered as the laptop booted directly to the home screen with no log-on required. Perhaps this would be easier than I'd expected. Fingers crossed, at least metaphorically, I got down to work.

It didn't take long to check the document and image files. Each held a trove of information. There were reports on my activities and contacts for the last several weeks as well as photos of me taken around town. That sealed the trackers' fates. They'd been following me and a strong argument could be made they'd done so with ill-intent. Now to see what their e-mail could tell us.

I almost laughed aloud as I checked the browsing history and went to the email site listed. Whichever of the trackers used this laptop had been a trusting soul. Not only had he left the documents on the hard drive, unsecured and unencrypted, to be found by anyone looking, but they had so conveniently checked the "keep me logged in" option on the e-mail program. That meant I didn't need to look for a password or try a hack.

Damn, how stupid could these guys be and thank God they were the ones Jennings had sent after me.

It didn't get any better—for them at least—with the second laptop. Oh, the emails were a bit more difficult to get to, but only because I had to work at finding the right password. Not hard to do since the guy made a note of it in a saved document. At least he hadn't saved the document as "password" or something equally revealing. But a quick global search found the information I needed. Then it was only a matter of logging in and searching for any emails to or from Jennings.

And that's when reaction hit. Reading e-mail after e-mail between them brought home just how lucky I'd been when Matt intervened and saved me. Jennings had finally grown tired of the chase. The trackers were under orders to do whatever it took to bring me back to California. The implication was that he didn't care how badly they hurt me as long as I was returned to him. Then he'd make sure I learned my lesson about how foolish it was to cross him. After that, he'd "teach me" exactly what my place was.

Fear and fury filled me. My hands above the keyboard trembled and I snatched them out of the range of the camera. I wouldn't give anyone the satisfaction of seeing how badly Jennings' words shook me. Damn him. I'd never give in to him and I would never again live in fear of him. If he wanted war, by God, I'd give it to him. But he would never lay a hand on me. I'd die first.

"That's enough, Finn." Matt's voice was gentle. "Shut it down. We have all we need to insure Jennings never bothers you again."

I nodded. I couldn't say anything, not yet. Not with so many conflicting emotions boiling inside of me. The man who'd tried to rape me in order to seal his place as clan leader was also the man I suspected of killing my parents. His emails to the trackers left no doubt that he'd authorized them to do whatever it took, including hurting me badly if necessary, to bring me back to him.

Now he would learn how foolish he'd been not to let me go. All I had to do was make sure the trackers revealed everything they knew. Then Jennings' head would be mine to take.

But first, for my own peace of mind, I needed to confront the trackers. I needed to hear what they had to say and I needed them to understand exactly how big a mistake they'd made by tying their lives to Michael Jennings.

CHAPTER FIFTEEN

"Finn, you don't have to do this."

In a moment that screamed deja vu, I looked across the car at Matt. Less than eight hours earlier, he'd said much the same to me as we parked in front of the trackers' motel room. Now, like then, I knew what he meant. I even appreciated the sentiment behind it. But he was wrong. I did have to do this. If I ever wanted to put my personal demons to rest, I couldn't avoid what lay ahead. I'd come a long way this past week or so. I'd accepted Matt as my mate and took my place in pride and clan. I'd even found the courage to call Jennings. But I wasn't fooling myself either. Much of what I'd done was out of my control. That's the benefit and the drawback to being a shapeshifter. There are times when the "animal" dictates your actions. Then it is up to you to find a way to live as a human with the consequences of your actions.

Which was exactly what I had to do now.

That meant I needed to face down the men who'd tried to forcibly return me to California and Jennings. I had to accept on an intellectual level, as well as on the emotional one, that they'd been willing to hurt me, drug me and kidnap me. They hadn't cared that I didn't want to return to the clan I'd grown up in. They'd simply accepted the job and then tracked me down like a feral animal.

Well, they were about to learn how foolish they'd been.

"Matt." I rested my left hand on his arm, glad we were parked. "Don't worry. I'm all right."

Or I would be when this was finally over.

For a moment, he didn't say anything. He simply looked at me, his expression concerned as he searched my face for any indication I might not be telling the truth. I couldn't blame him. I'd probably do the same thing if our roles were reversed. After all, it hadn't been that long since he rescued me from these same men. He'd seen me hurt and scared. The fact he'd not tried to dissuade me from coming before now said a lot. He understood, even if he didn't completely approve, my need to face the men.

"You're amazing is what you are." He released his seatbelt and pulled me as close as possible with a stick shift and console between us. I didn't mind the hug. I hated the rest of it, but I'd not tell him that. I'd be too worried he'd do something foolish like sell the car and it really was a nice car.

"Not really. I'm just tired of running." I smiled up at him. "And I refuse to let Jennings or anyone else drive me from my home."

"Good." He gave an emphatic nod before bending to lightly kiss me. "Shall we get this over with?"

Now it was my turn to nod. The sooner we dealt with the trackers, the better.

A moment later, I stood next to the Mustang and looked around. We were parked in front of what looked like any one of the innumerable warehouse districts that had sprung up around the DFW area over the last few years. Non-descript one- and two-story buildings that showed the signs of hard use since their construction. Some of the storefronts were vacant but most looked to be occupied. Loading docks were situated at the ends of the building and there were more in the back, unless I missed my guess. Because it was the end of the workday, men and women moved across the parking lot to their vehicles. Nothing pointed to the fact anything out of the ordinary might be taking place in one of the buildings.

Matt took my hand and led me around the corner. As we neared a door set into the wall next to the nearest loading dock, Tamara stepped outside. She paused and looked around, eyes sharp. I had a feeling she could describe right down to the color of my underwear, everything I wore. Good. That meant she wasn't likely to overlook anything where the trackers, or anyone else, was concerned. Not that it surprised me. I'd learned in our workouts that Tam missed very little. That's what made her so good as the clan's security specialist.

"Matt, Finn, let's get inside."

She stepped aside so we could enter. Then sameness of the exterior continued inside. White walls, linoleum floors that showed hard use over the years lined a dark corridor leading further inside the building. That all changed as we came to the end of the corridor and Tamara used what was clearly a top of the line security panel to open a second door, this one out of sight from the exterior.

The moment the door closed behind us with a very ominous click, lights came up. A stairwell led down to what I assumed was a basement. It might have been that once. Now there was no mistaking what it was—a high security tech center of some sort.

What the hell?

Matt watched, a slight smile on his face, as I moved from work station to work station, being careful not to disturb the four men and women working there. Computers were set up to monitor local, national and international newscasts. One seemed dedicated to monitoring local law enforcement broadcasts. A large flat screen monitor on the wall facing the workstations was divided into four sections. One section was black while the others showed three men sitting at tables in different rooms. The trackers.

But, damn, what was this setup? It looked a lot like the settings for some of the shows I'd seen on TV over the years. Private security, usually of the sort that contracted with the government, and their super-secret headquarters complete with cells and interrogation areas. And always having the best in cutting edge technology. Maybe that's what this had been inspired by. All I knew was that my parents hadn't had anything like this and it made me a little uncomfortable.

Well, there was no way to find out except to ask. So I did.

"This is the product of Danny's and Tamara's professional paranoia." Matt grinned as Tamara simply shook her head.

"Finn, you were right the other evening when you talked about the danger we all face from the advances we've seen the last couple of decades in technology and science," Tamara took up. "Danny and I went to Matt several years ago, not long after he took over clan leadership, to talk to him about how close we'd come on more than one occasion of having our existence revealed simply because some overzealous lab tech decided to process all the evidence found at a crime scene. Most scenes have a lot of trace evidence that has nothing to do with the actual crime. No matter how careful we are, we leave behind skin cells, hair and so much more. We'd been lucky and had managed to keep anything untoward from coming out, but we knew our luck was running out, especially if we didn't take steps to protect ourselves.

"Fortunately for all of us, Matt listened. Then he talked to some of the other clan leaders in this part of the country and they listened to him. We pooled resources, including manpower and finances, to build this place. Our cover, if you want to call it that, is that we do private security, including forensic testing. But our real job is to make sure none of our people are implicated in something that could bring about the public knowledge of our existence before we're ready. Everyone who works here is either a shifter or related to one, so they have a vested interest in making sure we're covered."

"Finn." Concern filled Matt's voice when I didn't say anything. "Are you okay with this? I probably should have warned you."

"No." I shook my head. "You've had more than enough on your mind. And yes, I'm okay with it. This is exactly what my parents would have done had they lived. Hell, Matt, I'll even help man it if you let me."

"Good." He grinned and then told Tamara how I'd dealt with the laptops, including the video precautions I'd insisted on. She nodded in approval and then smiled. So far, so good. Let's hope I didn't do anything to mess things up now. "Have you gotten anything from our *guests*?"

Tamara's smile turned sour. "Nothing but a headache. They spent the first hour or so threatening everything from lawsuits to criminal charges if we didn't let them go. One of them even tried to bribe me. When I pointed out they were wasting their breath, the two older ones got nasty. A word of warning, their control isn't great. The last time I checked on them, their features were blurring with the need to shift."

That wasn't good on several levels. One of the first lessons my parents taught me when I started shifting was that high emotion could bring on a shift if we weren't careful. They worked with me, sometimes in ways I didn't really appreciate, to build a control that would be hard to break. They metaphorically beat into my head how important it was that none of us ever lost control to the extent that we shifted in a public venue. To do so could sign the death warrant for our entire kind. That's pretty heady stuff for a girl to have to learn but learn it I did. It bothered me that Jennings had sent hunters, who should be the most controlled of all our kind, who were ready to start shifting just because they found themselves in a difficult situation.

"I assume you've taken precautions then." Matt sounded as unhappy with the news as I felt.

"They've been put in separate rooms as you can see. They're cuffed to the table and their ankles are secured to their chairs. We searched them for weapons and took their IDs. I've done a standard criminal history search on them and have to admit I am not impressed. The two older ones have a string of traffic tickets stretching across the country as well as drug possession charges with two convictions in California. The third one is clean. But he's young, and he's scared to death."

"Do you recognize any of them?" Matt asked, and I turned to look at the split-screen images again.

"No." Things had happened so fast at CJ's I hadn't really gotten good looks at the men. Even if I had, my emotions had been too high. Now, studying their images on the screen before me, I shook my head. I didn't know them, not that it surprised me. I doubted Jennings would dare send anyone who knew me or my parents. There would be too much of a chance they might not bring me back if they actually caught up with me, especially not if they gave me a chance to try to dissuade them.

"What do you want to do?" Tamara looked from Matt to me and then back to Matt.

"I think it's time they find out how foolish they've been to trespass on our territory," Matt said.

"Not without me." I spoke firmly, hoping he wouldn't try to stop me.

He inclined his head. "Of course."

"Who first?" I turned my attention back to the screen.

"The youngest one. Tamara said he's the weak link. Let's exploit it."

Tamara nodded in agreement. A moment later, she led us out of the control area and down a side corridor. She paused outside the second door and punched in a security code. There was a soft *click* as the lock disengaged. Her hand closed over the door handle and she paused, looking back at us.

"Just because he's chained doesn't mean he can't shift. So be careful. The first sign of trouble, I'm in there and putting him down. Hell, I might even use the same weapons they used on Finn."

There was no mistaking how serious Tamara was. Not that I blamed her. She was taking a risk letting either of us in the room with the tracker. If anything happened to Matt, the pride and clan leadership would be compromised. As for using the same Taser and knife they used on me, well, I liked that idea probably more than I should have. But there was something about knowing they could be made to hurt as badly as they'd hurt me that seemed right, somehow.

"One more thing. You need to know exactly what we found when we searched the duffels they had with them when we took them down." She went on to detail what could only be called kidnapping kits. Between them, the men had handcuffs, rope, duct tape, a ball gag, syringes filled with what she assumed was some sort of sedative—and she'd already contacted Stefan to get them tested—as well as two more Tasers with barbs that looked like they'd been tainted as well. No doubt about it. The men had been prepared to do whatever it took to subdue and transport me back to California.

Bastards!

Any compassion I'd felt for the three, any doubts about what their actual mission had been, was gone. I no longer worried about what we might have to do to get information from the,. They'd either blindly followed Jennings' orders or they enjoyed hurting people. Well, they were about to learn they'd gone too far.

Anger building, I stepped forward, ready to confront my would-be kidnappers. Matt's hand on my arm stopped me. When I looked up at him, I was surprised by what I saw. He wasn't watching me with worry—well, not too much. He wasn't going to try to stop me. Instead, there was a measuring look to him, as if he was gauging my temper and approving. Then he smiled slightly and nodded. Tamara opened the door and we stepped inside.

As the door closed behind us, blue eyes filled with fear focused on us. Blond hair tousled, a bruise darkening his left cheek, the youngest of the three trackers watched warily as Matt and I just stood there. I'd been prepared for the anger boiling inside me, especially after hearing what they'd had on them when our people took them. What I wasn't prepared for was the way my panther rolled over me, demanding release. It recognized the tracker as a weaker animal, one no better than a carrion eater, one any pack or pride would be well rid of. Not that I disagreed. But I needed information from him first. Satisfaction had to wait.

"Why are you doing this to me?" he finally asked, voice soft and high-pitched with fear.

Matt crossed the distance between us and the table with two quick steps. Without hesitation, he leaned across the table and backhanded the young man. The blonde's head snapped back. He'd have fallen to the floor if he weren't chained to the table. Blood trickled from his nose and the corner of his mouth and my panther roared in approval. She liked this approach to dealing with the tracker and so did I.

"Silence!" Matt roared. I felt his power and watched in fascination as the young man began to shake. An Alpha could fill a room with his power without trying. When he did release control, even a little, that power became a living thing, something you could almost see and that you most definitely could feel.

Mine, my panther purred inside my skull.

Ours, I corrected.

"You trespass on my territory. You attempted to kidnap my mate and injured her in the process. Then you tried again, endangering not only her but other members of my pride. If you wish to live, you will answer my questions without hesitation."

The young man didn't speak. He didn't need to. His fear filled the room. I could smell it, sharp and bitter. Tamara had been right. He was the weak link of the three.

"Your name."

"Answer him!" I snapped, easing my own control. Let him see he was in the presence of not one but two Alphas. If he had any sense of self-preservation, he'd start telling us everything he knew, whether we asked for it or not.

"Steve, Steve Marchant," he stammered.

"Your clan?"

"N-northern California."

Good, the first tie to Jennings.

"Pack or pride?"

"P-pride. Eureka pride."

"Jennings' original pride," I supplied when Matt glanced at me.

"Why were you after my mate?"

Part of me railed at being discussed as if I weren't standing right there but another part, the shapeshifter part, understood. As clan leader, it was responsibility to take the lead, at least for the moment. Obviously, the young man either hadn't accepted his claim that I was his mate or he simply was too scared to have realized how Matt referred to me. Fear does strange things to a person, as I well knew. Right now, it not only loosened Marchant's tongue but it turned his brain to mush.

"W-we weren't. We were sent to bring home our clan leader's mate."

Scared and stupid. Even though he'd seen me in the parking garage, not to mention CJ's shop, he didn't realize his target stood in front of him. Either that or he was wasting his acting skills and should be in Hollywood making movies. My money was on him being that scared and stupid.

"And how were you supposed to take her to California?" Matt moved away from the table and leaned against the wall near the door. I knew why he did it. I could read the fury in him. Whether the tracker realized it or not, Matt was close to the breaking point and distance kept him from putting hands on the young man and possibly killing him before we got the information we needed.

"We were to remind her of her place with the clan and convince her to return with us."

God, did he think we were that foolish? Or did he actually believe what he said?

"Convince her with Tasers and blades tainted with some sort of drug or poison meant to cause her pain and slow her recovery? Or is that what the handcuffs, rope and ball gag were for?" Matt demanded.

"T-those were just props in case she resisted. I swear it"

Matt opened his mouth and I placed a hand on his arm. When he looked at me, I gave a quick shake of my head. We needed more information before we showed our hand.

"Who told you to come here?" I asked. We had to get him to admit Jennings had sent him. The emails weren't enough.

"Our clan leader."

"His name."

"M-Michael J-Jennings."

"Did he tell you to come here and not inform me, the local clan leader, that you were here much less why you'd come?" Matt sounded calmer and I relaxed a bit.

"He said not to worry about it. He'd take care of it."

That sounded exactly like what Jennings would do. Of course, it wouldn't surprise me to find out he'd been more upfront with the other trackers. He'd have warned at least one of them what would happen if they got caught, reminding them it was an incentive not only to get the job done quickly but to do it before the local clan leader got scent of them.

"What happened last week in the parking garage?"

The blond looked down at the table, his hands fisted together and straining against the cuffs. "I-I don't know what you mean."

"Don't be a fool!" Matt snapped. "I was there. I saw you hunting her. I saw her get tasered and knifed and I saw the results of it all."

The young man just sat there, shaking his head. Whether he realized he'd been well and truly caught or he was still trying to deny he'd done anything wrong, I didn't know and I honestly didn't care. We needed to learn all we could about what Jennings had been up to—and what he might do in response to his trackers being caught—and learn it before the son of a bitch had time to respond.

My panther stirred, restless and angry. It didn't like this verbal sparring. Neither did I, truth be told, but I knew we needed more information. But this was taking too long. I needed to do something to loosen Marchant's tongue. Then my cat pushed against my control and I understood. It was time for me to act like the Alpha everyone said I was. More importantly, it was time to act as Matt's mate.

"Don't be a fool." I put as much disgust as possible into my voice. "Your clan leader knows you failed. Do you really think he's going to do anything to save you? He wouldn't dare. To do so would be to admit he'd ordered you to violate shapeshifter laws. You violated our territory and the territory of other clans without permission. You assaulted me and tried to kidnap me, twice. Think about it. If I were your clan leader's mate, would I be here willingly? Would I be proclaiming not only my role in pride and clan but reveling in my place as mate to the clan leader of this territory?"

Now I did sneer. "Would I have stayed away from the Northern California clan this many years, cut off all contact with people I knew, if I wanted to be part of the clan?"

"You?" His head snapped up. His eyes went wide with recognition a split-second before the color drained from his face.

"Yes, me. I felt the Taser and blade and suffered their effects. I know what you and your companions tried to do. We recovered the kits you had with you when our people captured you. We also have your laptops and cell phones. We know you came here to take me by force if necessary. That doesn't sound like you were here to escort me back to a home I want to return to. Now tell us exactly what Jennings ordered you to do."

"I-I can't."

"Are you willing to sacrifice everything for him?" I shook my head. Fear and not loyalty moved Marchant. I wasn't sure I could break through that. "He's willing to sacrifice you for his own obsessions. Why are you letting him?"

He didn't say anything. Instead, he studied his hands where they rested on the tabletop. At my side, I felt Matt stiffen and understood. Marchant was a fool. But he was still our best bet for finding out what we needed to know. Somehow, we had to force his hand and get his cooperation.

"Tell me this, what exactly did your clan leader tell you about me?" Maybe a change of tack would work.

"He said you were his mate and had been taken from him years ago. We were to locate you and rescue you. You belong with him." He continued to look at his hands. "He said you might not want to come with us. You'd been gone so long, he was afraid those who took you might have brainwashed you against him."

Wow. This just kept getting better and better. Now he was claiming I'd been kidnapped. I guess we were lucky he hadn't filed a police report along those lines. How stupid was this guy to believe him? Sure, the Stockholm syndrome was well documented but anyone who'd been in the pride or clan at the time I left would know I'd run away. There'd been no coercion and there sure as heck had been no kidnapping.

"Look at me."

I waited, wondering if he'd comply. The fool. Instead of doing as I said, he ducked his head even further. If he wanted to sacrifice himself for Jennings, that was up to him. However, he'd soon learn what a fool he'd been to blindly follow Jennings. No one insulted me and they sure didn't insult my mate.

"Look at me!" I repeated as I took Matt's hand and released the last of my control.

Marchant whimpered as he complied. His eyes wide, he looked at Matt and me. There was no doubt in my mind that, had he not been chained as he was, he would have fallen to the ground, exposing belly and throat in a show of submission. Instead, the sharp smell of urine filled the room. My panther reveled in it. This was what power was like. This was what it meant to be an Alpha.

"Now answer our questions."

He nodded, sweat dripping from his face. He couldn't start talking fast enough. By the time he stopped, there was no need to talk to the others. But we would. We'd make sure we knew everything we could about what Jennings had planned and what he might do now that his plans had been discovered. Then I'd be more than happy to turn the three back over to Tamara and Danny until the clan leaders met and a decision was made about what to do with them and what to do about Jennings.

CHAPTER SIXTEEN

"Finn, you need to calm down."

Calm down! Had he lost his mind? How the hell was I supposed to calm down when we now had proof of how far Michael Jennings was willing to go in order to force my return to California?

I closed my eyes and slowly counted to ten. Hell, I could have counted to one hundred or even one thousand. It wouldn't have helped. Since leaving the warehouse, my temper had built to what could only be called epic proportions. So had a fear I didn't dare voice, not to myself and certainly not to anyone else. Instead, I held the temper close to me, relishing it, nursing it. I had a feeling if I didn't, if I let myself really think about the fear lurking just below the surface, I'd take off again. Hell, that might be the best thing to do. At least it would keep Matt and his people safe from Jennings.

I leaned my forehead against the window and fought for control. Damn it, I'd given it voice. Now it was real, and I had to think about it. No, I had to deal with it. Somehow. But how do you deal with something so pervasive and soul-crushing?

I started nervously when Matt reached out to lightly touch my shoulder. Damn Jennings! In just a few short hours, he'd managed to turn me back into the frightened teen I'd been that night when ran away. Worse, he'd managed to do it without being near. All it had taken was seeing the preparations his trackers had made to take me, hearing them discuss what he'd told them to do if I wasn't "cooperative."

"Finn."

Concern filled Matt's voice as I lightly pounded my head against the glass. His concern only made it worse. I knew he wanted to help. He'd do everything possible to make me feel safe. I had a feeling if I asked him to, he'd call Jennings out right now and challenge him. But it wasn't his fight. Not really. I might be his mate, but this was my nightmare. I was the one who had to end it. The problem was I didn't know how.

God, running sounded so good just then. It would be so easy to say I needed to go for a walk to clear my head. All I'd have to do was take some cash with me and Matt, bless him, had insisted on giving me some just that morning. A short walk to get me outside the neighborhood and then I could hitch a ride downtown with someone. From there I could hop a bus somewhere, anywhere just so long as it took me away from Matt and the others. I had to keep them safe.

Except I didn't think it would. Not in the long run. Jennings had proven he had a long memory and that he held onto grudges even longer. He'd come after Matt simply because Matt had gotten in his way. If I ran, there'd be nothing I could do to help when trouble came. It would mean dealing with Jennings sooner, rather than later, but I'd been running long enough.

Hadn't I?

"Talk to me, Finn. What can I do?"

Matt rested his hands on my shoulders, just enough to let me know he was there and he cared. How could I explain to him I was scared, not only for myself but for him, for his sister and everyone else he cared for?

I did it by doing just that.

"Matt, I'm scared." I turned and wrapped my arms around him.

He held me close, his cheek resting against the top of my head. No passion now, just safety. "Until today, I'd known intellectually what Jennings wanted. I knew he was obsessed. Hell, as far as I'm concerned, he's more than a touch insane. But today brought it home. This is the first time I've realized just how far he's willing to go to get his hands on me and that scares the hell out of me."

"Finn, I won't let him near you. I promise. He'll never lay a finger on you again."

I shook my head. He didn't understand.

"Matt, I'd be lying if I said I wasn't scared for myself because I am. I'm terrified. God, I want to open the door and run. Just run. Get as far away from here as I can." I paused, trying to find the right words. "But that's because I want to protect you and yours. Jennings is going to come after you now. I know it just as surely as we both know he isn't going to stop coming after me until one of us is dead."

I swallowed hard. I'd never said that aloud. Hell, I'd never even thought it, at least not more than in passing. But I would not let him take me alive, especially not now that I had a pretty good idea what he planned once he had me.

"Finn, I'm no fool. I knew when you called him that I was painting a great big target on my back. I knew it and I accepted it." He tilted my face up so I looked at him. "I would have done it no matter what. No man should treat a woman the way Jennings has treated you. He's the sort of man my daddy taught me ought to be taken out and hung from the nearest tree. The fact I'm clan leader means I can't let him act as he has without taking action. He violated my territory and put my people in danger of discovery through the action of his trackers.

"That's enough for me to deal with Jennings. The man shouldn't be in any position of authority. He's a danger not only to those who look to him for leadership and protection but to all of our kind.

"Then there's you." Now he held me away from him, his expression serious. "When I realized what was going on in that parking garage, I knew I had to help you. It didn't matter who you were or who those men were. All that mattered was I knew you were in trouble. Then, when I knew you were all right, that they hadn't hurt you as badly as I'd feared, it was like the world stopped. I'd never thought to find a mate. Sure, I planned on finding a woman to spend my life with, maybe raise a family with. I know how rare it is to find a life mate. But there you were, on your knees before me, offering me everything I thought I'd never have."

I reached up and framed his face with my hands. Fortune smiled on me that day in the parking garage. But I didn't like knowing it had also put Matt on a collision course with Jennings, even if it seemed like he looked forward to it.

"Matt, I don't want you doing anything foolish."

"Then you understand how I feel." His hand lightly caressed my cheek. "You have to promise me no running, no anything without discussing it first with me."

"I promise if you do." I smiled, relief filling me, when he nodded. "There is one thing I want to do today if possible."

He cocked his head to one side and looked at me. "What?"

"Nothing serious, I promise." Now I grinned. In for an inch, in for a mile. "Will you call CJ and see if she can bring her kit over tonight? Her work with the two of us isn't finished, not yet."

"All right." He relaxed and pulled me into a quick hug. "Danny should be here soon."

I tensed again and then relaxed when I realized Matt didn't seem too concerned.

"Don't worry, sweetheart. He just wants to brief us on what happened after we left."

"And we have some things to discuss as well," my grandmother said from the doorway. How long she'd been standing there, I didn't know but it was a pretty good bet from the expression she wore that she'd heard at least some of our conversation.

"Go on. I'll call CJ and then I have to take care of a couple of things for work," Matt said and gave me a quick kiss. "And remember, neither of us is going to do anything stupid." Now he pinned me with a look I understood and was more than happy to turn back on him.

"You keep that in mind as well," I said. "Matt, I mean it. I'd never forgive myself if anything happened to you because of me."

"We'll both be careful. Now go see what your grandmother wants." He gave my butt a light swat.

Grinning, feeling a little better, I did as he said, doing my best to ignore the nagging voice at the back of my brain telling me it would still be better to run.

"So, Finn, when are you going to come to work for me?" CJ asked as she laid out her tools. "Your art is perfect for what I do and I promise it would make us both money."

Stripped to the waist, I lay on my stomach at the edge of the bed Matt and I shared. A moment later, CJ stood next to me. Hands gentle, she peeled away the bandage she'd applied earlier. I waited as she carefully cleaned the area and then applied more ointment. With my head pillowed on my right arm, I watched as she nodded in satisfaction. Then she checked the sketch I gave her when she arrived a few minutes ago.

"And I'm still waiting for an answer," she reminded me.

The corners of my mouth twitched up in a smile. For the first time in my life, someone wanted to pay me to do something I enjoyed. I'd never become a tattoo artist, at least I didn't think I would, but just being asked to design artwork for her sent a thrill through me.

"When I'm sure you're asking because you really think I can help and not because Matt prompted you or because I'm his mate and an alpha."

"I didn't say a word to her!" Matt protested from the door.

"Out!" I jabbed a finger in the direction of the living room.

"But I want to watch." He grinned and winked.

"You just like seeing me half naked."

"True." His grin widened, and I blushed as I remembered we weren't alone. "But I really want to see what you're having CJ do this time. You've gotten a lot of ink an a short period of time, Finn. Are you sure this is how you want to do it?"

He wasn't asking about the pain from the sessions. I'd done more than take on the markings of pride and clan. My design, expertly brought to life by CJ, showed my family's history. Our ties to the Oklahoma clan, going back to Kansas and Pennsylvania as well. Each of the dominant animals in our bloodline had been worked in. But this last, this was in many ways the most important. It was my tribute to my parents and their sacrifice. I had no doubt they died not only because they had doubts about Jennings as a pride leader but also because they refused to let him near me.

"Sit up," CJ said softly as she finished rebandaging the work from that morning.

"Matt, you'll see the tattoo soon enough. In the meantime, judging by how fast I hear your sister moving, I think Danny's here." The chiming of the doorbell and Sharon's soft, almost breathless, greeting confirmed my guess.

"What?" Matt's brow furrowed and CJ burst out laughing.

"Matt, you make a great clan leader, but you're blind where your little sister's concerned," she said.

"Are they? Are you saying?" He looked from us to the front of the house even though he wouldn't be able to see the front door and then back to us.

"Has he always been this dense, CJ?" I asked as she began prepping my lower arm for the new ink. By the time she finished, I'd have a full sleeve tattoo that also covered that shoulder.

"Only where Sharon's concerned."

He growled and turned to leave. Then he paused and looked back at us. "I still want to watch but I think I'll leave before you two completely destroy my sense of dignity." At least he grinned so I knew he wasn't mad.

"That will keep him occupied for a few minutes," CJ commented. She swabbed disinfectant over my skin and then waited for it to dry. "And I'm impressed you picked up on it. Sharon and Danny have been fooling just about everyone, themselves included, for almost a year now."

"That's pretty much what I thought when it finally dawned on me." At least CJ seemed to approve. That was good because I liked Sharon and was beginning to think Danny and I might become friends. If they could be happy together, I'd do whatever I could to help them, even if it meant running interference with Matt in big brother mode.

"And you still haven't answered my question, Finn. When are you going to come to work for me?"

"You sure you really want me to?"

"I am." She once again reached for my sketch and glanced at it. "Finn, I can't pay you a lot, not to start with. But I have a feeling we'll be able to work something out. A royalty agreement possibly. If you agree, I'd like you to update my book of sketches and add some new ones while you're at it. If you're interested, that is."

"I am. Let's talk about it next week."

"Sounds good. Now let me get this placed. Then you can see what you think. If you like it, we'll get started. This is going to take a while."

A while was an understatement. Almost five hours later, CJ sat back and sighed wearily. Then, as she stretched, lifting her arms over her head, she grinned. She clearly approved of her work. Hopefully, I'd be as happy with it as I was with the other ink she'd done for me. Otherwise, I'd voluntarily sat through a zillion bee-like stings as she worked for nothing. Being a shapeshifter might mean I healed faster than a normal, but I still felt pain. I also didn't like pain, so if I'd sat through all this only to hate what CJ had done. . . . .

CJ helped me up and watched as I moved into the bathroom. Standing before the mirror, I held my arm out and twisted it this way and that, doing my best to see every centimeter of the new tattoo.

Then I dropped my arm to my side and angled by body so I could see the full sleeve and shoulder tattoo in the mirror. Matt had been right. After so long of never even thinking about getting a tattoo, I'd gotten more ink in the last few days than most folks would consider getting in their lifetimes. The newest blended beautifully into what CJ had done earlier. The scene continued, transitioning to show a bear, a coyote and an eagle. The bear and coyote were among the animals some of my ancestors had changed into. They also had special meaning to the Cherokee. Now my original design felt complete.

"CJ, it's perfect. Thanks." I turned from the mirror and grinned in appreciation. "What do I owe you?"

"Not a thing." She shook her head. Her grin now matched mine. "Finn, I'm not doing this out of the goodness of my heart and, before you ask, Matt hasn't paid me for it either. I'm not going to charge you a dime for the work." She held up a hand to forestall any protest I might voice. "Trust me, I'm being selfish here. I plan on using you as a walking billboard for my work *and* I'm going to insist you do new art for me whenever you want."

For a moment, I considered her offer. Then I nodded. It was a good trade-off. Hell, it was a great trade-off, at least from my perspective. "You've got yourself a deal." I moved to stand before her and extended my hand, waiting until she took it. "Now I'm going to find something to put on so we can join the others."

"After I put some ointment on it and cover it," she corrected and motioned for me to sit on the edge of the bed. "And then I have a very late date. I'll leave clan politics to you and Matt."

"Thanks," I said without humor. Unfortunately, she was right. I needed to join the others and see what I'd missed.

When I entered the den a few minutes later, properly attired in jeans and tank top, I smiled to see Danny and Sharon sitting side by side on the sofa. Matt lounged in his favorite chair. Before I could ask about my grandmother, there came sounds from the kitchen. She was either cleaning up or cooking. My hope was that she was baking.

Some of my favorite memories as a child were of the cakes she'd bake whenever I'd visit.

"Well?" Matt asked as he stood and hurried to my side.

"Well what?" I knew perfectly well what he meant, but he didn't need to know that.

"When do we get to see the new ink?"

"Oh, I don't know. CJ said it needs to be covered for a while."

"Don't be mean, Finn," Sharon laughed from across the room.

"Well," I drawled and then danced out of the way when Matt made a grab for me. "If you're good, you'll get to see it later tonight. Everyone else can wait until the weekend."

He growled and then grinned. I smiled and took his hand, "So, what have you guys been talking about?" I slid to sit on the floor in front of Matt's chair. When I leaned back and rested my head against his thigh, his hand stroked my hair. To my surprise, my panther didn't object to our position. We were with family. The last conclusion they'd draw from where I chose to sit was that I was showing submission to Matt.

"We were just confirming the arrangements for this weekend," Danny said. "It looks like almost every clan will be represented."

"Your grandmother and I spoke with the leaders of the nearest clans. They'll be here and will bring support with them. It seems they've been thinking along the same lines as Irene and my big brother," Sharon put in.

"Oh?"

"Yeah. They agree we need to figure out a way for the clans to be more interconnected. We can't continue to isolate ourselves if we want to survive," Matt said. "So, after we introduce you as my mate and the clan's female Alpha, we'll meet with the other clan leaders to see what we can start hammering out."

"You have been busy."

I shook my head. Regret washed over me for a moment as memory of a snatch of conversation between my parents popped up in my head. It had been late and I was supposed to have been in bed and asleep. I'd gotten up for some reason, probably because I was curious about what they were talking about after a clan meeting. I'd crouched at the top of the stairs, hiding in the shadows, and listened. They'd been worried because a member of one of the local packs had lost control and shifted during the day. He'd been young and had experienced his first shift just a few months earlier. For whatever reason, his pack leader hadn't been able to teach him the necessity of controlling the urge to shift when his emotions ran high. Everyone had been lucky that day because the only normals around had been family members who knew about our kind. But it could have gone so wrong.

That night my parents discussed how that had been a prime example of why the clans needed to work closer together. Each clan had members with different specialties and resources. Surely there was a way to share those resources to protect our kind. Unfortunately, there were still too many who felt isolation, not only from the normals but from other clans, was the best way to protect our kind.

"You're awfully quiet, Finn," Matt commented.

"Sorry. I was remembering my folks talking about how the clans needed to start working together."

"I'm not surprised they felt that way." Danny leaned forward, resting his elbows on his knees. "Your mother was the first Alpha I heard say we needed to quit hiding our heads in the sand and realize the world was changing around us. We needed to adapt before we were discovered." He paused, and I had a feeling he had something else to say.

"What is it?" I asked finally.

"My friend emailed me the copies of the reports surrounding your parents' deaths." His expression hardened, and anger flared in his eyes. My heart beat faster and I reached for Matt's hand. It was obvious Danny didn't like what he'd seen and that worried me.

"And?"

"Let me start by saying I haven't had a chance to study the reports as closely as I'd like, but I've seen enough to be confident that neither your mother nor your father committed suicide."

His words hit me like a blow. I'd spent years convinced there was more to their deaths than we'd been told. Over the last few days, I'd finally allowed myself to admit what I'd suspected all along: that Jennings had something to do with what happened. But to hear Danny actually confirm my suspicion that they hadn't killed themselves, that they hadn't abandoned me, was almost too much to take in.

All those years I'd wondered in the back of my mind what I had done to make my parents take their lives. I'd been angry they'd killed themselves and left me alone. I felt betrayed they'd left me at the mercy of a bastard like Jennings. Now I knew they hadn't. No longer did I have to wonder if our happy home had been nothing but a lie. It hadn't been. They'd been taken from me and I had a pretty damned good idea by whom.

Tears stung my eyes and I scrambled to my feet. Before I could move away, Matt's arms went around me, and he pulled me onto his lap. He held me, comforting me as I cried. Sobs wracked me as all the emotion and all the fear surfaced. Then my grandmother was there, demanding to know what happened. I was vaguely aware of Danny telling her what he had said. She didn't say anything, not at first. Instead, she wrapped her arms around me, not trying to take me from Matt's embrace, but adding her comfort to his.

"God. Oh God." I scrubbed my hands against my cheeks, wiping away my tears. "You're sure?"

"Positive," Danny said. "We already knew the detectives weren't comfortable with the initial suicide ruling. The only reason they listed it as a possibility in their report is that a 'close family friend' told them your father had been diagnosed with an extremely aggressive form of cancer. This 'friend' said your parents came to him and discussed how they didn't want your father to suffer and how they didn't want to be separated by death. Even though things didn't quite add up, there was also nothing jumping out at them to contradict what Jennings said. So, barring anything to the contrary coming out in the autopsies, the suicide ruling would be entered."

I stared at Danny in disbelief. What did he mean they'd accepted the suicide explanation just because Jennings said my parents told him that's what they were going to do?

No, it didn't make sense. My parents wouldn't have kept something as serious as Daddy having cancer from me. They'd have told me. That he had been sick, possibly dying made no more sense than their committing suicide had. Damn, had the world gone mad or was it just me?

"Finn, there's more."

I breathed deeply, searching for calm. I wasn't sure how much more I could take.

"Your father wasn't sick. The coroner found no evidence of cancer or any other illness when he did the autopsies. Both died by gunshot wounds to the head."

I closed my eyes and instantly regretted it as the memory of walking into their bedroom after school that horrible afternoon and finding them. They lay on their bed. At first, I thought they'd been taking a nap. Then I'd scented the blood. A scream was torn from me as I saw it pooling on the bed and floor. Somehow, I'd made my way downstairs and called Aunt Jane. Then I'd run outside and waited, praying it had all been a bad dream.

"What about gunshot residue?" Matt asked.

"Traces were found, but not what you'd expect from self-inflicted wounds. The coroner made a point of noting there was no stippling around the wounds. He also speculated that the bodies had been posed after they'd been shot."

"Then why the hell wasn't the cause of death changed?" I demanded. I'd have surged to my feet if Matt hadn't kept a firm hold on me.

"That's a damned good question." There was a bite to Grandma's voice, an underlying current of anger I'd never heard before. My panther stirred, restless and worried. Not that I blamed her. I knew how close I was to shifting and had a pretty good idea Grandma was as well. Angry as we were, there was no telling the damage we'd do if we let our animals out.

"It was months before the coroner's findings were in. By then, the case was cold. The detectives tried to talk to Finn—who had already run away—and Jennings who continued to stick to his story they'd killed themselves. Since there'd been no evidence of a third person being involved, the best the cops could do was list the cause of death for both your parents as gunshot wounds, origin unknown."

"That's bullshit! Jennings had to have had something to do with it."

"I agree, Finn. Either he did it himself or he knows who did and is protecting them. The problem is we don't have any proof. Not yet at any rate. And, much as I hate to say it, you have to accept the possibility we may never know exactly what happened that day."

"I'll be damned if I accept it, Danny." I pushed out of Matt's comforting embrace. I couldn't just sit there. "That son of a bitch killed my parents. It doesn't matter if he did it himself or had someone else do it for him. He's responsible and he will pay for it."

"He will," both Matt and my grandmother said.

"Finn, if he shows up this weekend, he's going to pay for that and for what he's done to you. I promise you that as your mate and as clan leader. But you have to promise you aren't going to do anything foolish. You have to trust me, trust us to handle this."

"This is my fight," I growled.

"No, Finn, it's *our* fight," my grandmother said firmly. "And one we need to prepare for."

My lips pulled back, baring my teeth. My cat was so close to the surface I could feel the fur trying to spring from my pores. This was the closet to losing control that I'd been in years and I didn't care. No one, not Matt, not my grandmother, no one was going to deal with Jennings but me. He'd taken my life from me. Worse, he'd taken my parents from me. I'd see him dead, slowly and painfully, by my hand and to hell with the consequences.

"Finn!" Matt's voice brooked no arguments and I felt his power as Alpha roll over me.

"All right!" I snapped.

"Finn." Now he stood and moved to me. He was wise enough not to touch me. Angry as I was, I'd probably do something foolish. Oh, I'd regret it later, but just then anyone was fair game, especially if they tried to keep me from getting satisfaction from Jennings. "Sweetheart, I promise if we find proof he was responsible for your parents' deaths, you get to deal with him. Right now, however, we have to focus on what we do know, what we do have to use against him.

"But don't think for a moment we won't bring this up with the other clan leaders. This is yet another example of why we have to work together. It's clear Jennings is a danger to us and has to be dealt with."

I closed my eyes and drew a deep breath, holding it before exhaling. He was right, but that didn't make it any easier. I wanted Jennings' blood for so many different reasons now.

"All right," I repeated more softly. "Are you okay?" I looked at my grandmother, worried by the anger still reflected in her eyes.

"I want his blood just as much as you do, child." Now she closed her eyes and breathed deeply, much as I had a few moments before. "Matt, I recommend we spend the time between now and the meeting preparing what we're going to say."

"Agreed." He held his hands out to me, waiting. It was up to me to make the first move. Some of my anger receded. Thank God, he was so different from Jennings. When I put my hands in his, he drew me close. "Sharon, you're either to stay here or with Danny. I'm not risking Jennings or one of his people making a grab for you. This isn't open to debate."

For a moment, it looked like she'd argue. Then she cast a quick look at Danny before smiling. "Since you seem to approve of the two of us, I'll go with him and I'll be good."

"I'll take good care of her, Matt."

"I know you will, Danny."

Heaven help him if he didn't.

"Irene, I hope you'll stay here, at least until Adam gets back in town," Matt continued.

"Of course." She smiled as she moved to stand before us. Then she reached out, taking one of my hands and one of Matt's in her own. "I want to get to know my granddaughter better and we need to prepare her for the weekend."

And that probably meant more "lessons" with her. I groaned inwardly. She'd already proven herself to be a hard taskmaster.

"Finn, are you all right?"

Matt stood in the doorway to the bedroom, his expression concerned. In the time since Danny and Sharon left, we'd been talking with my grandmother. Neither she nor I had tried to mask our anger or our pain. To finally, after all this time, have our suspicions that there was more to my parents' deaths than we'd been told confirmed should have been a vindication. But it wasn't. All it had done was bring back the pain and fear I'd felt when I walked into my parents' bedroom and found them. Then Jennings had taken over the clan, claimed me as his mate and tried to rape me when I refused. He'd taken my family and my life from me. The years on the run were years I'd never get back.

Now, with Grandma retired for the night, Matt and I needed to talk. But I didn't have the words to explain what I felt. My emotions were still in turmoil. One moment I felt relieved, almost vindicated, to know my parents hadn't killed themselves. The next I was almost blind with the need for vengeance. Then came the pain of their deaths, washing over me just as strongly as it had so long ago. This was one rollercoaster I wished I could get off.

Matt stayed where he was, waiting for me to say something. I realized then he'd done basically the same thing all evening. Except for that one time when he'd let his alpha side come to the surface—

and I knew that was to remind me I wasn't alone and didn't need to do anything foolish—he'd not put any pressure on me. He'd been there for support, but he hadn't taken advantage. Nor would he.

"I don't know." That was the honest truth. "I've always believed there was more to what happened than I knew. In the back of my mind, I knew my parents hadn't killed themselves. But there was a part of me that wondered what I'd done—or not done—that caused them to do it and leave me behind. Then came the mess with Jennings and I had to run before I had any of the answers I so badly needed.

"Now I find myself wondering if the truth would have come out if I'd stayed in California instead of running away. Maybe if I'd stood up to Jennings and told the clan what he'd tried to do me, the investigation wouldn't have been dropped. Did I let their killer get away because I was too weak to stay?"

Tears ran down my cheeks. There, I'd said it. Had I betrayed my parents and all they stood for by not staying and pushing for the truth? How was I supposed to live with that?

"Finn, no!" He crossed the room and folded me in his arms, holding me close. "The last thing your parents would have wanted was for you to stay and become Jennings' next victim. You know that, just as you know they loved you." He tilted up my face and gently wiped away my tears. "You can't blame yourself for what happened. Remember, your aunt and uncle told you to run because they were that worried about you. When you ran into your grandmother that time, she told you the same thing. You did what you had to do. You stayed safe, exactly what your parents would have wanted."

"I don't know, Matt."

"I do." He rubbed his thumb against my cheek, soft and reassuring. "I'm not going to tell you to let it go. You couldn't, and I wouldn't ask you to. But I promise I'll make sure Jennings pays for what he's done to you and to your family."

"You certainly got more than you bargained for when you

stopped to help me in that parking garage." Somehow, I managed a slight smile.

"I did. I found a woman I admire and respect a great deal, even if we've only known one another a short time. I also found my mate, an alpha who is my equal. We're both proud and stubborn and that will cause us to butt heads from time to time. But that just makes life interesting."

"You are a strange, strange man." I couldn't help it. I laughed, the first time I'd done so in what seemed like forever.

"Of course, I am." He grinned and gave my shoulders a squeeze, releasing me quickly as I gasped slightly. We'd both forgotten the new tattoos and the pressure of his embrace brought it all home again. "Sorry. Did I hurt you?"

"No. But that did remind me I need to put some more ointment on the tattoos. Otherwise, CJ will have my head." I grabbed the hem of my tank top and pulled it over my head. My cheeks heated as Matt grinned down at me.

"So, do I finally get to see the new ink?" he asked as I walked into the bathroom to get the tube of ointment CJ had given me.

"Only if you help apply this." I tossed the tube to him and grinned as his left hand reached out to snatch up the ointment before it hit the floor.

A few moments later, I lay face down on the mattress, much as I had while CJ worked. Matt carefully exposed the tattoo. For a moment, he didn't say anything. I waited, not quite holding my breath. Suddenly, it was very important to know what he thought. Then a shiver went through me as his finger lightly traced just outside the edges of the tattoo. His soft whistle followed.

"Finn, it's gorgeous. Sit up so I can see the rest of it." he rested one hand at the curve of my waist. Then other reached for my hand and held my arm out so he could see my new *sleeve*. "I'm not sure I recognize all the symbolism but that doesn't matter. It really is wonderful, and I love how it blends so well into what you already had."

I relaxed to know he approved. That was important since I had designed it to tie into the pride and clan markings. But now was the time to explain what I'd had CJ do.

"The bear and coyote not only have meaning to the Cherokee, but they are also animals some of my ancestors shifted into. The background represents the Oklahoma clan and my own ancestry. The eagle is there as protection. This, along with what I designed for the pride and clan markings, represents who I am."

"I like it."

He placed a gentle kiss on my neck, just above the tattoo where it curved over my shoulder. A thrill of excitement ran down my spine. Then I tensed reflexively as he began gently rubbing the ointment over the new tattoo. After securing the bandage over it, he eased me down on the mattress. Then he slid down to lay next to me. It seemed right to shift slightly so my head rested against his chest and his arm went around my waist, holding me close.

"Matt, thank you."

"For what?"

"For caring." I lifted my head just enough to press a kiss against his jaw. "I hadn't realized how alone I've felt until these last few days. I'm not sure how much longer I could have lasted on my own. I was dying inside and didn't know it."

"You're selling yourself short again."

"No. I'm serious. My life had become nothing more than trying to stay ahead of the trackers just one more day. I can't tell you the last time I went to a movie or had drinks with a friend." I paused, biting my lip to keep my emotions under control. "Do you know I didn't get to graduate from high school? I did manage to get my GED. Figured my folks would come back to haunt me if I didn't do that much. But their deaths and then what happened with Jennings put an end to things like going to school and dreaming of the senior prom and college."

"What do you want to do now?" He tilted my head up some. "I meant what I said before. You can do whatever you want. If you want to go to college and get a degree, we'll do whatever it takes to get you admitted to any college you want to go to. If you want to work, you can do that. You have your life back now, Finn, and it is your life. I am not about to tell you what you can and can't do."

I smiled and leaned up on my elbow so I could kiss him. Then I settled back down at his side. "I told CJ I'd do some work for her."

"Good." His fingers ran through my hair.

"Matt, I don't get you," I said softly. "You have every right to push me out of your bed and onto the streets. You could demand almost anything from me as my Alpha. Yet you don't. Instead, you give. You give of yourself and you try to give of your money and not once have you asked for anything in return."

"Finn, I'm not the sort of man—or the sort of Alpha—who believes my position entitles me to take whatever I want. My folks raised me better than that. If I only wanted someone to share my bed, I'd go out and buy myself a whore whenever I wanted to get laid. But that's not what I want. I want a partner, an equal. I want someone who shares my values and beliefs and who will help me raise a family. I want you, but only if you want me in the same way.

"That means we go at your pace. I'll help you as much as you let me. I may feel like kicking you in the ass now and then because you're about as hard-headed as I am, but I won't actually do it." He smiled now, and I grinned back at him. "But I do insist on one thing."

"What?"

"If you're going to work for CJ, you're going to need some things. You'll need art supplies and a good computer or tablet. Maybe both. You'll need someplace you can work without interruption. So you'll let me outfit one of the rooms here in the house as your office."

Part of me wanted to object. I'd been on my own and had done for myself for so long that it was difficult to accept help from anyone. But he was right. I would need some things if I was going to try to make a go of my art. It might not be what I wound up doing for the rest of my life, but it was something I could do in the short term.

Not that I wouldn't repay every cent he spent, even if it took forever.

"All right."

He shifted, and I felt him looking down at me in surprise. "What, no argument?"

"Not this time." I grinned up at him. "Unless you want an argument."

"I have something better in mind than arguing."

"Oh, really?"

"Really." He grinned and shifted his weight. A moment later, I lay on my back, looking up at him. "But only if you're agreeable."

"Hmmm." I whooped in laughter as his fingers found my ribs. "Not if you keep tickling me," I gasped.

"I think I can find something you'll like better."

He stood and helped me to my feet. Without a word, he unbuttoned my jeans and unzipped them. Then he eased them over my hips. I stepped out of them and then my panties. Before I could object to him wearing too many clothes, he stripped. Things were definitely getting interesting.

"Lie down on your stomach."

"Huh?"

Okay, a brilliant conversationalist I'm not.

"On your stomach."

Not quite sure what he had in mind, I did as he said. The mattress dipped as he straddled my waist. My breath caught as his hands began slowly kneading the tension from my back. Careful of my new tattoo, he worked his way slowly from my neck and shoulders to my waist, his lips following.

"Matt."

"Shh. Relax and enjoy."

"You?" It was barely more than a breath and was all I could muster as his mouth followed his hands ever lower.

"I am enjoying." He looked up, grinning.

"God, so am I."

CHAPTER SEVENTEEN

"Matt, you've got to be kidding."

I stared at the leathers he'd laid out on the bed while I showered. When I first entered the bedroom, I thought he'd simply laid out the same leather pants and vest I'd worn the night he introduced me to the pride. But, upon closer examination, it was easy to see these were very different. Both laced up and looked like it wouldn't take much to shed them. But that was where the similarities ended.

I turned and looked at Matt where he stood in front of the closet door. When I arched an eyebrow in question, he actually blushed. God, he could be so cute. Then I felt myself blushing as one possible explanation for not only his blush but the need to quickly shed my clothes came to me. Surely not. . .

"No, oh God, no, Finn." He all but stammered it out. "Believe me, we are NOT having sex in front of everyone."

Thank God. It was one thing to undress and shift in front of others of our kind but it was something completely different to do so and have sex in front of them. I didn't even want to think about doing so in front of my grandmother and Uncle Adam. I might as well just dig a hole and bury myself because I'd surely die of embarrassment otherwise. Matt might be a wonderful lover but not only no, but hell no to having sex outside the privacy of our home.

"Then why?" At least I didn't have to explain what I meant.

"Finn, we don't know what's going to happen tonight. We've done all we can to make sure safeguards are in place. But you know as well as I do that nothing is foolproof. I want you able to shift and shift quickly if the need arises."

I didn't say anything. Instead, I nodded. He was right. Even if the only ones expected tonight were members of the clan, we couldn't be completely sure what would happen. There was always the off-chance someone would challenge Matt for clan leadership or even me for the role of his mate. By adding in the other clan leaders and those they brought with them, we increased the odds of something unexpected happening.

But I knew that wasn't what he was worried about. We still didn't know for sure if Jennings would show up. My money was on him being there. He'd put too much time and effort into finding me and forcing me back to California. The last thing he'd want was for me to be with another man. Well, I had a feeling there was one thing he feared more than that—at least if he had even a modicum of common sense. He ought to be afraid of what I would say to the other clan leaders.

The thought of facing Jennings again after so much time should have worried me. But it didn't. At least not at the moment. There was a thrill of expectation, of finally being able to face down the man who had caused me so much pain and fear for so long. It wasn't neces-sarily logical and certainly not sane. But I knew what it was. For the first time I'd be facing him as an equal, Alpha to Alpha. He'd learn I was no longer the scared and hurting girl he'd terrified.

"Even if it doesn't come to that, we very well may want the clan, as well as the other clan leaders, to see just how powerful an Alpha you are. That means you'll have to shift," he continued. As he did, he watched me closely and I knew he wondered how I'd react to that.

Well, that was easy. I moved across the room to stand before him. The towel I'd wrapped around me when I'd stepped out of the shower dropped to the floor as I reached up to kiss him. He needed to know I wasn't worried about what might happen tonight. I was confident in him as my Alpha and as my mate and I needed him to be confident in me.

"Matt, quit worrying." I brushed my lips against his once again before stepping back. If I didn't put some distance between us, we'd end up in bed and we didn't have time for that. "I will do whatever's necessary to secure not only my place with the clan but to support you as clan leader. I meant it when I pledged my life and my arm to you as clan Alpha."

"I know you did, and I meant it when I pledged the same to you." Now he pulled me close and I breathed in the scent of him. Standing there, in the protective circle of his arms, I felt safe and knew nothing would ever happen. "But there's more to it, Finn. I want the other clan leaders to know you are not only an alpha but are strong enough to be one of our leaders. If we are to survive in a world where it is becoming more and more difficult to keep our existence a secret from the general public, the clans have to work closer together than ever before. That means we have to respect one another and realize we can't continue to be ruled by the old ways. You understand that better than most. So you have to be accepted not only as my mate but as an alpha in your own right. Now, let's get dressed. I want to be there before the others arrive."

I nodded. We'd spoken of the need to plan for the future, to prepare for the day when we would go public with our existence. But I'd never realized until that moment that Matt meant to be one of those driving the decisions and he wanted me just as involved. It would be so easy to say "no" and slip back into the shadows. Our kind had become comfortable there, probably too comfortable. But, easy as it might be, we had to realize those shadows were shrinking and soon they'd be gone for good.

Besides, it wasn't as if what Matt implied was anything new, at least not to me. My parents had discussed it before their deaths. For as long as I could remember, they'd drilled two things into my head: the need to be careful to never betray my true nature to the normals and the need to be prepared for the day when our existence was finally revealed. They'd spoken at length more than once and with great passion about how it would be best for all involved if we determined the time and place to go public. If we planned for it, if we managed to lay the proper groundwork, much of the fear and knee-jerk reaction the normals would feel upon learning that "monsters" really existed would be blunted. If we were lucky, it would be blunted enough to keep our kind alive until we could be accepted as just another type of human.

For that to happen, our kind had to start working together. If I could help Matt facilitate it, I would—especially if it meant making sure Jennings and those like him were never allowed leadership roles in the clans again.

"Has Danny reported anything new?" I asked as I began dressing.

"Nothing solid. One of the teams he stationed at the airport reported seeing someone who matched Jennings' description leaving one of the terminals late morning. There were three others with him and none of them looked happy." He paused long enough to pull his shirt on over his head. "Unfortunately, our people weren't close enough to tell for sure and there were too many conflicting scents to be able to tell if they were shapeshifters."

"My money's on it being him."

And I'd feel a lot better if we knew for certain. At least our people said the four hadn't looked happy. That meant Jennings, if it was Jennings, wasn't as confident about what was going to happen tonight as he'd like. Good. A lack of confidence meant he'd be off-balance. If he was off-balance, he'd be easier to manipulate into admitting what he'd tried to do to me and, hopefully, what he had done to my parents. He would finally learn he had no control over me and absolutely no claim on me.

Matt watched as I pulled my hair into a loose ponytail. Normally,

I'd have braided it. Not tonight. Matt and the others might think they could control Jennings and avoid a fight. I wasn't so sure. The man I remembered had been hot-tempered and always ready to fight. That had been one of my parents' concerns about him. Instead of working with pride leadership to gain experience, he fought his way to the top. The memory of my father saying Jennings was a prime example of someone who believed in the adage "might makes right" came to me. Dad hadn't been complimenting Jennings at the time. Even then, he'd known there was something wrong with the younger man and had worried about it.

What Matt and I planned for the night would be more than a figurative slap in the face. Jennings refused to accept the fact I didn't want to be with him. He'd proven that time and again by sending trackers after me and not giving up, no matter how many years had passed. When he saw Matt and me together, when he realized what my tattooing meant—and what an insult it was to him since I'd refused to have anything tying me to the Northern California clan included in the inkings—he'd be hard pressed to keep control. If he figured out we had even more in mind than announcing my acceptance into the clan and the fact I was Matt's mate and an alpha in my own right, he'd fight. I had no doubts about it.

I planned to be prepared.

A soft knock at the door interrupted my thoughts. By the time I turned away from the mirror, Matt had opened the door and Sharon stepped inside. She looked first at her brother and then at me, nodding in approval. A slight smile touched her lips and, before I could say anything, she dropped to hands and knees and crawled closer.

"Get up," I laughed. "Save it for the meeting."

"Finn's right, kid." Matt reached down to help her to her feet. "While we both appreciate the sentiment—"

"Damn, big brother, you don't feel it, do you?" Sharon shook her head, eyes wide with surprise. He shook his head and looked to me. All I could do was shrug. "Neither of you are holding back right now, are you? You're both mentally getting ready for what might happen tonight."

I nodded.

"What you clearly don't realize is that you are also in full alpha mode. Your power hit me smack in the face when I stepped inside." She blew out a breath and then grinned. "And it's pretty damned awesome. I've never felt anything like that and I'll lay good money most of the others haven't either. But you might want to tone it down before we get to the ranch. Don't tip your hand too soon."

She was right, even if I hadn't realized Matt and I had been in what she called "full alpha mode." Matt was always so controlled. Then, looking at him, I saw the tightness to his expression, the steel in his gaze. He was ready for tonight, but he was also looking for blood. Thank God it wasn't my blood. There was no doubt he wanted Jennings' blood, just as I did. Well, we might have to flip for it because I wanted satisfaction from the man who had taken so much from me.

No, I needed it in order to move on with my life. I had to know he'd never come after me again.

"Have you heard from Danny?" Matt asked as he grabbed his wallet and keys from the dresser top.

"He called a few minutes ago to say everything's ready at the ranch."

Matt glanced at his watch and gave a decisive nod. "Then let's go. Unless traffic is lousy—which it very well may be—we should arrive with more than enough time to do our own walkthrough before the others start arriving."

"I also talked to your uncle, Finn. He said to tell you the others from their clan have arrived. They should get to the ranch shortly after we do."

"Thanks."

I felt better knowing he and my grandmother had some of their own people with them tonight. If the man our watchers saw at the airport really was Jennings, I had a feeling he'd brought more than just the three they'd seen. The Jennings I remembered wasn't one who let the odds be stacked in any way except in his favor. That meant he would have started sending people into the area almost immediately after I called him. One thing that reassured me was the fact Danny shared my concerns and was even more paranoid when it came to security than I was. He and Tamara had assured me I didn't need to worry, that they'd taken everything into account. I hoped so because tonight could turn bad very quickly.

"It's going to take about forty-five minutes to get to the ranch," Matt said as we pulled onto the highway.

"I don't remember it taking that long to get to Stefan's and Hannah's."

"It didn't, but we aren't meeting there tonight." He paused as he flipped on the turn indicator and changed lanes. "Because of the number of people who will be there tonight, we're meeting at a ranch my family owns mid-way between Fort Worth and Denton."

I didn't say anything. Part of me was glad he wasn't letting Jennings and his people anywhere near Stefan and Hannah's place. But another part of me latched onto his "ranch my family owns". I'd figured out pretty quickly that Matt had money, more than I'd seen in a very long time. His house, while not huge, was large enough to be comfortable. The furnishings were just as comfortable but there was no mistaking the fact they weren't thrift store quality. This car, a very beautiful Mustang, was no more than a year old and fully loaded. Add in the motorcycles in the garage, the expensive suits in his closet, which he'd assured me just the night before he only wore for business, and it all added up to money. But how much I hadn't asked and really didn't want to know. All that mattered to me was that Matt didn't appear to be ruled by it and neither did his sister.

"Don't worry, sweetheart." He gave my hand a squeeze and grinned at me. "The ranch has been in my family for generations. It's not as big as it once was. It's been divided between family members over the years and parts have been sold off. But it is large enough and secluded enough for what we need—which is why we've kept it.

Being a family filled with shapeshifters, it's important to have a place where we can be ourselves and not worry about being caught."

I grinned and shook my head. He'd done it again. He'd done his best to reassure me even though I hadn't said a word. The man was either a mind reader or there was more to being a life mate than I realized. Maybe a bit of both. Either way, and ridiculous as it was, I felt better knowing the ranch had been in the family for generations and wasn't something huge—at least it didn't sound as if it were. Besides, he was right. It would be nice to have a place where we could shift and roam in our animal forms without worry. That had been one of the few things I'd missed about Northern California. We'd been able to take advantage of the mountains and forests, shifting and knowing we were safe from prying eyes.

Besides, thinking about that kept me from thinking about the nerves forming knots in my stomach. This would be my first clan meeting since that terrible night so long ago when Jennings tried to claim me as his mate. I still woke up, covered with sweat and trembling in fear as the nightmare of that night returned. Maybe tonight I'd finally be able to put the nightmare to rest.

God, I hoped so.

At least Matt and my grandmother understood the need to bring the nightmare full circle. Grandma arranged for Aunt Jane and Uncle Lou to be there tonight, just as they had been that night I ran away. Should Jennings show up and try to claim me, they'd be able to tell the other clan leaders gathered what happened. It wouldn't just be my word against his. Even better, Grandma told me they'd contacted others who had been part of the Northern California clan at the time. Many had since left the clan. They'd be here as well. Jennings, if he was foolish enough to attend, would soon discover the tables had been well and truly turned.

If not, well, I might just have my chance to finally dance on his grave which was the closest I ever wanted to be to him.

Almost exactly forty-five minutes after pulling onto the highway, Matt pulled off the road and onto a gravel drive. A large sign near the gate advertised Vickers Tree Farm. Giving credence to the sign was a double row of trees that also served to obscure the area beyond the fence line. Adding to the illusion—heck, for all I knew, this really was a working tree farm—row after row of trees lined the drive. Illusion or not, they acted as a very effective buffer, not only preventing unwanted eyes from prying but also to muffle sounds coming from deeper onto the property.

We drove for another five minutes or so before coming to a large clearing. In the center was a sprawling ranch-style home. The porch stretched the length of the front of the house. A white swing and matching chairs with small tables invited people to sit and relax. Lights were visible from the front windows. A tire swing hung from one of the trees in the front yard. Closer examination showed a couple of bikes lying on the lawn, left perhaps in a mad dash to get to dinner.

"Matt?" I couldn't hide the concern in my voice. If he had worried about letting Jennings and other unknowns near Stefan's and Hannah's place, why wasn't he worried about letting them near here?

"Our brother lives here. So do our folks when they're in the country," he said as he parked in front of the house. "As for Jim, well, he's more than capable of looking after himself."

"What Matt's not saying is that Jim's the local police chief out here. He updated all the security around the place a couple of years ago. Last year, Danny and Tamara helped him update it even further. Believe me, no one can get within a mile of this place without Jim knowing about it," Sharon added as the front door opened.

Matt was a big man, tall and well-built. But the man who appeared in the doorway was massive. He had to stand at least six feet six inches and there wasn't an ounce of fat on him but there was muscle—a lot of muscle. It wouldn't have surprised me one bit to learn he could bench press a Volkswagen. He lifted a hand and waved before coming down the steps to greet us.

"Is he?" I left the rest of the question unasked.

"Oh yeah and this is going to be fun." Sharon definitely looked forward to what was about to happen. I needed to remember this. She had a warped sense of humor, not that I minded, but I'd much prefer not to be on the receiving end of it.

Jim Kincade quickly crossed the yard, grinning as Matt climbed out of the car. He punched Matt's shoulder good-naturedly and Matt countered with a soft swing to Jim's stomach. It wasn't difficult to imagine the two of them quickly turning this ritual into a wrestling match. While it might be fun to watch any other time, we had things to do to make sure everything was ready for tonight.

Before Matt could make it around the car, I opened the door and stepped out. The moment I did, Jim's head swung in my direction. The smile he'd been wearing disappeared, replaced by a look of surprise. Much as their sister had done when she'd entered our bedroom earlier, Jim dropped to hands and knees. He'd done so instinctively, without thought. The next move was mine to make, especially since Matt just stood next to his brother, grinning like a loon.

"Matt, help him up." I shook my head, grinning as he did. There was no mistaking Matt's pride just then, both in me and in his brother. "I'm Finn." I extended my hand, waiting for Jim to take it.

"Jim." His hand swallowed mine, but he was careful not to press too hard. "Damn, both Matt and Sharon warned me you were an alpha and a strong one. I guess I didn't take them as seriously as I should have. Sorry."

"Don't. To be honest, I didn't take them seriously when they told me I was an alpha."

He squinted down at me, his head tipped to one side. Well, that sealed it. That particular reaction seemed to run in the family.

"You didn't know?"

"It's a long story, Jim."

Before Matt could say anything else, the sounds of another car coming up the drive reached us. We paused, waiting, and the knot of tension in my stomach grew. Then the front door opened and Danny appeared.

"It's Tamara. Adam and your grandmother are just behind her, Finn," he called from the porch.

"You guys go on in. I need a few more minutes with Danny and Tamara," Jim said. "We'll talk later, Finn, over a cold one. There's a lot about my kid brother I can tell you."

Seeing the look that crossed Matt's face, I laughed. It was going to be fun watching the brothers try to outdo one another. But that would come later and it was something to look forward to, sort of a reward for making it through tonight.

"Now I see where your Uncle Stefan got the idea for his barn."

I stood just inside the door and looked around. Other than the fact this barn was so large it made Stefan's look small, there was little difference to how it was set up. There was one change, however, that looked to be recent. At the far end of the main room was a raised platform. Two wooden steps led up to the platform where two chairs with a small table sat. At least they were regular chairs and nothing fancy. But I had no doubt they were meant for Matt and me. Nor did I doubt they, along with the platform, were new additions to the room and meant to drive home the fact that we were the Alphas in charge of what was about to happen.

And, yes, the butterflies in my stomach just multiplied a hundred-fold.

"Very nice, Matt," my grandmother commented as she joined us. "I see some new additions since the last time I was here, but not many."

"Why mess with something that works?"

"You've been here?" I asked.

"Our clans have met together here several times, just as his has joined us in Tulsa on occasion."

Clan politics really were different from what they'd been when I was younger. Or was it just that they were different down here? Not that it mattered. I happened to agree with how closely it seemed these two clans at least had become and it helped me understand why

Matt was convinced this was the way all clans had to go if we were to survive.

"I have so much to learn."

"Not really. You already know it," Grandma said as she reached for my hand. "Remember what your parents taught you and trust your instincts. That's all you need." Now she paused. Her left hand reached up to her ear and I realized she was wearing a Bluetooth receiver. She listened for a moment and then nodded. "Excuse me. My people are here and I want to have a word with them. Matt, Adam said to tell you there are others starting to arrive as well."

"Thanks." He looked around and motioned to a young man I recognized from the warehouse. "Go tell Tamara and Danny we need to see one of them ASAP." The young man nodded and trotted off. "Sharon will give you a quick tour of the barn. If you have any questions, ask her. I want to make sure everything is set. I'll join you in a minute," he added as he turned to me.

"Go. Don't worry about me." I was worrying for both of us.

"Finn, relax," Sharon said softly as we moved away. "There's no way Jennings or anyone else can get within a mile of this place without us knowing it. Danny may be paranoid, but Jim makes him look laid back when it comes to security. Put the two of them together with Tamara and we probably have better security than the president."

"I can't help it." I looked over my shoulder to make sure we were out of Matt's line of sight. Satisfied, I stopped and leaned against the wall. For the moment at least, we were alone. "I need you to make me a promise, Sharon." I waited until she nodded. "If Jennings shows up tonight, and I know he will, there's going to be trouble. No matter how much Matt thinks we can keep this from disintegrating into a fight, we won't be able to, not unless Jennings has completely changed since I last saw him. I don't think he'll be foolish enough to call Matt out. My concern is that he's going to have enough people here to cause trouble. If that happens, you stick to your brother's side. Make sure nothing happens to him."

She frowned and then sighed, her frustration clear. "The only way I can promise that is if you promise not to leave his side. My big brother is very protective, and he's already told me my only job tonight is to keep you safe."

I shook my head, torn between affection and frustration. I should have realized Matt would have done something like that. He'd been too relaxed whenever we'd discussed Jennings today. I could tell myself I hadn't realized what he meant to do because I didn't really know him that well and didn't know what cues to look for, but that would be a cop out. Within an hour of meeting him, I'd known he was a man who took his duties as clan leader seriously. He'd take his role as mate even more seriously and would do whatever it took to make sure I stayed safe—whether I liked it or not. Well, he was about to learn two could play that game.

"Sharon, you'll do as I say. Please." I chewed my lower lip, wondering how to explain that I knew Jennings would try to hurt Matt. "I promise I'm not going to do anything foolish, but I have to know Matt is safe."

"Just as he has to know you are." She crossed her arms, a stubborn expression on her face.

"Neither of us is going to do anything foolish," Matt said as he joined us. He looked at his sister and gave a jerk of his head. She nodded and left, obviously relieved she wasn't going to have to choose which of us to disobey. "I mean it, Finn. We're both going to play tonight smart. This is our territory and our rules. Remember that."

Ours.

He'd never really understand what an odd concept that was for me. I'd been on my own so long that thinking of myself as part of a unit was hard. Maybe that's why I was so adamant that nothing happened to Matt because of me. Maybe it was part of the life mate thing. Whatever it was, I meant to follow through. He'd done so much for me already. I wouldn't let him be hurt because of it.

But, I couldn't tell him that. He was male enough, alpha enough, not to agree. He'd quite likely sic not only his sister but my grandmother and anyone else he could enlist to watch over me. So, I'd agree, provisionally at least, especially if it meant he promised not to do anything foolish.

"You have to promise me not to do anything foolish." I reached for his hands and looked up at him. I wanted him to see how worried I was.

"I do." He pulled me close for a moment before stepping back. "Here." He held out a Bluetooth receiver and watched as I slipped it into place in my left ear. "That ties you into the security net. I have one as well. It lets us monitor the security channel."

Which meant we'd know if anyone was trying to sneak onto the property—or worse.

"The others are beginning to arrive. Are you ready?"

Not really, but I wouldn't tell him that.

"Let's do this."

He smiled and bent to lightly kiss me. Then, with my hand in his, he escorted me back to the main room. We had no more taken our seats when he nodded to where Danny stood near the door. Danny nodded in return and then opened the door. Like it or not, ready or not, it was show time.

The next half hour was a blur of faces and names as Matt or my grandmother introduced me to either clan members or the other clan leaders and their mates. Tears burned my eyes on more than one occasion as someone mentioned knowing my parents and how glad they were to finally know I was all right. From time to time, I'd catch a glimpse of one of the pride members I'd already met moving among those gathered. There was a soft narrative running in my ear as security reported the next arrival, checking their names off against the list of clans invited to attend.

Throughout it all, Matt kept hold of my hand, a reminder that I was no longer alone. He beamed proudly as he introduced me as his mate. We'd agreed that we would both keep tight control over our animals during this phase of the gathering. Those gathered would be able to tell we were both alphas, but they wouldn't know just how strong we were together. Leave that until we knew for sure if Jennings was going to make an appearance. Since I wanted to see the look on his face when he realized I wasn't the helpless teenager I'd been the last time he'd seen me, I was more than happy to comply.

As everyone began to settle down so the formal "meeting" could begin, I relaxed a bit more as my grandmother and Uncle Adam led their people to chairs near where Matt and I sat. Joining them were six other clan leaders and their people. They represented Matt's closest allies. Then came the members of our own clan. They formed a buffer between the others who gathered, those who might not be as quick to join in on our side if Jennings appeared and tried to cause trouble.

Seeing Aunt Jane and Uncle Lou sitting just behind Grandma, I smiled. I'd only seen them once in all those years since I'd fled California. I hated being away from them and the rest of the family, but what choice did I have? Now I no longer had to stay away from any of them in order to protect them or myself. Those days were over.

I hoped.

Moments before the door opened again, Tamara's voice came over the Bluetooth receiver in my ear, warning of a new arrival. Her anger and frustration were clear as she reported that he'd refused to identify himself or his companions. The corners of my mouth turned up in what would have been a predatory smile if I hadn't controlled it even as fear licked at my composure like a flame. It is amazing how such contradictory emotions could exist at the same time.

Matt's hand tightened on mine as the door swung open. Years may have passed since I'd last seen Michael Jennings, but I'd have known him anywhere. He still strutted into a room like a bandy rooster, his expression haughty. His blonde hair had thinned, something you don't usually see in a shapeshifter. Even stranger, it was almost white now. There was a dissipation to him that surprised me. He reminded me of some of the drunks I'd crossed paths with over the years. But what surprised me the most was how I felt no real power to him. I doubted he was keeping it under wraps. That wasn't his style. He would want to awe everyone with just how powerful he was.

Could it be he wasn't as powerful as I thought? If so, how had he managed to hang onto power for so long?

When Matt glanced at me for confirmation, I nodded. Whether I was ready or not, it was time to face my nightmares. At least I wasn't alone. This time would be different. It had to be.

CHAPTER EIGHTEEN

J ennings stepped further inside and paused. At his nod, the three men with him split off and ranged around the room. I fought the urge to smile when I saw Danny signal for our own people to follow. That was enough to ease yet another layer of tension. This clan of mine—yes, mine. No one, and especially not Michael Jennings, was going to take it away from me—knew what needed to be done. Nothing was being left to chance. Precautions had been put in place and Jennings, should he decide to cause trouble, wouldn't know what sort of trap he'd walked into until it sprang around him.

Matt gave my hand another squeeze and nodded to my grandmother. She, in turn, signaled Uncle Adam. As they stood, so did the other six clan leaders and their mates or seconds who sat with them. Without a word, they moved to stand to either side of the steps leading up to the platform. As they did, I couldn't help but think they looked like an honor guard, a very serious and dedicated honor guard.

As the room fell silent, Matt stood and helped me to my feet. My stomach did a flip-flop or three and I fought the urge to lick my lips nervously. There was no way I'd let any of those gathered know how nervous I was. They needed to see me as being as strong as Matt. More than that, I wasn't about to let Jennings think he could shake my confidence. If he believed I'd either not recognized him or simply didn't care that he was there, he'd be off-balance and that was certainly preferable to me feeling that way.

"I welcome you, especially my fellow clan leaders, and thank you for coming tonight," Matt began. He sounded so calm and confident. His hand gave mine a quick squeeze and I smiled up at him, aware as I did that Jennings frowned angrily in our direction. "It has been a long time since so many of us have gathered together like this. The last time was when Adam Walkinghorse was married."

I breathed deeply, stilling my anger at the reminder that I hadn't been able to be there for Uncle Adam when his wife had been killed by a drunk driver. Our kind might be stronger and heal quicker, but we could still be killed, especially when involved in such a horrible auto accident. Neither my grandmother nor Uncle Adam had said much, but I'd done an internet search into the accident. Aunt Kelly's car had been struck by a farm truck. The force of the impact cut her car almost in two. I didn't need to read more to know she'd died almost instantly. The pictures of the accident spoke volumes. A good woman had died that night, leaving behind a family to grieve. The other driver survived, his blood alcohol level almost three times the legal limit.

"I asked you here today to meet the newest member of our clan. She has honored us not only by joining the clan but by agreeing to be my mate." He paused and grinned down at me. "Many of you knew her parents, clan leaders themselves. I ask you now to welcome Meg Finley to the Texas clan."

As Matt spoke, I kept my attention on Jennings. His face flushed as Matt drew me closer to him. At the announcement that I was his mate, I expected Jennings to interrupt. He opened his mouth as if to say something and his fists clinched at his sides. But, before he could do or say anything, the man at his side leaned in and whispered something to him. Jennings' head jerked once in acknowledgement. Before

I could signal Danny, he nodded and one of Tamara's pack moved closer in. The man who had spoken to Jennings hadn't entered with him. How many others here reported to him and we didn't know it—yet?

"I have given Matt and Finn my blessing," my grandmother said, climbing the steps to stand before us. She hugged first me and then Matt. "The saddest day of my life was when I learned of the deaths of my daughter and son-in-law. Finn's disappearance soon after left a hole in my heart I wasn't sure would ever be filled. I knew why she'd run from the only home she'd known. More than that, I agreed with her reasons. But she's home now, here with Matt and this clan. It is my hope that together they will bring our two clans even closer than before."

Tears filled my eyes and I blinked them away as she once again turned to me. We hugged once more and then she stepped back, making room for Jerrod Young, clan leader from New Mexico. One by one, the six clan leaders who'd approached the platform with my grandmother added their voices to hers. They welcomed me as a member of the clan and as Matt's mate. They spoke of the strong leaders my parents had been and their confidence Matt and I would carry on the tradition here. The fact that they, like my grandmother, represented some of the largest and most influential clans wasn't lost on anyone there.

That seemed to be especially true where Jennings was concerned. His face flushed a dark purple. The muscles of his jaw worked. It was easy to guess he was hard pressed to keep from interrupting. Part of me was thrilled to see it. Anger made almost everyone careless. But it also worried me because I had no idea what he'd do or say before the night was over.

I glanced to my right and signaled Sharon where she stood a couple of steps away. "If there's trouble, get my grandmother out of here. Matt and I can take care of ourselves," I said softly as she moved to my side. She nodded once and stepped back.

"Thank you," Matt said as the clan leaders returned to their places at the foot of the steps. "I'll admit I am a very lucky man to have Finn standing at my side. Not only does she come from one of the most respected bloodlines of our kind, but she is one of the most powerful alphas I've had the honor to know."

"You honor me by accepting me as your mate." I stepped forward and repeated what I had done that first day after he rescued me from the trackers. I dropped to my hands and knees, showing my submission to him as clan leader. This time, however, I looked him in the eyes. It was a show of equality. He smiled and knelt before me, his hands reaching out and lifting me to my knees.

"You need never subject yourself to me, Finn. You are my mate, my equal. Together we will lead our clan and protect our people."

We stood as one. It might have seemed like a scene out of a "B" movie, but it seemed right. I smiled and lifted my face to his kiss.

"No!"

Jennings' voice rose in challenge. As he stepped forward, Danny's and Tamara's people moved closer. Matt's grip on my hand tightened and he pulled me against him. I knew all that even as my focus narrowed to include little more than Jennings.

"Yes," Matt said simply. His calm response was a sharp contrast to the anger in Jennings' challenge.

"No," Jennings repeated firmly. "Everyone here knows of my claim on Meg Finley. She is my mate. It was witnessed and accepted years ago by our clan before she was taken from me by my enemies. I'm here now to reclaim what's mine."

His?

The man had lost his mind. It had been bad enough when he tried making that claim before the Northern California clan. But to advance it here, in my own home territory was beyond insane, especially since there were those here who could put the lie to what he said. Well, if he thought I'd go along quietly like a good little girl, he had another thing coming.

I gave Matt's hand a quick squeeze before releasing it and stepping forward. Finally, I had the chance I'd wanted for so long. I was about to take control of my life back.

"You're a fool, Jennings." Derision dripped from my voice and he stiffened. "You may have convinced yourself that's what happened, but it's so far from the truth to be laughable. Look around you. See the faces of those who were present that night, those who protested your attempts to violate shifter and normal laws by claiming me. Recognize that they are just as willing to speak against such action now as they were then."

I took another step and stared down at him.

"I was fifteen that night and my parents had been dead less than a week. You'd managed to secure clan leadership because the rest of us were grieving. When you tried claiming it was your right as Alpha to name me your mate, these people stood up to you. They reminded you of my age, of the deaths of my parents and the need to grieve as well as of the laws your claim violated. Your response was to say none of that mattered. You were clan leader and your word was law."

There were a few gasps an even more angry murmuring at that.

"You turned those who disagreed, those who did nothing more than try to protect me, out of the clan. That was enough to convince me that you didn't care about anything but your own desires. You proved that later that night when you cornered me in my parents' home and tried to rape me." Now I bared my teeth, daring him to deny it. "I'm sure you remember that night as well as I do. Especially since you see the scars I left you with every time you look in the mirror." He reached up and touched the scar bisecting his left eyebrow before pulling his hand down and frowning.

"My only mistake was that I let you scare me. I was young and hurt and didn't think anyone would believe me if I told them what you'd done. So, I ran. I cut myself off from friends and family because you proved yourself to be nothing more than a child molester, a would-be rapist. Your response was to send trackers after me and keep them after me all these years."

"Lies!" he bellowed.

"Which part?" Uncle Lou demanded as he stepped forward. "The part about you ignoring the fact Finn was only fifteen at the time or the part about throwing those of us who objected to your plans out of the clan?"

"Or perhaps it was the part about you saying your word as clan leader was law and not what all the clans had decided?" another man asked as he, too, stepped forward.

"Or perhaps it's the part about sending trackers after her and keeping after her all these years." Uncle Adam's voice was hard.

"You ordered your trackers to violate clan territory without permission," I continued. I needed Jennings focused on me. "When you finally felt they were close enough to actually capturing me, you ordered them to do whatever was necessary to subdue me and take me back to California. You approved them tainting the barbs of their Tasers and blades with a drug designed to slow our healing and to cause as much pain as possible. You equipped them with handcuffs and chains and other items to keep me under control. You even furnished a private jet for use when they found me."

Sweat pricked out on his upper lip but he wasn't about to lose face by admitting my accusations were true. Good. I didn't want it to be easy on him. I wanted everyone present to know what sort of a monster he really was. Then they'd support whatever needed to be done to be rid of him once and for all.

"If you had any proof, you'd have presented it by now." He stepped forward and turned to look at those gathered before turning back to me. "I don't know what this son of a bitch has done, but it's clear he's brainwashed you. Well, that's done with now. It's past time for you to come home."

"I am home, you fool. As for what Matt's done, he saved my life. If it weren't for him, I'd have fallen prey to your trackers."

Matt moved to my side. As he did, he glanced at Danny. Danny nodded in response and, as he turned to leave the room, Uncle Adam joined him. So far, everything was going exactly as planned. All I could do was hope it continued to do so.

"Here's your proof, Jennings." Contempt filled Matt's voice as the three trackers were escorted into the room. They were brought to stand between Jennings and us. The youngest cast a quick, terrified look at his clan leader before focusing his attention straight ahead. The other two looked almost as scared as did the first, but they refused to look at Jennings. Instead, they kept their eyes focused on Matt and me, dropping to their knees when Matt finally looked down at them.

The room was quiet enough to hear the men breathing and still enough to smell their fear. I realized then that Matt had been right. Instead of bringing them in in handcuffs as Danny and Tamara had recommended, he'd insisted they be free. He wanted everyone to see that they had not been mistreated. No one had laid a hand on them since their capture. He wanted no one to accuse us of coercing any information from the men.

Without a word, my grandmother moved to stand before the three. As soon as they acknowledged her presence, she began questioning them. Names, clan affiliation, clan leader were all quickly established. Even though she stood with her back to us, I had no doubt that her expression betrayed nothing as she asked why they'd been in our territory and why they hadn't let Matt know of their presence. When they explained they'd been told not to inform the local clan leader, there was an angry murmur from the crowd. Good, one more nail in Jennings' metaphorical coffin.

"What were you to do if you managed to corner my granddaughter?" she asked.

I held my breath. This was one of those situations where the saying, "never ask a question you don't know the answer to" could cause us problems. If any of the trackers suddenly decided their best bet was to stay loyal to Jennings, everything we'd planned so carefully could fall through.

"We were told to bring her back to the clan, no matter what," the man closest to her said softly. "He told us she might not agree to come, that she'd been turned against him and our clan. We weren't to listen to anything she said about not wanting to return. She was his mate and she belonged to him."

I ground my teeth and my nails bit into my palms as I forced myself not to react. Hearing him say it, even though I'd already heard it before, reminded me of how close I'd come to losing everything. It wasn't that I'd have lost my freedom. I had no doubts I would have eventually lost my life because I'd never have willingly submitted to Jennings. But it was more than that. I had a home now, somewhere I belonged and wanted to be. I had a man, a mate, who respected me and cared for me. All of that would have been gone if Matt hadn't appeared when he did.

"Are you admitting you violated the Texas clan's territory?" one of the other clan leaders asked.

"Yes, sir."

"At any time did you try to talk to your clan leader about what he wanted, try to remind him of clan law?"

"N-no, sir."

"Why?"

"If you want to survive in our clan, you learn not to question the Alpha, at least not if you're male."

That brought another murmur from those gathered and you could almost see everyone take a step back from Jennings. Yet it didn't seem to faze him. His anger was so great, as was his confidence, that he didn't realize he was in enemy territory. Either that or he didn't care. Had he always been this much of a fool?

"This is all bullshit." Jennings slashed the air with one hand. Before he could move any closer to the trackers or to the platform, Danny and Tamara were there to stop him. Neither so much as flinched when he glared at them, obviously surprised that anyone would dare lay a hand on him, much less prevent him from doing something he wanted.

"What's bullshit is the way you so willingly put all of us in danger just to assuage your ego." I was down the two steps and standing in front of him before Matt or anyone else could react.

"Because of you, because you couldn't get over the fact a fifteen-year-old might not want to be with you, you risked everything, including all our lives.

"When I came to Matt and offered myself to him as mate, I pledged my life and my arm to pride and clan." Seeing how Jennings' eyes widened in disbelief at my words, I grinned. Finally, I'd gotten past his bravado. "That's right. I knew as soon as I recovered from the drug your trackers used on me that Matt was my mate. His panther called to mine and there was no denying we belonged together. So, yes, I offered myself to him as mate on whatever terms he wanted, something I would never consider doing with you."

"You bitch!" He shook with rage. I'd not only insulted him by refusing to be with him, but I'd offered myself to another man on whatever terms that man wanted. I was playing a dangerous game and I didn't care. I had to shake his confidence enough that he admitted what he'd tried to do to me and, hopefully, what he'd done to my parents.

"I may be many things, Jennings, but a bitch I'm not." I smiled and took a step back. It probably wasn't a good idea to stand too close to him, angry as he was.

"I don't have to stay and listen to this crap."

Before he could turn, Danny laid a firm hand on his shoulder. I watched the knuckles turn white as he dug his fingers into the soft flesh between the bones. Jennings didn't say anything, but he paled slightly and a thin sheen of sweat pricked out on his face. I remembered Sharon telling me that Danny was a third degree black belt. I had no doubt he'd managed to find a pressure point or two and was using it to keep Jennings in line.

That was good, but I needed Danny focused on me just then and not our "guest". A nod was all it took for Tamara to change places with him. In her boots, she stood a good two inches taller than Danny and that meant she was at least three inches taller than Jennings. He'd hate being at the mercy of a woman, especially one who made him look even shorter than he really was.

Danny moved to stand before me. Without a word, he dropped to his knees, head bent. Just about every person there knew he was Matt's close friend and advisor. But that didn't matter. He was making sure they all understood he accepted me not only as a member of the clan but as Matt's mate and as his Alpha. I smiled and reached out to help him to his feet.

"You have had a chance to look into the circumstances surrounding my parents' deaths." It was a statement more than a question.

"I have, and I risked overstepping my bounds by asking for the records from California before consulting you about it."

I gave him a quick warning look. I knew what he was doing. He was trying to deflect Jennings from me to him. While I appreciated the sentiment, I couldn't let him do it.

"What did you discover?"

Before he could answer, Jennings tried to twist out of Tamara's grip. He gave a surprised yelp of pain as she kicked him in the back of his knee and twisted his right arm up behind him. A moment later, he knelt on the floor and she towered over him, using the leverage of her height to hold his arm close to the breaking point. If he tried to shift, I had no doubt she'd break his arm and then his neck before he was halfway through the process.

"Shall I tell them what he found?" I asked Jennings as I moved to where he knelt. I twisted my fingers in his hair and forced his head back. "Shall I tell them how it was you who told the police that my parents had come to you and revealed their plans to kill themselves because my father had been diagnosed with a very aggressive form of cancer? Or how about the way you told the police they'd named you my guardian and then how you continued to lie after the cops realized that wasn't the truth? Or maybe you'd like them to think about how the case was allowed to go cold even though the coroner found no evidence of cancer or anything else wrong with father? And let's not forget about how the coroner felt their bodies had been moved and the scene staged after they'd been killed. Who besides you, the one pack or pride leader they had concerns about and who so quickly moved to fill the void in clan leadership, had anything to gain by their deaths?"

Now I was the one shaking with rage. Matt took a step in my direction. I shook my head and released my grasp. I needed to put some distance between Jennings and me or I wouldn't be responsible for what happened next.

God, it was so tempting to just reach out, grab his head in both hands and twist.

Instead, I forced myself to turn and walk away. That had to be one of the hardest things I'd done since that night so long ago when I took one last look at the bedroom I'd grown up in before I slipped out into the night, never to return. This time, though, I had someone waiting for me. Standing there, just a few feet away was Matt, pride and approval reflected in his eyes. I focused on him, remembering that I was no longer alone.

I stepped onto the platform and held my right hand out to Matt. His hand closed over it and he waited, letting me move to him. It was such a simple way of proving to not only those watching but to me as well that ours was a partnership. We chose to be with one another, something very different from what Jennings had planned for me.

"Gun!"

CHAPTER NINETEEN

For a moment, the world stood still. Tamara's warning disappeared in the explosion of sound that followed. I didn't move. I didn't even breathe as I waited for the pain I knew would follow. But it didn't. Dear God, it didn't.

I spun around, my eyes searching for Tamara, for Jennings, for the gunman. Relief filled me to see how she and Danny were wrestling Jennings to the ground. On the floor in front of them lay a gun. I recognized it as a 1911 and growled deep in my throat. How in the hell had he managed to bring a weapon into the gathering?

A moan had me spinning back to the platform. My breath caught and fear caused my knees to try to buckle. Matt lay on his back, Sharon kneeling at his side. Blood soaked his shirt and covered his left side. Then his chest rose and I heard him draw a ragged breath. He lived.

Fury coursed through me and I spun back to the rest of the room. "Hold that bastard. If he tries anything else, if he so much as opens his mouth, break his legs." Part of me hoped he did try something. I wanted him to hurt as much as Matt was hurting now. But I had to think. I had to remember I stood for the clan with Matt injured. "He came with at least four others—the one standing next to him and three more. Find them and bring them to me. And for the love of God, search them." I thought for a moment. "Clan leaders, identify any here you can't personally vouch for. They are to be held apart as well."

With that, I turned back to the platform. A flicker of relief ran through me to see Matt now propped against his sister. Pain etched deep lines on his face and he groaned softly as Sharon pressed a cloth she'd gotten from somewhere against his wound. Tears ran down her face as she tried telling him he needed to lie back. He shook his head and held a bloody hand out to me.

I dropped to my knees at his side, grasping his hand in mine. I lowered my forehead to his and then tilted my head so I could brush my lips against his.

"Finn." Fear and anger filled Sharon's voice as she looked across her brother at me.

"Take care of him. I need to deal with *this*." I glanced over my shoulder to where the other clan leaders as well as some of our own people were quickly bringing Jennings' companions forward.

"Finn." Matt's hand tightened around mine.

"Shh." I brushed my lips against his again and then sat back, trying to smile in reassurance. As I did, Stefan appeared with his medical bag. "I remember my promise not to do anything foolish, but I do need to deal with this, for you, for the clan and for myself. Trust me."

"Always." He gave my hand one last squeeze and then let go.

Fury unlike any I'd ever felt before filled me as I stood and turned back to face Jennings. Danny and Uncle Adam held him on his knees, his arms pulled behind his back. Tamara stood behind him. Her hand fisted in his hair. She pulled his head back, baring his throat to me. It would be so easy to step forward and slit it—or rip it out. But not yet.

"Let him go," I ordered as I stopped a few feet away and bent to retrieve the gun.

"Finn?" Danny looked at me in concern.

"Do it!" I snapped.

"Yes, Alpha."

As I waited, my grandmother and the other clan leaders Matt moved to stand behind me. But my attention was on Jennings, wondering what he'd try next.

Danny and Uncle Adam reluctantly released their holds on Jennings and stepped back. Tamara took a bit longer. She bent and whispered a warning not to try anything else in his ears. Then, with a shove that sent him sprawling onto the floor, she stepped back. One look at her face was enough to know she'd not hesitate to kill him if he tried anything else.

Not that I blamed her.

"You bitch!" Jennings rasped as he surged to his feet and spun in Tamara's direction.

I had to give him at least a little credit for not trying to close the distance between them. Maybe he wasn't a complete idiot after all. Not that it would help him. He'd destroyed any hope he had for support among the other clan leaders when he brought a gun into the gathering. By actually using it, he was lucky not to already be dead.

Well, the time had come for him to realize just how big a mistake he'd made.

"On your knees!"

My voice carried through the room as I loosened my control. Gasps of astonishment were followed by many of those present doing as I ordered. Jennings' eyes widened and the color drained out of his face. His body reacted instinctively and his knees buckled. I saw how he fought the need to do as I'd ordered. The corners of my mouth twisted up in a bitter smile when he finally sank to the ground, the only clan leader to do so.

Well, well, well. My suspicions had been right. He wasn't an alpha, at least not a very strong one. That was why he'd been so desperate to control me. Mating with me would legitimize his claim to clan leadership. As long as I was out there, I was a danger to him. How many people had he coerced or blackmailed just so he could hold on to his position?

"You've violated our territory. You tried to rape me and then you hunted me like an animal. Whether you admit it or not, you had something to do with my parents' deaths," I said as I moved to stand before him. He trembled as he looked up at me, fury reflected in his eyes. "But that pales in light of what you just did. You violated our laws and brought a weapon to a meeting of clan leaders. You used that weapon to harm my mate, you bastard."

My hand flashed forward, catching him across the jaw with a full-strength backhand. There was a fleeting moment of satisfaction as he fell back, blood flowing freely from his busted lips. His muscles tensed and I braced, ready for him to launch himself at me. Then I remembered who I was. I was the daughter and granddaughter of clan leaders. I was mate to my own clan leader and an alpha in my own right. Jennings was nothing more than a blight I needed to deal with now, making sure everyone realized what a cancer he'd been.

"Don't try it." My voice was soft, the threat clear. For a moment, it looked like he'd ignore the warning. Instead, he reached up and wiped at his blood before spitting on the floor, barely missing my feet. "The only reason I'm not turning you over to the authorities to answer for my parents' deaths is the fact I have no doubt you'd shift and betray our existence to them. You've proven over and over again that you don't give a damn about anyone but yourself."

Now I turned my attention to the other clan leaders. It was time to drive home the point.

"This man has violated our laws and the laws of the normals. That is bad enough. Worse is how he flaunted it. He didn't care if any of you knew or not. Why? Because he knew you weren't talking to one another. You didn't know he was sending trackers into your territories over and over again in an attempt to find me. You didn't listen when others came to you, asking if you'd heard of any trouble.

Instead, you turned a blind eye and kept telling yourselves that the best defense was to keep your heads down. If you didn't pay too much attention to what was happening in the world outside the clan, that world would never intrude.

"Now we have a clan leader who decided he didn't need to follow our laws to challenge another in a fair fight. He brought a gun into our gathering and shot an unarmed man. He shot my mate!"

Now I was shaking in fury. I drew a deep breath, trying to calm down. I couldn't lose control, not now. I had to finish this, had to make the others understand we couldn't remain isolated from one another any longer.

"She's right," my grandmother said as she stepped to my side. "The Oklahoma clan has already pledged to work closely with the Texas clan. We will share resources and information with them as well as with the clans from New Mexico, Arizona, Kansas, Colorado, Nebraska, Montana, Wyoming and Missouri." As she spoke, those clan leaders joined her.

"But that leaves us with what to do with this bastard. I will not let him get away with his attack on my mate."

"She's right. We have to do something."

The speaker was one of the clan leaders who Matt had identified earlier as trying to straddle the fence. While she didn't exactly advocate our kind completely isolating ourselves from the world-at-large, she also didn't want to think about how best to insure that, when our existence was finally discovered, we weren't hunted down and killed out of fear. To have her step up now and support action against another clan leader had to be a good sign. I had to believe that.

"Before we do, I want to know what happened to my daughter and my son-in-law." There was no mistaking the anger in my grandmother's voice now.

"As do I," Uncle Adam said before I could speak.

"I don't have to explain anything to you," Jennings rasped. "I'm a clan leader. That means I answer to no one except the members of my own clan."

"Or someone who challenges you for leadership," Jeremy Gibbs, head of the Colorado-Nebraska clan said.

"Or if the majority of other clan leaders charge you with violating our laws, laws we have all sworn to uphold in order to protect our kind," Matt rasped from where he lay.

"Or when it becomes clear that your actions have put of our kind in danger without cause," I added.

My fists clinched at my side and I breathed deeply, trying to still my rising anger. It would be so easy to shift. All it would take was the merest thought about changing and the shift would begin. It wouldn't surprise me to look at my hands and see the nails lengthening, changing into claws. I could almost feel the fur sprouting from my pores. But I kept control. I couldn't give in to the animal yet. I had to prove to everyone present that I had the control all alphas were expected to exercise. I had to prove to them I was a worthy mate to Matt. Most of all, I refused to give Jennings the satisfaction of seeing me lose control.

"What happened to my daughter- and son-in-law?" my grandmother demanded, her voice brooking no disobedience.

Jennings jerked once, his jaw working as he tried to stop himself from speaking. "Go to hell."

"Answer her!" I snapped, my power once again flowing full force from me.

His jaw worked and sweat ran down his face as he fought to keep from speaking. Every muscle seemed to tense. Much more and he'd either break free of my control or he'd stroke out. I wouldn't shed a tear if it were the latter.

"I said answer her."

"I-I killed them."

Just hearing him say the words was all I needed. That admission cost him his life. He might walk out of the barn, but he'd never leave the property, at least not of his own accord. Our kind had gotten very good over the centuries making sure the bodies of those who violated our laws were never found again.

"I think we've heard enough," Gibbs said coldly. "We have more than enough clan leaders here to deal with the matter."

"No!" Jennings struggled to his feet. I quickly waved Danny and Uncle Adam back before they could stop him. I wanted to see what he did next. Heaven help me, part of me hoped he tried an attack then and there. "I killed to claim my place as clan leader. I claim Meg Finley as my mate as is my right and I challenge any other claim for her."

"Your right?" I threw my head back and laughed. He might think he was being smart by trying to invoke our laws to protect himself, but he was about to learn how wrong he was.

Jennings might have called upon an ancient, and rarely used, provision of our laws but he hadn't really through it through. In the past, when such challenges had been issued, the clan leader answered them. With Matt injured, it was easy to guess Jennings felt he'd have to forfeit. If Matt insisted on answering the challenge, Jennings could kill him. That was something I wasn't about to let happen.

Besides, I'd done my research. I knew that particular law inside out. Although tradition had the clan leader—or pride or pack leader—answering the challenge, it was actually the female who was challenged. She could choose to answer the challenge herself or she could name her champion. Under normal circumstances, if there was anything normal about it, I'd have gladly let Matt stand for me. But not today. This was my fight. Jennings just didn't know it yet.

"Finn, it would be my honor to stand for Matt against this bastard." Danny stepped forward, determination reflected on his expression.

"As would I," Uncle Adam put in and moved to stand next to Danny.

I smiled, touched, as voice after voice joined theirs. Not only did the various pride and pack leaders of our clan offer to stand for me, so did a number of the other clan leaders. Jennings' eyes widened in surprise before his sneer was back in place. He still hadn't figured it out. He continued to think he held the upper hand.

It was time to prove how wrong he was.

I climbed the platform and knelt next to Matt. I cradled his head between my hands and lightly kissed him. He knew what I planned, I could see it in his eyes, and he didn't approve. At least he wasn't going to try to stop me. Still, I had a feeling we'd be having a very long discussion about this when it was over.

"I know what I'm doing," I said softly, so softly no one but Sharon and Stefan could hear me.

"Be careful."

"Always." I kissed him again and then turned my attention to Stefan. "Take care of him."

"The best medicine for him is for you to be careful."

I nodded and stood. A sense of calm settled over me as I moved to stand next to my grandmother. Jennings watched and the first hint of uncertainty shadowed his expression. He wasn't used to not being the one in charge. All his bluff and bluster hadn't helped him today. Now he was about to learn how his lack of knowledge and respect for our laws had just signed his death warrant.

It might not be by my hand and I might not live to see it, but he would not leave this place alive.

"I demand justice for my parents' deaths and for the wrongs done to all of us by this man." I pointed to where Jennings stood. "But that is up to all clan leaders to decide. However, for what he did to my mate, I claim his life."

"You can't!" Jennings actually laughed. "I've called challenge."

Now I smiled, confidence filling me. "But I can. My decision is as mate to the clan leader, Alpha to his Alpha. The clan has accepted me and that gives me the right and the authority to claim your life. But don't worry. I haven't forgotten your challenge even if it is obvious you've forgotten our laws. Matthew doesn't have to be the one to accept. I can choose any of those who have offered to champion me or I can choose someone else."

My grandmother's gasp told me she understood what I was about to do. I patted her arm in reassurance as I stepped past her. Then I drew myself up to my full height and stared down at Jennings. Time for him to learn just how foolish he'd been to come here.

"I accept your challenge. We'll fight here and we'll fight now."

As I spoke, most everyone gathered began stepping back, forming a circle around us. Several of those who had offered to fight for me remained where they were, ready to protest the moment I looked in their direction. Instead, I waved all of them but my grandmother back. She might not approve of what I was about to do—then again, she probably did approve. I had a feeling she'd love nothing more than to face Jennings down herself—but she would also make sure that, no matter what happened next, Jennings didn't leave here alive.

"I'll make sure he pays for your parents if anything happens to you," Grandma said softly. She pulled me into a quick embrace, her lips pressed to my ear. "Don't hesitate. Don't play with him. Just do it. He'll try to draw it out and tire you or force you into doing something stupid. Strip and shift and as soon as he's done the same attack." With that she stepped back, joining Uncle Adam on the platform where Matt sat propped against his sister, watching us.

I quickly toed off my boots. As I reached up and loosened the lacings on my vest, my focus narrowed to Jennings. He looked like he'd just been presented with a gift. Did he really think I'd let him force me into conceding the fight to him? If that were to happen, he'd have every right to force me to return to California with him. That assumed, of course, he managed to get past my grandmother and the others alive. He'd still have to answer for what happened to my parents and what he'd done to Matt. But it was obvious he either wasn't thinking that far ahead or he just didn't care.

"I've been looking forward to this for a very long time, Meg." He actually smiled. "You're going to learn how foolish you were to leave me. But I promise that before you die, you—well, your cat—will learn what a truly powerful lover I could have been."

My blood ran cold as I realized what he meant. He'd rape me, either in human or shifted form, given the chance. Well, I had no more intention of letting that happen now than I had that horrible night so long ago.

"I remember your shifted form, Meg. Such a pretty little cat. It won't be much of a challenge to me."

Well, Grandma had pegged that one right.

"But my cat, like me, has grown, Jennings." Now it was my turn to smile. "Besides, I remember your cat as well. It always surprised me that someone with such a small cat as their animal could actually be clan leader when there were so many larger, stronger cats among us."

Fury suffused his face. I'd scored the first point. Good.

"Now, if you're done talking." I dropped my vest to the floor. My trousers followed.

"Down!" someone yelled from my right a split-second before the sound of a second gunshot filled the room.

Damn it, not again.

Instinct took over and I dove to the right. Pain radiated from my left arm. But the fury that followed overrode it. I rolled to my feet and looked around. Danny, Uncle Adam and several others had Jennings down on the floor. From the right came the sounds of scuffling. A moment later, several of Tamara's people shoved someone forward.

Meehan!

My lips pulled back and I growled softly. My cat was so close to the surface now it wouldn't take much to release her. I held her in check, barely. I had to deal with this before I let her have her satisfaction. Then I'd gladly let her loose, let her deal with Jennings and anyone else who tried to stop me.

"This stops now!" I closed the distance between Meehan, held firmly between two very burly members of Tamara's pride. Without thinking, I backhanded him much as I had done Jennings earlier. "Tamara, Danny, I don't care what you do to him. Just make sure he understands that this sort of betrayal will not be tolerated. Then mark him so any pack or pride he goes to will know how he turned on his own."

"Y-you can't!"

"She can and so can I," Matt said. I turned to see him struggling to his feet. "And know that if you ever cross into our territory again, it will mean your death. Now keep him secure until Jennings is dealt with."

As Matt spoke, Stefan moved to my side. I tried waving him off as he reached for my injured arm. The arm hurt, but I could tell I'd suffered only a flesh wound. It wouldn't slow me once I'd shifted. For the moment, it reminded me not to trust Jennings and not to drop my guard.

"Uncle Adam, let that bastard up." I waited until he and the others who'd been holding Jennings down did as I said. "Shift," I said simply as Jennings climbed to his feet.

I released the last of my control. Pain rolled over me as muscles contracted and bones began to reshape. I dropped to my hands and knees. My head went back and my mouth opened. What started as a moan turned into a roar. My fingers dug against the floor, nails turning to claws. My vision blurred and for that one short but interminable moment, I was lost in the shift.

A growl sounded deep in my throat. Not far away, Jennings stood there, staring at me in disbelief. Why hadn't he finished undressing and begun his shift? Had my anger been so great that I'd shifted faster than usual? Or was it something else?

I swung my head, sniffing. Everything always seemed so different when I was in this form. Scents were stronger, colors brighter. And there were so many scents around me. Different shifters, some familiar, others not. Emotion hung in the air like a heavy fog. Fear, expectation, surprise.

Blood. Mine. Matt's—mate.

I turned to look for Matt. My body felt wrong. Heavier, bigger. Stronger. A step and a flash of orange, black and white caught my eye. No, that was wrong. So was the size of the paw. My paw, but big, so much bigger than it should be.

The human part of me that always remained after a shift didn't know whether to laugh or scream in terror. I was a panther. I'd always shifted into a panther. The colors and markings I saw as I twisted my head this way and that were most definitely not what I should be seeing. The long body and long, thick tail belonged to a tiger.

Was this a dream—or a nightmare?

A hand lightly scratched between my ears, drawing my attention away from my fear and confusion. I knew that scent. Grandmother. Elder. Alpha. I rubbed my head against her thigh once before turning my attention back to Jennings.

He remained motionless, as if rooted in place. His hands remained at his shirt front, fingers on buttons, but he made no move to undress. His chest rose and fell in quick breaths while his eyes dilated. My tiger—my new cat—reveled in the fear in him. Let him see what a mistake he'd made in trying to destroy my life. Let him know that he was now the hunted. There was no way his cougar could best me now.

"Wait," my grandmother said softly as my tiger-self took a step forward. "Let him shift."

I roared and gloried in how he cringed in fear. I was the predator and he the prey.

"T-that's not her!" He took a step back, only to come to a stop as Tamara's men blocked his escape. "I've seen Meg Finley's shifted form. It's a panther."

I roared again. He needed to shift. I was tired of waiting.

"You fool." Humor and pride filled my grandmother's voice. "You forget our family history. It's rare but not unheard of for our alphas to shift into more than one animal. They, and others like them, are the source for the skinwalker legends."

"You issued the challenge, Jennings. Shift now or sacrifice your life," Uncle Adam said.

My tiger waited. That felt strange. The panther had always been a part of me. Even before my first shift, I'd known I would turn into a panther—if I ever shifted. It wasn't a certainty that I would, not even with both of my parents being shapeshifters. One of the reasons there were so few of us was that we don't always breed true. Yes, it was more likely that a child of two shapeshifters would also be a shapeshifter but it wasn't a guarantee.

I paced. The human part of my brain was surprised at how quietly the large tiger moved. That part of my brain also wished I had time to learn just what this new body of mind could do in the short time it took Jennings to shift. I knew my panther form, its reactions and reflexes as well as my human body. But not this one.

A groan pulled my attention back to Jennings. He'd fallen to his hands and knees and was in the midst of shifting. Good. It was past time to get this over with.

A few moments later, a fawn colored cougar stood where Jennings had knelt. My tiger roared even as its confidence increased. The smaller cat would be no challenge. It was the mouse to my cat and my cat always won. It didn't matter what form we happened to take. We were Alpha and we would win.

The cougar answered my roar and paced forward. It was as much of a fool as its human counterpart. Otherwise, it would be submitting, recognizing my dominance over it. But that's not what I wanted. I wanted, I needed satisfaction for everything Jennings had done to me and to my family. I needed to make him pay for what he'd done to Matt. The tiger understood that. The tiger knew the importance of protecting territory and family.

The cougar leapt.

Move! I screamed at the tiger. It did but not quickly enough. The cougar's claws raked down our right flank as we twisted away. The fight was on and it had drawn first blood.

Our flank. Our blood.

That was it. I needed to release control. I trusted my panther and I needed to trust this new tiger of mine.

Remember the Alpha's lessons, the tiger-mind thought at me.

I gave a mental nod and quit fighting for dominance. As I did, I reached for the link that tied the tiger to the panther and to me. We were one. We needed to trust. We needed to fight and we needed to win.

Fur flew and blood sprayed. The human part of the *us* resisted the tiger's insistence that mercy couldn't be shown. I knew it, intellectually at least, but this was new to me. I'd never seen a fight like this between two shifters, much less taken part in one. Unfortunately, the cougar had no more scruples than its human form did. That put me at a disadvantage, one I had to overcome quickly or the larger size and greater strength of the tiger wouldn't mean squat.

The cougar raced in again, confident in its skills. At the last moment, it leapt, jaws opening. As if I were watching a movie, a large paw cut through the air, swatting the cougar to the ground as easily as if it were swatting a fly. Stunned, the cougar lay there. That was long enough to act—and act I must if I was going to end this.

It was over almost as quickly as it had begun. Tiger jaws are weapons unto themselves. The cougar's neck snapped and blood filled the tiger's—my, our—mouth. Part of me wanted to be sick but I refused. This was no innocent I'd killed. It had been the monster responsible for my parents' deaths and who knew how much more.

But now that the fight was over, every injury inflicted by the cougar ached. Still, there was one thing I had to do. I closed my jaws carefully around the cougar's neck once again and dragged the limp carcass across the floor to where my grandmother stood. It landed with a muffled thud at her feet. Then I forced my tiger-self up the steps onto the platform and collapsed at Matt's side.

His hand reached out to stroke my heaving side. I lifted my head. I needed to shift but I was so tired. Maybe I could just rest here for a few minutes.

"Lie still, sweetheart," he soothed. "Don't shift yet."

As Matt spoke, Stefan knelt on the other side of my tiger-self. His hands were gentle as they probed a set of deep scratches down my flank. "He's right, child. Just stay there. You'll heal faster if you don't shift yet."

I moved slightly so my head rested in Matt's lap. It was over, finally. I'd never have to run again.

CHAPTER TWENTY

Sun streamed in through a crack in the curtains. As if that wasn't insult enough, somewhere just beyond the window a zillion birds chirped happily. No one and nothing should be that happy this early in the morning.

Morning.

Memory of the events of the past day returned in a flash. I rolled over, twisting around to see the other side of the bed. It was empty. I ran my hand over the sheet and frowned. It was cold. At least it looked like Matt had slept there. So where was he? Had he taken a turn for the worse and I didn't know it?

Worried, I sat up and tossed back the sheet. Pain caught at my side and left thigh. Then I saw the bandages and remembered the cougar sinking its teeth into my leg near the end of the fight. Then it felt like he was going to rip my leg off. Now it merely ached like a bad toothache, enough to remind me of what happened but not enough to keep me in bed. Even if it had been worse, I'd be up. The memory of Matt lying there, bleeding from the wound in his side, haunted me. I knew we'd gone to bed together, under strict orders from Stefan to rest. So where was Matt and why hadn't I realized he'd gotten up —or worse?

Fear and worry can make a person do things they'd normally not do. Add in the fact I'm not a morning person, never have been and never will be, and was it any wonder I left the bedroom without thinking about the fact I wore no more clothes than I'd been born in? All I cared about was finding Matt and making sure he was all right.

I stepped through the door into the kitchen and came up short. Matt sat at the table, a mug of steaming coffee held gingerly between his hands. Sitting with him were Uncle Adam, Danny and Uncle Lou. Sharon was just coming in through the back door. My grandmother and Aunt Jane worked side by side at the stove. It was a homey scene spoiled only by the fact Matt looked pale and pain etched deep lines in his face.

Then heads turned to me and my grandmother smiled and shook her head. Only then did the fact I was nude hit me. God, talk about embarrassing. A blush started at the tips of my toes and worked its way up to my hairline. It didn't matter that each of them had seen me naked the night before. That had been different. I'd been about to shift then.

With a groan, I turned and started out of the kitchen. Two weeks ago this never would have happened. Two weeks ago, I'd never have thought I'd be sharing my bed—well, his bed—with a man I knew down to my bones was my mate. It didn't matter that we'd known one another such a short time. Such a short period of time and it had changed me in so many ways, as this morning proved. My concern for Matt made me forget a simple thing like modesty. Now I might just die from embarrassment.

I shut the bedroom door behind me and crossed to the closet. Maybe I could climb in and hide for the next year or two. At least by then my blush would have subsided—I hoped. I could still feel the heat of it. Damn and damn and damn again.

A soft knock sounded at the door. Before I could tell whoever it was to go away, the door opened. My blush deepened to be caught standing there, staring at the closet just as buck-naked as I'd been when I'd burst into the kitchen. Well, I could stand here and wish for whomever it was to go away, or I could turn around and act as if I was the confident Alpha and mate to the clan leader I'd been the night before.

That closet looked awfully inviting.

"Finn."

I didn't need to turn around to know Sharon was smiling. I heard the humor in her voice and felt my blush deepen again. God, if it kept doing that, I'd be turning purple before long.

She cleared her throat and tried again. "Finn, relax. We all understood."

"Understood what? That I'm an idiot who couldn't remember that she went to bed naked?"

"No, we understood that you woke up and realized Matt wasn't there and were so worried about him that you came in search of him without thinking about anything else."

She moved to stand beside me. Without a word, she reached into the closet and withdrew Matt's robe. As she draped it about my shoulders, I shook myself. Maybe she was right. Maybe that's what they thought. God knows, it was the truth. Not that it made it any less embarrassing.

"Matt?" I asked, sliding my arms into the sleeves and pulling the robe closed. Once I'd tied the belt, I felt slightly more ready to face the world, even if the robe swallowed me. "You were right. I couldn't think of anything but finding out if he was okay when I woke and realized he was gone."

"He's fine. The bullet went cleanly through his side. He'll be sore for a few days and that will make him grouchy, but he's going to be fine."

I relaxed to hear the truth in her voice and see the confidence reflected on her expression.

"And both your grandmother and I read him the riot act for getting out of bed. Not only did we think he ought to have slept in this morning, but we knew you'd worry when you woke and found him gone. I have a feeling he's getting another earful from Irene right now." She grinned at that and I shook my head, a smile touching my lips. Maybe I wasn't the only one feeling more than a bit embarrassed this morning. "Now, how are you feeling?"

"Other than still suffering from a terminal case of acute embarrassment?" She simply tilted her head to one side and cocked an eyebrow at me. "All right. I feel like I've been through the wringer, but it's tolerable."

"If you're up to it, let's go to the kitchen. You could use some coffee and I know everyone has more than a few questions about what happened last night."

Me included.

Sharon linked her arm through mine and together we left the bedroom. I had to give it to the others. As we entered the kitchen, they acted as if I hadn't come barging in wearing nothing but my birthday suit just minutes earlier. Instead, Matt smiled almost apologetically and motioned for me to take the seat next to him. As I did, my hand reaching for his, Uncle Adam pushed a mug of coffee across the tabletop in my direction. A moment later, Grandma set a plate of bacon and eggs before me. Aunt Jane served Matt. Once everyone else had been served, they crowded around the table or leaned against the counter.

For a few minutes, we ate in companionable silence. I discovered that acute embarrassment had done nothing to take the edge off my hunger. I finished what I'd been served. Almost before I'd managed to put my fork down, Sharon was there with seconds for me. As I thanked her, the memory of my father telling me that I'd always be hungry after a shift came to me. He'd gone on to explain that if I was ever seriously hurt either while shifted or if I shifted after being hurt so healing would be sped up some, I'd need even more food, especially protein, to recharge my system. Since eating an entire package of bacon as well as a dozen eggs sounded pretty good just then, I assumed he'd been right.

When I finally leaned back and wiped my mouth with a paper napkin, Matt slid his arm about my shoulders and leaned close. "Are you all right?"

"I ought to be asking you that." I reached up and cupped his cheek with my right hand. "I've never been as scared or as angry as I was when I realized that bastard shot you." Just the memory of that moment had my mouth going dry again.

"Then you've got a pretty good idea how I felt to have to watch you fight that son of a bitch."

"Since you've brought up what happened last night." Uncle Adam leaned back in his chair and snagged the coffee carafe from off the counter behind him. He refilled first my mug and then Matt's before topping off his own. "Would you mind explaining what happened?"

I didn't need to ask what he meant. My shifting into a tiger was the proverbial elephant in the room just then.

"I don't know." And that was the God's honest truth. I rubbed my face with my hands. "I wanted to kill Jennings after what he'd done. It was bad enough to finally know for sure he was responsible for my parents' deaths. I wanted vengeance for that and for having to be on the run for so long. But seeing Matt lying there bleeding was too much. I didn't care if I died in the fight as long as Jennings died before me.

"Then I shifted. At first, I didn't realize anything was different. You know how it is those first few moments after a shift. You're there, in the back of the animal's mind, but still slightly disoriented. I realized Jennings was looking at me like I'd sprouted a second head or something but figured he was just surprised by how quickly I'd shifted. It wasn't until I moved and realized I felt different, bigger, heavier, stronger. Then I saw the different fur and color patterns and the human me turned into a gibbering idiot. Then you were there, Grandma, scratching between my ears. You weren't surprised, were you?"

She smiled, her pride obvious. "No. Your mother never shifted into anything except a panther to the best of my knowledge. But she'd never really been pushed and certainly never like you had been. Even though you'd said you'd never shifted into anything but a panther, I had a feeling that if you were pushed hard enough, you might surprise us all." She reached across the table and patted my hand.

"Matt, I swear I didn't know." I looked up at him, worried what he'd think.

"Sweetheart, don't look so scared." He grinned and carefully pulled me close. I wrapped my arms around him, careful not to squeeze too hard and aggravate his wound. "You're my mate and what happened yesterday just proves we're well suited. The panther is my predominant shifted form, but I've been known to shift into a lion on more than one occasion."

I shook my head, amazed at my luck. But there were still questions I needed answered and I swallowed against a sudden bubble of nausea. "What about Jennings?" Memory of how my tiger had dragged the dead cougar across the floor only to drop it at my grandmother's feet returned and I closed my eyes as I focused on not throwing up.

"Stefan took care of the carcass," Matt said. "He'll do a necropsy on it and then dispose of it."

"I-I don't understand."

"He didn't shift back after you killed him. That doesn't happen often. Stefan wants to know why and I agreed. Once he's done, he'll make sure the carcass is taken far from here and taken care of. No one will ever be able to trace Jennings back to us."

"His people?"

"It was amazing how quickly they were ready to turn on him once he was no longer a danger to them. They'll be watched and they know it. Don't worry, they'll not cause us any more trouble," Danny replied.

"Is it really over?" Intellectually, I knew it was, or at least that it was close to being over. But emotionally, it might take me a long time to believe it.

"It is," Matt assured me.

"Some of the other clan leaders will be here for lunch. We'll be discussing what happened last night and what led up to it. We'll also start talks about how to make sure it never happens again," Grandma said. "But that will only happen if you and Matt get some rest. Stefan was adamant about that when he checked on you two earlier."

I wasn't tired, not now, but one look at Matt was all it took to agree. I could see the pain in his eyes. So, I nodded and carefully stood. His hand slipped into mine and I waited as he slowly, painfully stood. Even as I slid an arm around his waist, he slid his around mine. We leaned on one another as we moved slowly out of the kitchen.

"It's been a hell of a couple of weeks, Finn," he said as he settled on the edge of the bed a few moments later.

"It certainly has," I agreed. "And I wouldn't trade it for anything." I bent and lightly kissed him. As he leaned back, I slid out of the robe, tossing it across the foot of the bed. Then I slid beneath the sheet at his side. We might both be too sore for loving, but that didn't mean we couldn't cuddle.

"Are you sure?" he asked softly.

"About being here, with you?"

He nodded.

"More sure than I've ever been of anything in my life." I leaned up and kissed him. "Get some rest. You need to be at your best when the other clan leaders get here."

"You too."

I shifted so my head rested on his shoulder and my hand on his chest. This was home. This was where I belonged. Now it was up to both of us to make sure nothing else threatened it or those who looked to us for leadership and protection.

REQUEST FROM THE AUTHOR

It has long been said that the best form of advertising is word of mouth. That is especially true when it comes to books. Friends and family members trust reviews and suggestions for books that come from people they know.

That word of mouth goes even further in this digital age. If you enjoyed this book, do me a favor. Spread the word. Tell people on your various social media accounts. Leave a review on Amazon. If you're a blogger, write a post about it. All that does help. Besides, it is the one way we, as authors, know you really enjoyed our work.

Thanks!

AUTHOR'S NOTE

I've had so much fun putting this expanded and updated edition of *Hunted* together. The characters have been favorites of mine from the very beginning. Getting to come back to revisit—and expand—their stories has been a joy.

This expanded edition is the first of the re-releases for the series. *Tracked* (previously released as *Hunter's Duty*) and *Prey* (previously released as *Hunter's Home*) will be released over the next six weeks. As with *Hunted*, each of them has been re-edited and, in some instances, parts have been re-written.

All this is in preparation to relaunching the series with a new book, *Snared*, which will be released next summer (of not sooner).

I hope you enjoy returning to the world of Finn & Company as much as I have. Please check out my Facebook Page for further information about upcoming books.

ALSO BY THE AUTHOR

Slay Bells Ring

Witchfire Burning

Light Magic

Wedding Bell Blues

Coming Soon:

Tracked (Stalker's Moon, Book 2)

Prey (Stalker's Moon, Book 3)